REBECCA
BRYAN

The Sand Bar

A NOVEL

outskirtspress
DENVER, COLORADO

The Sand Bar
A Novel

v5.0

Outskirts Press, Inc.
http://www.outskirtspress.com

ISBN: 978-1-4327-8827-8

Library of Congress Control Number: 2012902357

PRINTED IN THE UNITED STATES OF AMERICA

For Mom and Dad. I count my lucky stars every day.

Accolades go to my husband and children who have patiently watched their wife and mom spend countless hours at the computer living in a fantasy world. You all deserve a trip to Disney Land— but don't hold your breath. Second, thanks go to my wonderful editor, Val Serdy. The Sand Bar wouldn't be a tenth of what it is today without your fabulous prose. Honestly. On a more serious note, if you suffer from Postpartum depression you're not alone and it is treatable. Call your doctor. Lastly, thanks to the Fremont County Search and Rescue Team, who spend countless hours on boats, snowmobiles, and other crafts rescuing complete strangers in some of the most amazing and unforgiving country in Idaho. It is no small thing. Thank you. To make a donation go to fremontrescue.org.

Chapter One

Red and blue lights flashed in my rearview mirror.

"Perfect. Just perfect," I muttered under my breath.

A tumbleweed bounded across the barren Idaho highway. It skipped in front of me and smashed against a fence, lodging itself into the barbed wire. I gripped my steering wheel. Beads of sweat gathered on my forehead. My car was becoming a sauna as I waited for the inevitable knock on the window. In the distance, a mirage lake rose from the steaming hot pavement. I unwrapped my sweaty, stiff fingers from their chokehold. My heart pounded, and my hands shook as I moved a potted plant (whose leafy vines spilled from an open cardboard box), shoved the fast-food leftovers aside, and rummaged under a pile of killer stilettos—all vying as potential weapons—to look for my wallet.

Now with the annulment finalized I realized I didn't know what to call it or myself. With nothing to show for the past eight years besides a dusty diploma, a lot of emotional baggage—Gucci, thank you—and a really great collection of Jimmy Choos, I was surrounded by everything I owned, including my never say die lemon geranium; all piled in the Mercedes given to me on my twenty-fourth birthday by the man I once called husband. Could I consider myself a divorcee? He wasn't dead, so I knew I wasn't a widow. I really didn't know. It was as if the marriage had never taken place. Eight years of my life up in a puff of smoke. My eyes stung, my head pounded. My lungs burned. I slowly blew out the hurt. I was sick of crying; tired of being the poor pathetic reject.

I dug through my purse. An orange 1978 Dodge truck crept

past. My face burned at the sight of the thing. I'd been stuck behind the ancient heap of junk whose tailgate read like a bad tweet—"Keep Idaho Green," "The Gem State," "Feed the birds, not the bears,"—for a mile, while a van loaded with unrestrained kids sucking blowfishes against a filthy window—infected with who only knew what kind of disease—blocked me from the left. As soon as the van edged in front of the truck, I'd slammed on the accelerator and blasted between them both like a slick cobra. The engine growling beneath my Jimmy Choos had released a certain euphoria—a rush that had lasted nearly thirty seconds—like an itch being scratched. That's when I'd passed the state trooper strategically hidden behind a large juniper tree in the median, and most assuredly gunning me. I'd checked the speedometer. I'd been going ninety. I'd sworn and slammed on the brake.

This was certainly not the first time I'd been stopped by an Idaho state trooper. Idaho was famous not only for its potatoes, but also for the plethora of state troopers staked out to fill the local tax coffers with speeding ticket revenue, especially by out of state license plate holders. It might have sounded like I was nursing a grudge, but honestly, the statistics spoke for themselves; in the previous eight years I'd received six tickets while traveling this road—nearly one ticket for every year. I could travel over six hundred miles unscathed, but as soon as I entered this little stretch of highway, boom; on came the lights, out came the ticket.

I stared out the window. He was certainly taking his time. Farm fields and pockets of old lava beds and wild sagebrush stretched as far as the eye could see; a sight that would have seemed surreal in San Francisco. I tried to think of happier places, like Stinson Beach. One of the few places I had felt real peace since moving to San Francisco eight years earlier to attend Stanford. I could almost feel the soft breeze blowing off the ocean. I closed my eyes and imagined seagulls circling overhead for abandoned crumbs. I dug my toes into the pretend cool, wet sand.

A rap on my window pulled me from my daydream. The California seagulls disappeared, as did the sand between my toes. The very outline and existence of that beautiful white city by the bay vanished, leaving only the nasty Idaho desert wind that had spun my hair into a tangled knot worse than stored Christmas lights, sagebrush, juniper trees, and a navy uniformed patrol officer in my view. Except he didn't seem so bad: tall, chiseled, and wearing sunglasses like Tom Cruise in *Top Gun*, except with blond hair.

"Officer," I began, handing over my license and registration, "I just came from San Francisco to see my sick father. I only sped because I had to get around a dangerously slow pickup."

"Dangerously slow?" he seemed to chide, taking my information and examining it.

I bit my lip and glared out the windshield. Slow and steady Dodge was now a speck of burnt orange in the distance. I had to plead my case. Something about having my license suspended if I received any more tickets spurred me on.

"Did you see that toaster van? At least a dozen kids and not a single one restrained. Why don't you go stop that driver and demand their kids be put in car seats?" I was leaking lighter fluid, and he was the match. I turned away and bit my lip.

"Toaster van?"

"Yeah, the one that looks like a big toaster." Jeez, where was this guy from?

He laughed a little, still studying my license. "I just haven't heard them called that in years."

"Listen, I just really, really can't get a ticket," I pleaded. My eyes welled with tears. I squeezed them shut and bit my lip harder. I tasted blood. I was a mess.

"Marlo Leavitt Kensington?" the officer said, more like a statement than a question.

"Um, no, not anymore. Just Marlo Leavitt." My face flushed.

He raised his eyebrows and stared at me for a moment. "Oh."

Before we were married, Courtney's parents insisted on our signing a prenuptial agreement. At first I was offended. But it was never about their vineyard money. So I signed the papers. Then we had our marriage annulled, and the prenup became void anyway. It didn't matter. Like I said, I was never in it for the money.

I figured if I got desperate for the money I didn't get from our failed marriage, I could always sell off my Vera Wang collection.

He cleared his throat and pointed with his pen. "You got yourself a serious collection of shoes there, Marlo."

I glanced over at the open box. Stilettos, wedges, ballet flats. You name a designer: Manolo Blahnik, Michael Kors, Nicole Miller, Gucci, and I probably had one of their pieces; all there from all the wine tasting parties I hated to go to. I had no idea what I'd do with them now. Or what I'd do with my Tiffany lamp from the San Francisco furniture market or the Gorham china or my favorite hand-loomed rug from Chinatown, all stuffed in the back trunk.

How had I ended up with these things? I'd never had a fetish for shopping before I met Cort. I'd never had any money. I was a girl from small-town Idaho living in California for the very first time and way over my head.

Instead of a savings account, I had a traveling yard sale.

"Don't worry, I don't plan to use them as weapons," I promised.

He leaned into my window and smiled. Sort of. It was actually more of a smirk. I glanced over his features. Nice lips. Tan skin, but with the reflective sunglasses I couldn't see his eyes. What I could see looked nice enough, but I did not place his features among any old friends.

"Where you headed, Marlo?"

"Home," I stated shortly as embarrassed tears welled again.

"Where's home?"

Holding my nose with my hand to stop the tears, I managed a small, "St. Anthony."

"That's a pretty short skirt for those parts, don't you think?"

I glanced down. My pink Ann Taylor jersey skirt had inched its way up to the tops of my browned thighs. I started to pull the material down, but my sweaty legs were like suction cups against the black leather seat, and they made an awful sucking sound as I lifted them. It left me feeling irritated that we were discussing my choice of wardrobe.

"Are you giving me a ticket for my short skirt or my speeding?"

"They were always nice, but wow," he said, still taking a gander.

I coughed in my throat a little. Tears were definitely gone now. I could feel my hands shaping into fists of hardened clay.

"Are you seriously talking about my legs?" Who was this jerk?

He started to laugh. He leaned into the window and rested his arms on the door.

"I'm just giving you a hard time. If you were trying to get home, you ought to have come through an hour ago, though."

My fists relaxed a little. This guy was playing with me. I didn't know whether to be flattered or offended.

"Do I know you?"

"You used to," he explained, flipping his wrist to look at his watch. "That was, until you went all uptown on us." He turned his attention back on me. "You just might as well take it easy, 'cause it will be awhile before you can get anywhere."

"Why?" I demanded, my irritation growing by leaps and bounds.

He scrunched up his nose and leaned in closer. "How could you forget the Twenty-fourth of July Parade?" It was obvious by his crooked smile he was finding this all rather comical.

"I didn't forget. Today's the twenty-fifth."

"Changed to the first Saturday closest to the twenty-fourth about six years ago."

"Oh," I frowned.

The Twenty-fourth of July, or Pioneer Day, was in commemoration of the Mormon pioneers who crossed the plains and settled in the Salt Lake Valley in July of 1847. Many families continued on and created settlements in other places. Southeastern Idaho was a recipient of this expansion; therefore, it became fitting to celebrate along with Utah. Unlike Utah, however, it wasn't an official holiday here, but had always felt like it with the parade and all the festivities.

This had always been a source of discomfort for me and Cort. I wasn't exactly a practicing Mormon, but I did have pioneer roots. Every time this came up I would get the same questions. Were my parents polygamists? How many wives did my dad have? Just how many brothers and sisters did I have? It was sort of funny the first time, but over time, I realized Cort's friends were not making pleasant banter, but were making fun of me. We learned to skate around those issues by never bringing them up.

"Still don't recognize me?" he asked again.

I frowned. I thought I knew his voice, but I still couldn't place him.

"Maybe if you took off those shiny sunglasses I could tell who you are," I quipped sweetly while displaying a less-than-genuine smile.

He pulled them off. The faint smile lines surrounding his dusty brown eyes caught a cord. They did look familiar, and yet, it couldn't be. This was a strong, grown man with a square jaw and laugh lines. I searched for his name tag. Dawson. It finally came to me, though I couldn't believe how handsome and tall he had become.

"Luke Dawson?"

We had dated in tenth grade. If you could call it that. I think I had been as tall as him at the time, and our dates usually consisted of calling each other on the phone after school. I probably hadn't talked to him since.

"Wow! You're a man!" I squeezed my eyes shut and shook my head. That had sounded ridiculous. "I mean, I haven't seen you in a really, really long time, and you've grown up," I backpedaled.

"Graduation night. You were fighting with that boyfriend of yours. I offered to take you home."

I sat with my mouth hanging wide while the memory tugged behind my eyes. "Wow," I shook my head. "How do you remember that?"

"I remember everything, well, at least the interesting stuff," he said, tapping his head with his finger. "So . . . leaving the big San Fran?" he asked, examining the boxes and bags piled all around me.

I choked a laugh. "For a while. Long story."

He smiled pleasantly, "Yeah, I think I caught that."

"Oh yeah," I said meekly.

"From the looks of things, he took pretty good care of you."

I feigned a laugh. "Sure. This and a checking account with seventeen dollars is everything I own in the world." I waved my hands to show off my bounty.

He turned and looked down the road. "I heard about your dad. How's he doing, anyway?" he asked, changing the subject.

In a small town nothing is left private. I was sure the story of my dad having a heart attack in the middle of the grocery store had gotten out to every person, child, dog, and cat in the entire upper valley, even before the news reached me.

"He's home from the hospital. So I guess that's the good news."

It had happened one week ago. After the big split, I hadn't planned on coming home. In fact, that was the last thing I wanted to do. I had a degree in history I hoped to dust off and put to use once I got my teaching certificate. Then I got the call. My mother's usually quiet voice was barely audible as she explained my father had suffered a massive heart attack. He had lived, thank God, and was having quadruple bypass surgery as she spoke. There was no doubt what I had to do. I didn't know how long I would be gone, or if I would ever come back to San Francisco, but I wanted nothing more in the world than to see my family again. And especially to see my father and tell him how much I loved him. Make up for the way I had treated him since I'd married Cort.

"Glad to hear it," Luke said, bringing me out of my thoughts. "You'll be coming to the big party tonight, I hope?"

"Party?"

"I take it you're not in the social networking scene?"

I rolled my eyes. "Definitely not." When you have nothing to show for your life except a ruined marriage and a nice collection of shoes, one is less motivated to reminisce with old friends.

He wrote something in his notebook.

Seriously? He was going to give me a ticket? I must have been some lousy girlfriend.

He ripped it from his tablet and held it out to me. "It'll be quite a crowd. And if it's any consolation, you really look great."

Reluctantly I took the paper from his hands. The time and place of the party was hastily scrawled across the page. I let out a sigh of relief. I recognized his chicken scratches. His handwriting hadn't improved much since the tenth grade.

"Thanks. I'll think about it."

An awkward silence stood between us as we looked at each other. He really was handsome, with full lips, an angular tan face, and soft brown eyes. I wondered briefly why I hadn't paid more attention to him in high school. We'd even been in the same English class our senior year. But I had been too enamored with my boyfriend, Brandon Jensen, to pay poor Luke much attention.

"This is when you tell me that you're going to give me a warning, but that I need to take it easy on these lovely Idaho highways. Then you're going to tell me to have a nice day, which, by the way, is the last thing someone who has just received a ninety-dollar ticket wants to hear. Just so you know."

He laughed pleasantly again. I'd always been able to make him laugh. His laughter had the gentle effect of water bubbling over rocks.

"Got a bit of a lead foot, huh?"

"A bit."

"After all these years, you still have me wrapped around your tiny finger."

I smiled and readjusted my skirt again, my foul mood lifting.

"Any suggestions where I should park?" I asked.

"Maybe by the gas station. The parade runs down Bridge Street."

How could I forget the location of the one stoplight in town?

"When was the last time you were here?"

"I haven't been here for the Twenty-fourth for a really long time, but I came last Christmas to go skiing at Targhee with my husband." Something churned in my stomach when I called Cort my husband. "I mean ex." Foul mood hovered again.

"Well, anyway, try to make it tonight. It would be nice catching up."

"Yeah, it would," I agreed with little enthusiasm. In some ways I would have liked to see him again, but mostly the idea of "catching up" with old high school pals left a thick bloated mass in the bottom of my stomach. Luke was one thing, but what about all the others? What about Brandon? I could barely manage to think his name.

Brandon and I had dated my senior year of high school. He had begged me not to go to Stanford. He'd even proposed marriage, though I never told a soul since there hadn't been an official ring or anything. But how could I face him now?

"Thanks, again," I said as I shook his hand through the open window.

"Don't forget about tonight," he added.

I stared at our hands intertwined. Luke noticed and quickly withdrew his hand. He nodded, turned, and walked back to his patrol car. I watched him in my rearview mirror. He disappeared into his car. I blew air through my mouth, fastened my seat belt, and started the car with shaking hands, taking another deep breath as I crept out onto the highway.

Chapter Two

I watched a documentary once on homeless people. A lady, standing in line waiting for a place to sleep, had commented, "Most people are one month away from being homeless."

I remember looking around at the things in my beautiful row house—the antique hutch, our wedding china, the white sofa with the down cushions, the shag carpet, the oil paintings of the city proudly hanging on our sparkling white walls, and our nearly bottomless bank—and felt safely out of harm's grasp. But before I could register what was happening, I returned early one day to find Cort in bed with another woman. My tennis partner, Cheri. I haven't picked up a racket since. The pain and disgust I felt was unimaginable. My life became an upside-down cake, and I was the pineapple under a pile of uncooked goo. I felt like the Game of Life left abandoned on the table; all the little faceless bodies with their yellow and white convertibles going nowhere fast. Did they have a space in the game for days like this? *Your marriage failed; go back fifty spaces and try again.*

I passed a sign announcing St. Anthony was eight miles ahead. My eyes burned. I gripped the steering wheel and blinked hard. Four years ago I would have never guessed I'd be in this position. Even six months ago I would have denied I'd ever return home like this. My friend Clay had offered me his place while I looked for a job. But then my dad got sick and I was flat broke and the look in Clay's eyes told me he wanted more than a roommate.

Clay had been my saving grace at Stanford. At home I'd been one of the brightest. At Stanford I'd been just another number. Clay tutored me through statistics and nursed me through a number of letdowns.

He'd been a good friend. Then I met Cort. I fell head over hills for the handsome and rich fraternity brother who bought me new clothes--matching handbags and shoes-- and took me to expensive restaurants. I'd had my first real seafood with him, not trout like we caught in the streams in Idaho, but seared tuna and calamari, at a fancy little place just across the bay near Sausalito. He taught me how to sail, took me on fabulous day trips down Highway One in his Maserati, and introduced me to scuba diving—though I was a dismal failure.

He was one continuous thrill ride, and I fell in love. My life had seemed like a fairy tale.

The St. Anthony exit sign rose into sight. My stomach flopped like a dryer with loose sneakers bouncing around. I wasn't sure what to expect. Would I run into old friends who had happy, successful marriages and adorable babies? I had neither. But why should that have bothered me? I'd attended a prestigious university. I'd lived in a beautiful home and had more money than most of these people could ever dream of having. Even though it had been short term, it had, for a moment, been wonderful, and someday I would get that old life back. *Yes,* I reminded myself, *this town is a short-term fix*. A tiny dot on a map. A place you filled up on gas and grub before heading up to Yellowstone National Park. Not a place you come back to.

The sign announced the population had not changed in thirty years; hovering over 3,000, depending on what was happening over at the funeral home or the local hospital. St. Anthony was a place to have moved from or through. Its influence was like a tiny atom exploding in a million different pieces. Seven degrees removed and you could find someone who'd grown up in Fremont County. It was like Kevin Bacon. I'm not kidding. The stories of running into someone across the country from good old St. A were endless.

While its fame included not only an NFL player, and the birthplace of 1985 Miss America's husband, *and* a small grunge band member, it's most impressive—not to mention legitimate—claim to fame was that of Andrew Henry, the explorer who erected the first building by an American in the present state of Idaho in 1810, just five miles south of town against the Henry's Fork of the Snake River. He occupied it for one winter, and word is they nearly starved to death and resorted to eating some of their mules to survive. They abandoned the fort the next spring, never to return. One thing this town was not for: the faint of heart.

I turned into a gas station and parked between a small Geo Metro and a red Blazer reminiscent of the one Britney Cline drove into a ditch right after she got her license. I barely had enough room to inch my body between them, getting my olive Prada bag stuck on the Blazer's mirror more than once. Luckily no one seemed to notice. I yanked the bag firmly over my shoulder and set the alarm. The sun was high overhead. I adjusted my Kate Spade shades and examined my surroundings, aware of how ostentatious the Mercedes seemed next to the other cars; their rusted bodies and dented fenders looking sheepishly apologetic. I shook the feeling and held my head high. I would not allow their poverty to make me feel guilty for the few things I still owned.

Crossing the bridge near the veterans' park, I recognized the familiar green "dough boy" soldier standing tall on his platform. Stoic and focused, he seemed to watch me. Recognize me. I hadn't realized it before, but I always looked for him when I came home. It gave me comfort and made me feel protected.

"Yes, it's me. Don't laugh too hard now," I admitted to the statue. Spray from the Henry's Fork river below cooled my sweating face. My legs shook like they were on one of those fat gyrators, like the whole world was staring at me. It wasn't true, of course. All eyes were toward the parade down the street, and yet, I couldn't shake the feeling. I closed my eyes and blew out nervous air. This was no big deal. I'd just get through the crowd and quickly walk home. The rush of the rapids encouraged me forward.

The crowd ahead blocked the roads and sidewalks on either side. I looked for an opening, but it was elbow-to-elbow bodies. I grimaced. I'd have to just make an opening then. I attempted to squeeze through a small space. It was smaller than it looked, or I was bigger than I thought. I became stuck between two heavyset women, all breasts and thighs and plump legs. It was like I'd been dropped into a bucket of Kentucky Fried Chicken. I willed myself thinner, but I remained wedged between their love handles. My movement caught their attention. They both turned and stared at me with their blue eye-shadowed glares and matching Aqua Net dos, throwbacks to the seventies. I felt like a paperback novel between two bookends. They eyed my stilettos and miniskirt with disdain. I remembered what Luke had said about wearing short skirts

It was no use. They weren't budging. I wiggled back out. I pushed my long, blond hair away from my sweating neck and readjusted my shades. My bangled wrists clinked musically. Several faces, all unknown to me, turned to see what the commotion was about. I smiled faintly and shimmied my skirt as far down as I could without exposing too much tummy.

"Give a hand to our grand marshals, Mr. and Mrs. Bennett," a speaker to my left boomed. A balding, heavyset gentleman and his tiny, black-haired wife waved from a black surrey, "spit shined like a dandy's shoes on a Sunday morning" as my aunt Bert used to say. They smiled at the crowd. All the unwanted attention around me turned back to the parade.

I took another step backward and searched for another escape route. My heart thumped like a native's drum when I recognized an athletically built man resembling Brandon's frame. Something rose in my throat. My knees felt hollow. *Please don't be him, please don't be him,* I prayed, certainly not prepared to see him yet. How could I admit that he had been right all along? That I never fit in with the high-society city people. That Cort and I had been like oil and water for most of our marriage. The idea of facing him was frightening. I'd rather jump off the Fun Farm Bridge. Of course, it was pride, but all I wanted now was a long bath and a cup of my mother's soothing hot chocolate, even if it was ninety degrees outside. The man turned sideways. I froze and prepared myself for the shock of it. Except, the man's face was not Brandon's. He was at least ten years older, and his outline was completely different. A rush of relief blew through me. I shook out my arms. Paranoia was really getting to me.

Along the curbs children swarmed like flies around taffy, Tootsie Rolls, and Dum Dum sucker droppings. They stuffed their pockets with their treasures and hollered at the fire truck—crawling with little boys in baseball uniforms—to throw more. From the kids' perspective, the parade seemed to be a great success. I had loved the parade as a kid. It had been the highlight of my summer. Of my year, almost. Once again, that sense of nostalgia burned in my chest. I blinked several times and took two big breaths to clear my head. I was turning weepy again.

What was I nostalgic about anyway? Certainly not this backward town. Once upon a time it had been a happening place. During the prohibition years, the town boasted pea seed factories, lumber mills, mercantiles, jewelry stores, several banks, a theater called the Rex, and a couple department stores—the kind where the clerks brought you clothes to try on, and then wrapped them in special boxes tied with ribbon, all for free. The town even supported two grocery stores and a couple drugstores with ice-cream fountains where I used to ride my bicycle for an Ironport cherry soda or a bubble gum ice-cream cone.

My sister Melissa and I used to lie on the mahogany stools and count the colorful mountains of chewing gum stuck underneath the counter. It was like a collection of squished rocks with teeth marks. Dating back twenty years at least. I think we stopped around two hundred. Then, feeling as rebellious as the kids who spray painted initials or the year of their graduation on the water tower or on one of the abandoned sugar beet factories outside of town, we added our wads to the mix.

Unfortunately, most of the old brick buildings built over a century ago had fallen victim to decay; abandoned for the bigger department store, the fashionable mall 45 minutes away, leaving the local merchants with old inventory and little hope for survival. But memories of my Norman Rockwell-like town were always close to my heart, in spite of how backward it seemed to me now as an adult.

My heavy heart thumped for home. That was all I wanted: to go home and see my father. Wrap my arms around him and listen to him recount stories from his childhood, even though I'd heard them a thousand times before.

The two large women shifted, and an opening appeared. Determined to get through, I wormed my way between them. But like before, the hole sealed up just as I was halfway through. My feet hovered off the ground. My chest was jammed against the ladies' sweaty, large arms. I reached my foot forward so I could shimmy my way out, but there was no ground beneath it. I slipped. My sparkling silver Jimmy Choos went flying, leaving one heel stuck in the crack of the sidewalk and the other getting smashed beneath someone's large boot. The two women turned. The hole expanded. I fell to the ground. My Kate Spade sunglasses went flying across the cement. I caught myself with my hands as I landed hard on my knees. Everything went quiet. My hands stung. I felt a thousand eyes on my butt. I knew my skirt was up around my hips. I prayed I wasn't wearing my black lacy underwear.

The crowd parted around me. My knees burned. Reaching between one of the women's legs, I searched for the shades.

"Excuse me," I apologized, silently praying that I wouldn't touch her. My fingers swiped the edge of the shades. The woman took a step backward. My face contorted in pain as she rested all her weight on my now splintered hand.

"Excuse me!" I yelped, trying to keep from howling like a crazy person. She didn't budge. Pain shot up my wrist. My body did a little spasm. I groaned.

"You're standing . . . on my . . . ouch!" I yelled. She took a step forward.

"What the hell?" she gasped when she recognized me kneeling beneath her. She lifted her foot. I scooped up my nearly flattened hand and what remained of my three hundred-dollar shades and pushed myself up. No sorry, no apology from the big fat lady as I adjusted my now skiwampus shades onto my sweating face. I dusted my scraped knees off and slipped my sweaty foot back into one of my sandals. I swung my designer bag back over my shoulder. It smacked one of their elephantine arms.

Talk about making a grand entrance.

They both turned back to me and glared. I mumbled another apology as I hopped on one foot while stretching the other backward in hopes of easing back into my sandal. Naturally, it didn't work. My foot only groped the tip of the sandal as it had turned sideways, preventing my toes from hooking the shoe.

"Dammit," I murmured under my breath. Hot tears flooded my eyes. I gave up looking graceful, hobbled over to my shoe, yanked it out of the crack in the sidewalk, and shoved it firmly onto my foot. Then I readjusted my skirt and pulled my hair back from over my eyes, and tucked it smartly behind my ears. The two women gave each other a knowing look. That raised eyebrow that I had seen a lot in my life and had learned to ignore. I stumbled away from them, feeling the familiar pink flush warming my face. I was the biggest klutz. It was like I had been given two feet that had identity crises. They seemed to have a way of making grand and very ungraceful entrances.

There was a gap in the parade. I quickly crossed the street. A young girl around twelve handed me a paper. An advertisement for a local dance studio. I folded it up and looked for a recycling container. There was nothing resembling even a garbage can. I stuffed it in my bag. I started walking. A red-haired boy around eleven handed me another flyer. I tried to refuse it, but the kid kept pushing it in my hands. I gave in and took it. Day care advertisement. It joined the dance studio in my bag.

A skinny blond-haired boy around ten wearing a skater hat and shorts that just barely hung on the edge of his hips blocked my path. He chugged a melted Otter Pop, and then let the wrapper flutter through his fingers. It flew through the air and smacked against my newly scuffed shoe. "Hey!" I yelled, "Little dude!" I pointed to my Jimmy Choos now streaked with red sticky syrup. The boy shrugged and turned back toward the parade.

I bent down and swiped the loose wrapper. Then I pushed through a crowd of kids and tapped the boy on the shoulder. "Excuse me, but you just littered on my . . . my shoe." I almost told him how much the shoes had cost me, but held my tongue. I hadn't forgotten how unbelievable it would have sounded in a town that did most of its shopping at the dollar store.

"I don't know where a garbage is," he whined, pushing his shoulder away from me and turning back to the local town commissioner who was offering free bubble gum.

I moved in front of him and bent down to his level. "Then put it in your pocket," I explained with a smile that did not match my eyes. I held the empty wrapper out to him.

"Is there a problem here?" a heavyset man demanded, stepping from off to my left. He seemed vaguely familiar, like someone in my older sister's class. Someone you didn't want to mess with then, and by the looks of those button earrings and his lower lip filled with something I was pretty sure wasn't Big League-chewing gum, you didn't want to mess with him now either. My face turned hotter than it already was. I stammered that his son had littered, and I had suggested he put his garbage in a garbage can.

"Braxton!" he yelled.

The boy turned and yelled back, "What!"

The father's face turned brick red. "You get your butt back here and pick up your garbage!"

He turned back to me. "Jeez! Kids these days!"

I caught the boy's father eyeing my legs. I pulled at my skirt and wished it were longer. The cotton fabric stuck to my hands. Great! Now I was a walking Q-tip. That syrup was worse than tree sap.

I nodded and looked for another escape route. I couldn't believe I had just gotten after that kid about littering. I was more afraid of what the father might do to him. It had been a long time since I had been around kids. Maybe they all acted like that. Maybe I had stepped out of bounds. I rubbed my fingers together. The syrup had smeared all over my hands. I needed soap, water, and 90 proof hand sanitizer. Preferably one I could drink from. I reached into my bag and grabbed one of the advertisements to wipe the sticky mess off. It only smeared it worse. It would have to do until I got home. I looked for a trash can. The boy was right. Not a receptacle in sight. I wadded up the paper and shoved it into my bag, all the while thinking I would have to decontaminate it and myself as soon as I got to my parents' house.

I glanced around. The crowd was staring me down again. Not grateful, happy that I had stopped a new generation from littering stares, but rather, looks of perturbed parade goers whose perfectly happy festivity was being ruined. By me.

My feet ached. I stumbled toward a small set of stairs on the side of an old building to hide and rest my feet on until the parade was over. I plopped down on the second stair and closed my eyes. The heat of the sun burned against my skin. I scratched at my neck, wiping the perspiration away. So far this day was not going my way. Actually, this past year had not gone my way. I still couldn't believe that I was in this situation. Divorced, broke, alone. How did I not see this coming? If only I could go back to the Marlo of eight years ago, I'd tell her to run away from Cort as fast as she could.

There were signs, to be sure. The first forewarning there would be trouble was our names: Marlo and Courtney. Put it on an invitation, a piece of mail, a class list, some sort of registry, and nearly 100 percent of the time people got us mixed up. I couldn't blame them. My father had always wanted a son, and when daughter number two was born and my mother was forced to have a hysterectomy, the only thing my dad had power over was my name. And instead of Marley, like my mother had suggested, he stuck to his guns and insisted on Marlo after my Grandpa Marlo Leavitt. Made him feel more complete, I supposed, and my mother—feeling like she had let him down by failing to produce a son—didn't argue. It wasn't until I discovered Marlo Maples during a history project in high school that I realized the sex appeal of my name. If it was good enough to seduce a president, then what did I have to be ashamed of? Not that I had any aspirations of seducing anyone, let alone a president.

And Courtney, well, his name only made him more interesting. More desirable, if that were possible. So for four years I played the game of perfect housewife. I took meticulous care of the apartment, dropped off his laundry, cleaned the house from top to bottom, bought seafood from the little corner meat market on Wednesdays because he thought that was when it was freshest, paid the bills, and planned elaborate dinner parties for our friends. His friends, I realize now.

Sometimes, gloved up to my elbows, scrubbing the floors till I could have served dinner on them, I'd stop and wonder how I'd become this person. I had left my backward-thinking small town and joined the ranks of women capable of anything. Then I met Cort, and I only wanted to please him. And to do so meant I had to become the woman not unlike his own mother, who was still the most particular housewife in all of Sonoma County. She had people come clean, but she followed behind them pointing out any blemish or spot they might have missed. I never could measure up to his mother's scrupulous OCD, and for all my scrubbing, manicuring, lessonings, and stylish dressing, I never fooled anyone. I played Bunco, bought the magazines, and wore the clothes, yet after all that, I was still the small-town girl from Idaho who couldn't seem to scrub the sand from under her fingernails.

The crowd sighed in unison. I opened my eyes. A giant carousel, crepe papered in blues and pinks and mechanically wired to turn counterclockwise, floated by. *No Rose Bowl Parade, but not bad,* I thought even as I realized I was biting my nails, an old habit that reared its ugly head when I was nervous or stressed. Cort would have a fit if he saw me gnawing away in public.

I turned to the side and spit out what remained of my thumbnail. It barely missed an old-fashioned black boot. I followed the worn boot up to find it attached to an older-looking woman in a flowery muumuu dress. She had salt-and-pepper hair pulled back in a tight bun, weathered brown skin, and sagging eyes that watched me curiously. She smiled slightly, her teeth pleasantly white under her thin lips. Despite her weathered skin she was a pretty woman. I didn't recognize her, but then again, I didn't recognize most of the people milling about. She nodded like I should know her. "Nice day?"

"Not that great. Not really the best year, either," I informed her.

"You need treat." She held out a Tootsie Pop. She waved it in front of me, coaxing me to take it. I was staring at it like I'd never seen a sucker before. Fact was, I couldn't remember the last time I'd eaten one. I reached out and took it from her hands.

"Thanks."

"You live here?" she smiled.

"No."

Again, "You live here?"

"No. I . . . my parents live a few blocks that way," I tried explaining, pointing down the road with the sucker.

Her eyes brightened. "Is a good place." She nodded. "You find answers here."

Her accent was unfamiliar to me. She looked Asian, or Native American, but the accent seemed Hawaiian. I simply nodded in agreement and hoped she'd be on her merry way. She winked and disappeared into the crowd.

My temples pulsed. I buried my head between my knees.

Nearly ten years ago I had escaped this low-budget town, vowing to never return, promising myself bigger and better things, and yet, as I watched the parade pass by, a wash of relief swept over me; a feeling that I was home again.

I pulled my head up from between my knees and wiped my brow. Then I pulled out the chocolate-flavored Tootsie Pop and plopped it in my mouth. I held up the paper to block out the glaring sun. I searched for the shooting star and Indian with the arrow on the wrapper. *That's what I need; a shooting star of my own,* I thought. Some kind of good luck.

The crowds parted again. There was no time to dawdle. I wadded up the wrapper and dropped it next to the other scrunched up papers in my bag, crossed the street, and made my way down the neatly manicured and tree-lined street toward home. Places I had passed by a million times as a kid; neighbors I had known and loved all my life. Three blocks down I turned the corner and caught sight of the beautiful turn-of-the-century white colonial where I spent my childhood. I sighed in relief. The old lady was right about one thing. This was a good place: a good place to visit and help my mother nurse my father back to health, a place to get answers, but after that, I was out of here.

Chapter Three

"Marlo? Marlo, is that you?" I heard over the clanking of dishes and shuffling of feet.

My mother appeared in the kitchen doorway, pink dress shirt and an apron around her waist, a dish towel thrown over her shoulder. She wore white golf shorts and the same white tennis shoes she wore when I was in high school. Her brown hair from a bottle was cut just under her chin in a no-nonsense bob and had grown out a little, revealing the relentless greys she can't seem to get rid of. Her large brown eyes smiled as she recognized her youngest daughter. She was immediately at my side, fussing over how long my hair had become, asking about the drive, and worrying that I was hungry.

She was a welcome sight.

"You're too thin, Marlo. You haven't stopped eating meat, have you? I know how those San Francisco hippies are," she said in her sing-song voice. She could tell someone to go to hell and they would probably thank her. I'd never known anyone that could get away with more political incorrectness than my mother.

"Yes, Mom, I still eat meat. I just don't eat as much these days."

"It looks to me like you don't eat much of anything these days. What you need is a good elk steak. That'll cure those hollow cheeks."

Her eyes swept down past my outfit, landing on my shoes.

"Those are some fancy shoes. What do you call them?"

"High heels?" I suggested, certain she didn't care about name brands.

"Oh, I thought maybe they were called hooker shoes." She laughed lightly. "Robert!" she sang out.

“Mom, don’t make him get up. I’ll go see him.”

“You might want to pull that skirt down a bit. Don’t want to give the old man another heart attack,” she said softly, a teasing sparkle in her eye.

My dad sat in his beloved recliner, remote in one hand, iced tea in the other. He looked pretty good despite just having had heart surgery. He wore a pair of blue sweats and had on a black and gold University of Idaho T-shirt. His alma mater. He’d grown up on a farm, but was more interested in the machinery than cows and sheep. Now he worked at the local dairy factory where they made cheese and other products. He managed people. That was all I knew. His receding hair wisped across the top of his head; technically a comb-over, but it worked for him. His ruddy complexion made him look as though he’d just finished some heavy exercise. Rosacea. He’d had it for years. Besides, his protruding stomach gave away the truth of the matter anyway.

“How was the parade?” he asked, slowly attempting to sit up.

I shrugged. “It was the parade; lots of candy.” I gave him a quick hug and sat on the arm of his recliner.

“How ya doing, Mar Bar?” he asked, tapping my arm with his pudgy, calloused fingers.

“I should ask you that question.”

“Why? My heart’s fixed. I want to know how yours is doing.”

I wrapped an arm around his shoulder and patted him gently. “I’m doing okay. Glad to be home.” I couldn’t believe it, but I honestly meant it. There was nowhere I’d rather be than with my family.

“Well, good, ’cause your mom there has planned a welcome home party for ya.”

“What?” I turned to my mom who was standing in the doorway watching us. “Oh no, Mom, please, I’m really not ready for parties.”

She threw her hands up in protest and crossed the room. “Now, Robert, don’t tease her. It’s only family, honey. Melissa and Troy, and your aunt Bert and uncle Stewart. Just a small group.”

Still too big in my opinion.

"What are you making?" I asked, noticing her hands were covered in dough.

"Oh, I just thought I'd throw an apple pie together."

I smiled. My mom made a killer apple pie. It was my favorite, and she knew it. I could taste the sweet cinnamon mixture now. "I'll help," I said, jumping up and following her to the kitchen.

The kitchen was a mess. Not a gross "I can't eat in here" kind of mess, but the organized, chaotic kind. My mom worked fast and furious, usually leaving a path of destruction to rival a tornado. We used to call her Tas, for the Tasmanian devil.

I always admired my mom. Always wanted to emulate her, but after spending four years around Cort's mom, Diane, I had begun to believe Diane was her superior. Diane was sophisticated, smart; a woman to contend with, but she had little room for the simple things that make life so meaningful. Cort said he couldn't remember a time she had sat on a couch and read him a story or tousled his hair. Everything had been scheduled. Including her love. Nothing got to my mom. She loved to feed people. And she did it through opening her doors to anyone. My mother-in-law saw a great need to feed the homeless and did it through large cash donations and service hours in different capacities of her choosing, all while staying crisp in her linens and pearls, which made for good publicity shots. My mom quietly served her family, digging in and helping out. Watching my mom smile at me—only joy and relief upon her simple face—I knew that there was nothing Diane Kensington could hold over Linda Leavitt.

I got lost in my mother's quick hands as she rolled out the dough and had it neatly fluted around the top of the pie pan and into the oven while I just stood and watched. So much for helping.

"Hon, would you mind pulling the steaks out of the fridge? They're in that glass casserole dish."

"Sure."

My mom glanced at the window. "Parade must be over. Bert and Stew just drove up."

I glanced out the window. My uncle Stew, a smallish, thin man, was holding the car door open for Aunt Bert who was struggling to get her large frame out of her Cadillac. I frowned. I knew I would have to face people sooner or later. I just didn't think it would be within an hour of returning home. But I didn't want to disappoint my mom. She thought she was doing me a favor. She seemed to read my face. She turned to me and rested a hand on my shoulder.

"Don't you worry about a thing," she assured me. "They're family, and they are so thrilled to have you home again. Now go open the door for Bert. I think she's got her cane stuck in the screen."

I stifled a smile.

"Hello, hello! Anybody here?" Aunt Bert called from the side door leading directly to the kitchen. She was holding a Tupperware bowl in one arm while supporting her large body with a cane in the other.

"I brought potato salad," she announced.

I hinted at a smile and took the salad from her.

"Oh my lands! You sweet thing." Aunt Bert tugged and patted like I was a freshly wounded bird that only needed some stretching and plucking to be made whole again.

Bert was my father's much-older sister. Unlike me, she was tall and big-boned like my father, and she'd easily gained fifty pounds since I last saw her five years ago, and added twenty years to her age. My uncle stood behind her and said nothing. He was bald with a beaklike nose and rarely spoke of anything that was not mechanical or science related. He usually only spoke to my dad. He disappeared in the living room. Some things didn't change. Including Aunt Bert. She was always happy. She saw everything in life through an optimistic lens: every lost job a new opportunity, every sickness a chance to learn compassion.

"Well, I'm just pleased as punch to see you back, dear," her big voice boomed, much the opposite of my mother's sweet lilting voice that was now arguing with my dad about his staying in his chair while she cooked the steaks. Aunt Bert didn't seem to hear them.

"You wait, dear. You're gonna see this old town through fresh eyes, I just know it." She fell into one of the comfortable corduroy sofas in my parents' living room with a soft grunt. There she was, making lemonade out of my life. I wished I could share her enthusiasm.

I sat down opposite her and looked out the window, wondering how I'd see anything with fresh eyes. My eyes felt tainted and prejudiced. "I don't know about that," I answered softly, still staring out at the blue sky.

"When I returned from college," she began, giving me the *listen and learn* stare, "I went to church one Sunday and looked around at all those old, white-haired knuckleheads who'd been stuck in this town for years and I thought they were dumb as sticks. I didn't understand why they would choose to live here on purpose, so I figured they were just ignorant old sheep."

She chuckled to herself. "College graduates are the ones that don't know diddly-squat. They've learned a few things from a book or listened to the ranting of some ideological professor, and they think they are mightier than a king and his army. But you can't beat experience out of a book." She smiled like she'd just shared the wisdom of the ages with me.

I loved my aunt Bert, but sometimes she talked in riddles, and on days like today, when my head was barely staying attached at the neck, I didn't want to beat anything out of anything or anybody. I just wanted to sleep.

"I don't plan on being here too long. Just long enough to help nurse my dad back to health. Then I've got to get a job, and I don't think I'll find anything decent around here."

She raised her blue eye-shadowed, deep-set eyes in surprise. "Oh? Well . . . decent jobs are hard to come by, but they're out there." She clumsily pushed her way to the edge of the sofa. "I'll tell you this. I've done my fair share of traveling, and there is never any place that feels as good as home."

"You're right about that," I had to agree. I just wasn't quite sure where my home was.

The patio door blew open from a breeze. The wafting aromas of grilling meat interrupted our conversation.

"What's he doing out there? You burning my steak, Robert?" she yelled hoarsely. She gave me a quick wink and heaved herself out of the thick sofa and hobbled to the back patio to check on my dad.

I remained on the couch, staring at the walls. Not much had changed. Not my aunt Bert or my dad refusing to listen to my mother and stay in his chair instead of cooking steaks, despite his doctor's warnings. Not even this room with its white walls and built-in bookshelves, the roller shades with the decorative fringe hanging off the ends; all the same. Not even the painting depicting a ship out to sea hanging over the fireplace had been moved.

My parents had purchased the oil painting on their honeymoon in Spain. The vibrant greens and blues twisted from the stormy sky and stretched toward the water, causing the sea to shift violently. As a young girl I stared at the painting for hours. If I glared hard enough, the boat seemed to come alive, and I could almost hear the waves crashing against the bow as it threatened to crack the stern and take it down. I wondered where the captain was. Had he taken shelter down below with his crew? Was there light or had they doused it from fear of starting a fire? My life felt a bit like that storm. Like I was taking cover in the hull of the ship, waiting for the tempest to break. Needing protection.

I stood and admired the curved ceiling and built-in bookshelves. One of the first homes ever built around here, it was probably a hundred years old. My father used to tell the story of the man who lived here years ago. He'd been a prominent banker, until one particularly grey day, just after the crash of twenty-nine when he made his way over to the city park, just across the river, took off his shoes and socks, his watch and his grey bowler hat, and flung himself into the raging waters. I was thirteen when I first heard that story. For a long time afterward, I had nightmares that a certain a man in a dripping suit was standing over me. Eventually I overcame my fear and learned to love the unique character of the old white clapboard house with its tall ceilings and quaint parlor that overlooked the river.

I glanced out the sliding door toward the sunroom my father built some years ago. I used to sit and listen to the river rush by, the air thick with geraniums, hostas, and other plants my mother insisted on growing, even though the harsh Idaho climate wouldn't tolerate them. In the sunroom she could have any kind of rainforest she wished for. As I started toward it, the sound of a car pulling into the driveway caught my attention.

I recognized my sister Melissa's Land Cruiser. Melissa and her husband Troy were sitting in the front. They had three kids. Two girls and one little boy. Troy was a local boy who farmed with his father. It was one of those rare stories where the farmer was actually prosperous. Potatoes equaled French fries equaled McDonalds. Who knew?

I wiped my hands nervously on my skirt. Though Melissa and I had been very close when we were young, we grew apart when Melissa went to college. During her second year, she dropped out of school and married Troy. Everyone thought she was pregnant, but she just wanted to get married. When I was accepted to Stanford, Melissa became even more distant. Sometimes I wondered if she'd have been happier if I'd held myself back; stayed home, attended the same community college, and gotten married and pregnant by the time I was twenty-one.

With no other option than running out the back door, I met them at the front door.

"Melissa!" I smiled. Melissa stood in the door, pulling at her striped blue and white blouse and eyeing my outfit. She shifted her feet and flipped her shoulder-length brunette hair around. Her lips were set tight in worry. Her deep-set eyes looked tired. She was heavier than the last time I'd seen her. I was embarrassed to notice it, but there it was. I figured it was because of the baby, even though by the looks of him he wasn't a baby anymore.

She only stared back at me in surprise. "I didn't see your car out there."

She seemed put off. Surprising her was not a good way to get back in Melissa's good graces.

"I got in a little earlier than expected and couldn't get through because of the parade. It's parked at the gas station."

"Oh-oh, lead foot's back in town," Troy teased, pushing past Melissa who was still stuck in the doorway. Troy was athletic built, with dirty blond hair, blue eyes, and a smile that never dimmed. He gave me a big hug.

"Funny story, actually," I said, as we made our way to the kitchen. "I got pulled over by none other than Luke Dawson."

Melissa set down a covered casserole dish and opened the fridge. "He always had a crush on you," she said without looking up.

"No, he didn't."

"Yes, he did. He asks about you all the time. I saw him a few days ago and told him you were coming home." She opened and closed a drawer in the fridge.

My mouth dropped. A thousand thoughts ran through my head. He knew I was coming home? He had totally played stupid. Once again, I didn't know whether to be flattered or offended.

"He probably was waiting for you. Looking for an excuse to pull you over," Melissa said smugly as she grabbed a carrot and took a loud bite. She closed the fridge door.

"Well, I bet he didn't have to try very hard with the way you drive," Troy added with a grin as he leaned around me and grabbed an olive from the relish tray sitting on the counter.

I glanced down at the two little girls that looked just like their mom, Maddy and Maura. They blinked their wide blue eyes at me. They didn't know me. I searched my brain to remember which one was which.

"Hi. I'm your aunt Marlo. Do you remember me?" I asked stupidly.

They didn't answer, but clung tight to their mom's legs, grocery sacks full of candy wrapped snuggly around their fingers.

"Marlo, they haven't seen you in a year and a half. That's like a lifetime to a child," Melissa reminded me as she pulled Maura or Maddy off her leg.

My face turned the color of current wine. I hadn't been a very good aunt to the girls these past few years, if ever.

"And look at this little guy." I leaned in to get a better look at Brayden. His eyes were as big as bowling balls.

I scrunched my eyebrows and pulled away. "What is that smell?"

"He pooped his diaper on the way over. I was going to go change him," Melissa smacked shortly.

"I'll take him, honey," Troy offered, taking the diaper bag off of Melissa's shoulder.

"He's not potty trained yet?"

"Marlo, he's not even two. That's pretty normal," Melissa muttered, the frown on her face evidence that I had hurt her feelings somehow. Though, like always, I had no idea what I'd done this time.

"Oh. Well, I don't know this stuff. When do kids get potty trained?" I tried, hoping to ease the tension.

"When they're ready," she answered sharply.

"Hello, hello!" my mother called from the sunroom. Her sweet voice melted the cold air between Melissa and me. She appeared in the doorway. Her once white apron was now smudged with brown steak stains.

"How do you like your steak?" my dad called through the screen door.

"Just carry mine through a warm kitchen," Troy yelled with a smile.

I wrinkled my face at the mental picture. "Well done for me, Dad!" I yelled, hoping he wouldn't offer me the same steak as Troy's.

Maddy and Maura, who up until now had been too enthralled in our banter to go looking for Grandma, tore around us and nearly knocked my mom down with their hugs around her knees.

"Time to eat, everybody!" Bert called from the back patio.

"Here, would you take this?" my mom asked, giving the relish dish to Troy, and the basket of cornbread to me. Troy hesitated.

Melissa grabbed the relish dish. "He's going to change Brayden's pants," she explained.

"Okay, oh yes, I think I caught wind of that," Mom smiled. "Yep. Why don't you go do that, Melissa, and let Troy take the relish tray?" Mom said.

"Troy offered to change the diaper," Melissa snapped. The room went quiet. Troy took the baby from Melissa. "I brought brownies," Melissa stated loudly, probably wanting to get the attention off Braden's soiled diaper and needing accolades.

We stared at her, trying to separate the visual image of Brayden's diaper and the pan of hot brownies now sitting on the counter. I wondered what Cort would have done if I had made him change the poopy diaper, but I already knew the answer.

My mother was the first to speak. "Thank you, dear. That was sweet of you."

"How was the parade?" my father asked his granddaughters as they hurried out to the picnic table. The girls cheered, showing Grandpa their grocery sacks bulging with candy.

Outside was a spinning wheel of activity. Bert barked orders about where we should sit, and my uncle Stew dominated my father's attention with shop talk about a broken piece of machinery he was working on. The girls ran up and down the grass. They stared over the lava wall that overlooked the river before running back to the patio where they hopped and squealed in delight. I set the cornbread on the table. I kept thinking about Luke. He knew I was coming. I had to suppress a grin. I sat where Aunt Bert assigned me. A blessing was offered by my father, thanking God for my safe return and our family for being reunited again. I sneaked a peak at the family: My aunt Bert, head erect, eyes shut tight. Uncle Stew, head buried in his chest, eyes open. The little girls stealing olives. Melissa, head bent, eyes open. Her mother and Troy, both intent on listening. I finally managed to shut my eyes as the prayer ended, amens echoing into the beautiful afternoon.

Chapter Four

"This steak is great,"Troy said, still chewing.

"Don't thank me. I couldn't get your father to sit," my mother quipped.

"Did you hear that Beatles remake? I've got it in the player," Dad said, not listening.

"I have it too!"Troy beamed. Troy was like the son my father never had. They both were addicted to football, liked the same kind of music (Beatles, Creedence, Led Zeppelin, etc.), and fished like they couldn't breathe unless they were hip high in waders on the river.

"Bob, you stay right where you are." My mother attempted to hold down his forearm when he shifted to get out of his chair. "You need to take it easy."

"I am taking it easy. I'm just going to turn on the CD player," he grumbled.

"I'll do it, Dad,"Troy insisted as he pulled back his chair and disappeared through the sunroom door. Within a minute, Paul McCartney's distant voice filled the parklike backyard. My parents' backyard was one of the best-kept secrets in the whole town. The soaring trees provided shade, the river, a soothing hum, and the roses that lined the back patio, a sweet fragrance. Because of its position, there was a natural and sweet-smelling breeze that drifted through the open windows, providing a cheap alternative to air conditioning. Many summer evenings, we'd climb into the canoe or just sit down on the dock and fish while we ate beef jerky and drank Dr Pepper until the sun went down. All possible, just steps from our backyard.

When the old-timers settled this place there was nothing but sagebrush and sand and lava from ancient volcanoes. This house—being among the first to be built—sat high above the river. Today, the cottonwoods, heavy with foliage, soared into the sky even as the nearby river resonated through the leaves that shaded the large backyard and provided a wonderful canopy in which to protect us from the hot summer heat.

My dad sighed happily and leaned back in his chair. No one moved from the patio table. I played with my steak while Aunt Bert rattled off the latest gossip.

"Remember that girl, oh . . . what was her name, Coralynn? She just got married. And Lee Carter has three children. They live just behind me, the cutest little troublemakers you have ever seen. You probably heard, but that cute little patootie you used to chum around with, the violinist?"

"Bridget?" I said.

"Yes, that's right. Bridget. She got pregnant and ended up marrying some basketball player at the university, but then he started up with her sister, oh, Melissa, what was her name?"

She snapped her fingers in Melissa's direction. Melissa was busy cutting up bits of hot dog for Brayden, who banged his legs noisily against the high chair. Melissa's strained face looked like she was ready to crawl off the table.

"Luann. Maddy, don't stick your hands in the peas," Melissa said softly, pulling Maddy's hand out of the bowl.

"That's right, Luann. So Bridget was heartbroken and took off for a while leaving her parents to raise the baby. Now here's the funny thing. Are you listening, 'cause here it comes. Bridget couldn't get it together and took off to Vegas. Now this little girl's parents are really her grandparents, her sister is really her mother, her other sister is really her aunt, and her uncle is really her father. Got that all?" She leaned back in her chair and crossed her arms, a big smile spread on her face. "I think somebody needs to call Oprah."

"I think somebody needs to call social services," my mother grinned.

In some ways I was thankful that Cort was not here. I wanted this life to be a small, very minuscule part of me, something distant that I could reflect on as I lived in my other world; the one with friends and money and exotic vacations. But those friends were gone, gone alongside the money. And so was Cort. And this life, gnawing my dad's chewy steaks and choking down my aunt Bert's potato salad with too much mustard, seemed to be my new reality unless I could make some changes after Dad was well.

"So, Troy," I had to change the subject, "I hear you're working as a search and rescuer."

"Sure am."

"How's that going?"

"It's dangerous, and he gets called out at all hours of the day. I hate it," Melissa interjected while simultaneously spoon-feeding Bert's potato salad to Brayden. He squished up his nose in disgust and spit it back out. I wanted to do the same.

"Honey, it's not that bad. I get called out probably once every three months. Winter is busier than summer, but then, you never know. Keeps me on my toes, and that's what I like about it."

"Please keep your potatoes in your mouth, Brayden! Troy, would you help me with him? Maura, stop banging your fork against the table." Melissa seemed exhausted.

"They're okay, honey," my mother promised.

"Can we go play on the hammock?" Maura asked, appearing desperate and hopeful at her mother.

Melissa sighed, "Yes, but stay right around here and keep Maddy with you."

"Yeah!" they hollered as they jumped from the table.

"Keep away from the wall or you'll have to come sit by me!" she yelled after them. "They love playing sink the pirate ship on the hammock. Remember how we used to play that?" Melissa stated more than asked. I turned and watched the two little girls run to the hammock and clamber on. I tried to remember how old Maura was. She was a toddler when I had gotten married. She was probably six now. I didn't dare ask. I smiled as they lay side by side and pushed and pulled the hammock until it began to swing back and forth like a rocking ship. Their giggles were infectious. Everyone around the table smiled. Melissa and I had played the same game. Two damsels taken captive by pirates. We spent hours and hours traveling the world on our imaginary ship.

"I love children," my mother said smiling at her granddaughters. "All they need is a hammock and they are halfway around the world on a pirate ship. See, Bob, we don't need a swing set."

Melissa stood up. "Anyone want brownies?"

There was a chorus of "I dos" from the "pirate ship." Brayden lifted both hands in the air and yelled his own approval. Melissa stood and began gathering plates from everyone.

"I'll help." I followed her around the table, wishing I had thought to help before she had.

"You don't need to. You're the guest. I can do it by myself," she called over her shoulder.

"No, I don't mind. I need to get up anyway." I followed her to the kitchen. I didn't like being treated like the guest. I was in my parents' house, the same as her. I didn't want special treatment, and I was determined not to let it happen.

"So, not lovin' the new gig?" I asked once we were safely out of earshot.

"The Search and Rescue thing? It's fine. He loves it, so I support him. It's just he has three little kids to think about, and sometimes he just goes out there like Superman. Like he's invincible."

Melissa searched through the drawer for a knife. "How did you like Aunt Bert's gossip wrap-up?" she smirked.

"I love Aunt Bert, but her stories are exhausting!"

"At least she didn't get Dad on one of his 'we were so poor' stories."

I couldn't help but laugh.

"Do they still have those 'What's happening around town' columns?"

"Of course. 'Sally Luvgren had John and Trish Petersen over for dinner on Sunday. And the Kings were in Utah for the weekend picking up their son from school,'" Melissa mimicked.

I laughed out loud. "Don't forget the one where they talked about the Jorgens having someone over to measure for new cabinets!"

"Yeah, that worked out real well, because Mr. Jorgen had no idea they were getting new cabinets."

"That's because they weren't!" We both laughed out loud at the memory.

"Yeah, little towns," I agreed once the laughing subsided. It felt good to laugh with her. It had been so long since we'd spent any time together, it was like we hardly knew each other anymore, and it was nice to be with her again. Maybe my failed marriage would make her like me better.

"I wonder what they'll write about me."

"I don't think you've made the 'What's happening around town' column yet, but I could make it happen if I talked to the right people," Melissa snarked as she cut the brownies in perfectly equal squares, then set the knife down and started opening and closing drawers looking for something.

"I'm sure it'll be all over town by morning." I swiped leftover frosting and brownie off of the knife and licked it off my finger. "How is Dad?" I swallowed and looked back toward the patio. "He's certainly putting on a show that everything is normal. And no one has mentioned the heart attack. Is it something we aren't talking about?"

"Actually, he asked us not to mention it when you came home. He wanted this to be about you, not him."

"Why?"

"Thought it would be too much for you to deal with in one day, but don't worry; we've taken very good care of him."

"I'm sure you have," I said, feeling a sting to her words.

"Here it is," she pointed out, reaching for a small spatula. Melissa moved across the room and pulled out a new garbage sack from under the sink.

"You've probably already heard about the big party in the park."

"I did hear about that." I sighed, fishing through my pockets for the paper that Luke had given me. It was then I remembered my car parked over at the gas station.

"My car! It's still at the gas station."

"Do you need someone to drive you?"

"Seriously, I walked farther to get my laundry in San Francisco . . ."

"And it was uphill both ways, I'm sure," Melissa finished, rolling her eyes as she tossed the empty garbage sack over her shoulder and picked up the brownies.

"Let me help," I insisted. Reluctantly she allowed me to take the brownies from her hands. When we returned to the party, my father was plucking on his mandolin and my mother was humming along to some folk tune. Melissa went to empty the garbage can. Troy was swinging the three kids back and forth on the hammock. The girls giggled, and Brayden shouted unrecognizable orders. They caught sight of the brownies in my hands and squealed happily, jumping from the hammock and running straight for me. It was the first time they didn't seem deathly afraid of me.

I set the brownies down and watched the kids snag a piece. Melissa broke the spell when she dangled a full garbage bag in front of me. "Mind throwing this in the can on your way out?"

"No problem," I said taking it from her outstretched hand.

"Where are you going, dear? You just got here," my mother inquired with a wrinkled brow.

I explained about the car. My father insisted that I get a ride.

"Dad, it's only a few blocks away. I really don't mind. It's good to get out and exercise," I hinted. What I really needed was a break from trying to pretend that I was just as happy to be there as everyone else seemed to be. I wanted to belong to this family, to enjoy their stories and love the food, but instead, I became lonelier as I watched Troy and Melissa care for their children. More in the way as my mother catered to my father's needs. More alone as Aunt Bert told us stories about people I no longer knew or really cared about, while sopping up baked beans with her cornbread. Cort's mother would have delicately winced.

I watched my uncle Stew squirm in his chair and realized I had more in common with him than anyone else at the table. The thought sent a shudder down my spine.

"Hey, Marlo, I'll give you a ride. I've got to head out anyway," Troy said, staring at his phone.

"What?" Melissa asked.

"I just got beeped. Sand Dunes. Somebody got lost around Egin Lake. I shouldn't be too long, but I better head out."

Melissa's face crumpled.

"There's always at least one accident at the dunes on the twenty-fourth," Dad said, sneaking another bite of steak from off my mom's plate.

"Don't worry, we'll bring Melissa and the kids home if it gets too late," Mom promised.

"Thanks, Troy," I said, watching Melissa's face, "but I'd rather walk, and you need to hustle anyway."

"Thanks, Mom and Dad, for dinner," he called, grabbing his Coke and replacing his baseball cap on his head. "Great to have you back, Marlo."

I never called Cort's parents anything other than Diane and

Richard, and even then, I had avoided having to say that. Listening to Troy, I wondered why I had done that. Or had Cort's parents implied that was their wish?

I walked down the front steps and crossed the street. I walked everywhere in San Francisco: to the meat market, the little fruit and vegetable stand, my favorite bakery between Market and Fifteenth Street where they made the most delicious croissants every morning. With each step away from the house a burden felt lifted. It wasn't that I didn't love my family. I just felt so out of place. Plus it felt good to stretch my legs again. I grasped the straps of my bag and pulled it tight over my shoulder. I could smell the savory bakery as I traveled down the parade-littered streets, but soon realized the delicious scents were coming from the city park where late crowds lingered for a last-ditch hot dog or hamburger from one of the temporary booths.

The Henry's Fork of the mighty Snake weaved postcard-worthy around my neighborhood, and then cascaded into rippling waterfalls through the center of town. I longed to stop and watch. I leaned over the bridge and watched the river gush over boulders and rocks with magnificent force, turning the green waterway into caps of white waves. The sound of rushing water filled my ears with its pleasant white noise as a local folk singer played over the speakers at Keifer Park. The park was an island. On one side was a swift but silent canal, and on the other side, dangerous but breathtaking rapids bounding over volcanic rock. The smell of wet moss mixed with grease was a familiar signal of celebration from Pioneer Days to Fisherman's Breakfast to the weekly summer farmer's markets. I closed my eyes and allowed the familiarity to take me back in time, reliving moments of my childhood that were far more hopeful and innocent than anything I felt today.

A couple holding hands strolled across the bridge. As they passed they smiled and said hello. I murmured a shy, "Hello," back, wondering if I should know them. I watched them continue down the sidewalk and decided they didn't really know me but were just being friendly. I pulled my bag over my shoulder and crossed the street. I could just make out the outline of my car. I shook off the nostalgia and hurried toward it.

My car was all alone in the gas station parking lot, but something wasn't right. It seemed to have sunk. My stomach dropped.

My tires were flat. All four of them.

"Those sons of—"

"Is this your car?" a stocky man with bowed legs called from the doorway of the gas station.

"Yes," I acknowledged in shock.

He threw a hand through his dust-colored hair and yanked up his pants. "I noticed it about an hour ago. There were a bunch of kids loitering after the parade. I don't know if it was any of them, but it looks pretty suspect. Lucky for you there's a tire store next door." I glanced over at the tire store looking busy even on this holiday that wasn't officially a holiday. The man was already walking across the parking lot. I ran to catch up.

A young mechanic leaning over the engine of a truck stood when he saw us coming. The man explained my predicament. "Think you could get somebody over there?" the man asked.

"Sure thing, Raymond," the early twenty-something man agreed before disappearing into the building.

"Jim will get you all set up," "Raymond" assured me. I couldn't place him. When you grow up in a small town you expect to know everyone. Even in San Francisco I was constantly looking for a familiar face. Some habits die hard.

"Thanks for your help. I think I can take it from here." I turned to shake his hand.

"We've had a problem with kids loitering around the store for a while. I'll check around and see if I can find out who did it."

"Thank you. That is really nice of you," I said, touched by his kindness.

Raymond shuffled uneasily. "Well, I better get back. Young lady, let me know if I can do anything else to help you."

I watched as he made his way back to his station.

"So, someone slashed your tires?"

I turned toward the voice. It was Kale Brady, a guy I had a crush on throughout high school, but had never had the pleasure of dating. My first instinct was to turn away. I wasn't ready to face people like Kale. But it was too late. We stared at each other for several seconds. He looked older, more mature, obviously, and had grown a small goatee. His dark hair flipped out from under his grease-riddled red Cardinals baseball cap, and his bright aqua blue eyes sparkled like sapphires.

A smile edged his lips. "Well, I'll be. Marlo Leavitt? I didn't recognize you at first. You look all city girl and stuff." He examined my outfit. I pulled my skirt down a little. First thing when I got home I was going to change. He stared at my shoes. I wondered if he was going to call them 'hooker shoes' too.

"How do you walk in those things?"

"You get used to it." It was true to some extent. To be honest, my feet were aching. I would have to change shoes before walking home.

"And your hair got really long."

I touched my hair with my hand. I don't know why I did that. Like I was acknowledging his comment with physical touch. It had never been past my shoulders in high school. I'd finally let it grow down my back a few years ago. Cort liked it long.

"Let's go take a look." As we walked, Kale asked, "So what have you been up to these last eight years?"

I sped through the main points. School at Stanford; failed marriage. I cringed at having to spit out the failed part. I prided myself on never failing, never giving up. It was how I'd won every spelling bee from fourth until eighth grade. It was how I became head of the debate club and editor of the school newspaper, and how I was able to stay on the honor roll even while working at the local diner, and was, of course, what had made attending Stanford on a scholarship even possible. I abhorred failing.

"How about you?" I asked.

"National Guard. Not married. I've been dating a girl name Amanda for a while, but that isn't really working out."

"Sorry."

"Don't be."

We stood behind my car. He smiled at the sight of it. No, salivated might be a more accurate description.

"Mercedes AMG CLK55 series convertible. 5.5 liter, 362 horsepower with a V8 engine. 0 to 60 in 4 seconds." He whistled softly as he slowly caressed the hood of the car. He's response to seeing my car made me smile.

He squatted down and examined the tires. "Yep, all four tires slashed. How long you been back anyways?"

I checked my watch. "About three hours."

He laughed. "You make enemies fast. But with a car like this I don't think you had to try very hard." He turned back to me, squinting in the direct afternoon sun. "You don't have four spares in your trunk, do ya?"

"Nope. I do have a lot of other stuff though. In fact, everything I own is in that car." My face drained of any color. Kale read my thoughts. I fished for my keys and popped the trunk with one push of the button.

Everything was exactly how I'd left it; bags filled with clothes, boxes full of shoes and books, and a few miscellaneous last-minute throw-in items. I went around to the front and opened the door. Everything was still there, not even a missing pair of wedges, though the potted plant was wilting just a bit.

"You got a lot of junk in your trunk!"

I laughed at his double entendre.

"You're lucky they didn't get a hold of this."

"I don't think they did it for what I had in my trunk."

"The guys are going to love working on this baby."

"How long do you think it will take to get it fixed?"

He let out a breath of air as he adjusted his hat. "Tomorrow's Sunday so we won't get some new tires sent to us before Monday or Tuesday. Sorry, Marlo, but it's going to be a couple days."

I stared at the car in disbelief and rubbed my temples. I could feel a major headache coming on, and the hot sun wasn't helping.

"In the meantime, why don't I give you a ride home?" he asked.

"Are you sure? It would be good to take some of this stuff now. I'll come back later for the rest."

"No problem. We'll just have it parked inside the shop tonight. Is that okay?" he asked. I nodded gratefully.

Kale unloaded the two bags I pointed to while I grabbed the potted plant, and together, we returned to the tire store.

"Did you hear about the big shindig tonight at the park?" he asked as he helped me into the cab of his truck.

"I did actually." *Once or twice*, I thought to myself. This must have been the biggest thing since Nathan Craig had a huge bonfire out at his barn and nearly burnt the whole thing down. Not much happened around here.

"You remember Jenessa Barnes?"

How could I forget her? She had nearly run our school. My mother had mentioned a while back she ran the town now that her husband was mayor.

"Didn't she marry Trever Keaton?"

"Yep. He was sworn in as mayor a year ago. Jen apparently got some Pioneer Day money to fund the party. Might be worth going just to see what she comes up with."

"She had some great parties when we were young."

"Now she has the purse strings to go with it." He pulled into my parents' driveway and asked, "So what's next for you?"

"Honestly? I don't have a clue." I let out a laugh. "One thing is sure. I certainly don't plan on staying here too long. Talk about a wrong turn."

"Wrong turn?" His blue eyes instantly turned on me, his face far from vulnerable.

I swallowed, feeling that I might have just offended him, as I had offended my aunt earlier.

I peered out of the window, unsure of what I meant except that I didn't want to live in this little town.

"I do believe that somewhere along the way I made a wrong turn." I didn't want to end up buying my shoes at Wal-Mart like everyone else, but was pretty sure that actually saying this would ruin any sort of friendship we might have in the future.

"Sometimes wrong turns are like taking the scenic route."

"Look at you waxing poetic," I teased.

"It's true. Most of us are trying to figure it out. And most of us make a lot of mistakes, but that's what makes us who we are in the end," he said.

That was the problem. I didn't know who I was. I'd never felt like I belonged in California, but now, back in my hometown, I was no more near finding myself than I had been anywhere else. I shrugged.

"Anyway, I'll give you a call when the car is done," Kale said before he jumped out and pulled the bags from the back. We hugged, and then he was off, disappearing around the corner. I stood in front of the door and stared up at the house. I was officially home.

Chapter Five

As the afternoon wore on, the wind picked up, bringing storm clouds with it. I decided to bag the party. Not because of the turn in the weather, but because I had lost contact long ago with all my old girlfriends, and frankly, I couldn't handle seeing another old flame. I knew going to a party with everyone in town invited would be a lot like playing Russian roulette. Guys like Brandon Jensen were sure to be in attendance.

The late afternoon sun shown warmly across the kitchen table. I sat eating leftovers when my father walked in and sidled down beside me. I stabbed a piece of rubberized steak with my fork and stirred it in tiny circles in a blob of A-1 sauce.

"Hey, there," he said gingerly. "Mind if I join you?"

"Sure." I grabbed a celery stick, dipped it in ranch dressing, and handed it to him.

He bit off a small corner and chewed.

My father has a "white" personality. This is how my mom often started conversations with us when she wanted us to understand where he was coming from. Dad hates confrontation, especially when it involves one of his feisty daughters. My mom didn't just use this on Dad; she used it on all of us. "Melissa's a red, so you have to give her room. Troy's a blue. He just wants everyone to be happy," she often reminded us. I was a white/red, constantly at war with myself, and Cort had been a little bit yellow, a little bit white. Some days he was one thing; other days he was something totally different.

I could see that Dad didn't want to eat the celery or talk about his health, but I pushed forward anyway. "How are you feeling?" I asked.

He looked out the large kitchen window overlooking the circular drive and stared at the birch trees or the lamppost down the street or the neighbors' neatly trimmed hedges across the yard.

Finally he said, "Sore. Tired. But besides that I feel good." He rubbed his hands in his face, and then gave me a big smile.

"I'm glad the surgery went well. What do the doctors say?"

"That I'm doing better than they expected. The heart seems to be taking its new additions on well, and my blood pressure is stable. You know, same old same old."

He leaned his elbows on the table and rested his chin on his clasped hands. Then he gave me a stern look. "The real question is how are *you* doing?"

I flinched and looked out the window. "I'm doing great, seeing as how I am sitting here in this kitchen with you." I jumped up and made my way to the fridge. "Can I get you something to eat?"

"Maybe something to drink."

I grabbed two Cokes and popped the top of one before handing the other to Dad.

"Hmmm," he said, taking the soda and setting it on the table. He rubbed his belly and ignored the relish tray that was sitting in front of him. "How 'bout a piece of that jerky too?" he pointed to a sack of homemade jerky sitting beside my elbow.

"Are you sure that's a good idea?" I questioned, holding the bag away from him.

"Just one little piece. I didn't even eat the steak. Did you see that colossal-sized salad your mother made me eat? I'm starving." He looked at me with puppy-dog eyes. I tossed him the bag. He took one small piece, showed it to me, and then took a big bite as he closed his eyes and slowly chewed the salty meat. I laughed.

"Melissa says you aren't going to the big party tonight," he said reaching for the jerky bag.

"Oh no, you don't," I insisted, grabbing the bag and zipping it shut before throwing it onto the counter.

I glanced out the window and watched as Melissa helped the little girls into their car. I needed to talk with her. She had been moody ever since I came home. *I'll deal with her later,* I promised.

"It sounds fun, but I just got home, and I'd rather be with you and Mom," I tried.

"Just remember, most of those people don't live here, and when they leave, well, there won't be a lot of kids your age to hang out with. This isn't San Francisco, you know."

"You got that right," I muttered under my breath.

I pushed my cold meat aside and leaned back in my chair. "So why did you ask everyone not to talk about your heart attack when I came home?"

He stopped midswallow. I thought he might have another attack by the way his face turned beet red.

"Where did that come from?" he choked, as he washed the remains of his jerky down with his Diet Coke. He sat for several moments looking very uncomfortable. Finally he cleared his throat. His deep-set grey eyes looked suddenly very old. "I didn't say they couldn't talk about it. I just asked that they be sensitive to your situation. You've been through a lot lately. My thing is no big deal, Mar Bar. People wouldn't know except I had it in the grocery store. Aisle five, among the mops and brooms and laundry soap," he rolled his eyes and growled in self-contempt. I suppressed a smile.

"You had so much going on with your divorce and all that I wanted today to be about you."

I tapped my foot anxiously. "If I didn't think I could handle talking about your heart attack I wouldn't have come home." My hand pointed toward the window. "And besides, what about Melissa? She says she has been taking good care of you. She's totally bogged down with her three kids and Troy working so much. Didn't you worry about being *sensitive* to her situation? Or am I the only daughter that can't handle things?"

Dad sat hunched in his chair, a look of disbelief on his face. "This doesn't have anything to do with you not being able to handle it."

"But you're asking them not to talk about it with me has everything to do with me not being able to handle it. I can't believe you thought I was so weak. Or worse, so self-centered!"

My eyes stung. I blinked hard. I hated that my eyes teared up whenever I was mad or embarrassed. I hated worse that I had become the poor self-absorbed daughter who couldn't handle one more problem. I pushed my chair back and made my way toward the stairs.

"Marlo, it is not like that!" Dad called after me.

My dad and I had been close all my life. He'd never admit it, but I knew I was his favorite. Now I was an outsider, like I had lost my father's admiration or trust. It was childish perhaps, but it hurt. I ignored him and continued up the stairs.

I slammed the door to my childhood room and looked around. Not much had changed. It was still like a sauna when the window was closed. The drawn shades created a reddish glow against the mauve-striped wallpaper. My small bed was pushed against a corner, the mauve-and-green-flowered quilt lay draped over the top. My corkboard still hung over a slightly cluttered desk now covered with scraps of discarded fabrics, scissors, and other sewing paraphernalia. Other than the sewing machine now tucked away on the bookshelf and the fact that my Zac Efron poster was missing, it hadn't changed much,

I leaned against the closed door and let out a sigh, relieving the elephant that was pressing the life out of me. Why was I mad at my dad? Why had I run away to my room? Wasn't that the opposite of what I was trying to prove to him? That I could handle it? Hiding wasn't going to make it all better. I was twenty-six years old, or would be this September, but I was acting like a teenager. I could handle stress. Hadn't I been married to Mr. Perfection for four years?

Beads of sweat gathered on my brow. Moisture prickled between my breasts. I pulled the shade up and opened the window wide. A breeze instantly fluttered across my sweating skin and into my suffocating room. Laughter and animated voices drifted like brightly colored ribbons across the river, luring me in like the Pied Piper. Through the trees a large group of people mingled at the park. *Maybe I should go over for a little while. Dad is right. This town will be dead come morning.* I glanced down at my pink skirt. It would never do. I pulled out a pair of designer skinny jeans and some black over-the-knee boots, threw on an oversized grey sequined top that hung a little off one shoulder, pulled my hair back into a low ponytail, and headed out before anyone had the chance to ask where I was going.

I knew Jen was a great party planner, but as the new mayor's wife, she far exceeded my expectations. From top to bottom, everything was lit up like a Christmas tree. Burning torches outlined the bridge and walkways leading to an open grassy park where canopies of tiny white lights crisscrossed the giant cottonwood trees. Bordering the park, red and white Chinese lanterns swayed rhythmically between branches while a Police classic rang out over speakers tied to trees. It was all very festive, like a dream. Hundreds of people mingled—their sounds rolling like waves through the unusually humid air. Smells of barbeque filled my nostrils. My stomach grumbled. The leftover steak I'd nibbled on at home had been less than satisfying and I could go for one of the burgers being cooked.

I stood behind one of the large trees, a chameleon hidden from sight, as familiar faces passed by. My heart pounded in my chest. I pressed my hands against the bark of the tree, wishing I could blend in. My eyes flitted from face to face. No Brandon. No Luke. I breathed a sigh of relief and relaxed a little. It was sort of nice to be here. Watching but not participating. There were so many memories in this park. Some of the greatest were during Fisherman's Breakfast, where the city offered free breakfast to passing fishermen on the opening day of fishing season. In the beginning, before the superhighways of today, it had been fresh coffee and doughnuts to passersby, as all traffic heading to Yellowstone traveled through town. It grew so large that the city council members proposed the event be moved to the park where everything from the pancake mix to the sausage was donated and cooked up to feed a thousand mouths.

Because we were real fishermen, or rather, because my dad was, he took the opening day seriously. We always knew what day it was by the fishing hat pulled down around his ears and his khaki vest covered in old fish stains and pierced with extra flies. He'd have us at the front of the line the minute the first pancakes started bubbling on the grill. I could still smell the sausage and pancakes wafting through the air; the anticipation of not only getting out of school, but of spending the whole day with my dad.

As I grew older, my love for fishing waned. Right around the time I turned fourteen and discovered boys. I no longer stood alongside my dad at six in the morning for steaming hot chocolate, pancakes, sausage, and hash browns smothered in syrup. Instead, I'd tell him I didn't want to go fishing. Melissa and I would take turns standing in line for two hours so the other could go off and flirt or walk around with our friends.

Once the news crew interviewed me for Fisherman's Breakfast. I had innocently touted that it was a tradition to come here for breakfast with my dad before heading out for the opening day of fishing season. When they asked where he was I had to point to a nearly empty picnic table where he sat quietly eating his pancakes. Shame stung me when I saw him all alone. The reporter made a joke about it not being cool to sit with him anymore and everyone around us had laughed. I'd laughed too, but inside, my heart burned with shame. That girl wasn't me. I wanted to run over and give him a hug, apologize for ditching him, but when the interview was over, I found myself surrounded by all my squealing girlfriends who were ecstatic that I was going to be on TV. I caught my father's hunched figure walking alone out of the park and another pang of regret jabbed me.

Sometimes it was easier to believe I was the person in my head rather than acknowledge the one staring back in the mirror. He never said anything about me missing opening day or choosing my friends over him at the breakfast. Tonight I searched for those old friends, but I couldn't find my place, the gap that you recognize, the one waiting for you to fill. It was gone, taken by another, or filled in altogether. A delete button ridding itself of wasted space. I knew it was not intentional, but all the same it had happened. With so much time passing and little or no contact with those I grew up with, I had allowed the natural progression of my life to nearly erase my past.

I turned to leave. I shouldn't have come. I didn't belong here anymore than I belonged in San Francisco. I didn't belong anywhere.

"What are you watching?" a deep voice said behind me.

I spun around to find Luke standing there. No longer in his police uniform, he stood smiling, wearing a pair of jeans and an indigo polo. His freshly washed hair was still wet along the tips. He noticed my outfit.

"You changed."

"So did you. You were right. That skirt caused all kinds of commotion."

He laughed. "Wish I could have watched, but those boots and that blouse are going to cause a small tidal wave themselves."

I glanced down and noticed my black bra strap was showing. I pulled the blouse back over my shoulder, wishing I'd gotten a smaller size. "Do you always offer such fashion commentary?"

"Only when girls from the big city come around." He couldn't seem to stop smiling. "Go ahead; I'll just sit back and watch."

"You're a real piece of work, ya know that," I said with a smirk.

I turned to leave but stopped when I remembered what Melissa had told me about Luke. I swung around to face him. He stood inches from my face. And was a good six inches taller than me. I opened my mouth to speak, and then closed it again, trying to remember what I had wanted to say. He raised his eyebrows. Then I remembered.

"You knew I was coming home today?"

He stammered a little. A small upturn of his mouth gave away his suppressed smile. "Not technically. I didn't know what day exactly, but I did see your sister."

"That's what I thought," I answered. "You do realize sisters talk?"

"So I've heard."

"All that stuff, my dad, you already knew?"

This time his eyes narrowed. "I knew about your dad and that you were coming home for a while. She only hinted to a divorce."

"Annulment," I corrected him.

"Right."

We stood staring at each other in silence.

"Hey, look," he said, pointing toward a large pavilion. "There's Brandon. Let's go say hi." He took my arm and started walking. Just hearing Brandon's name sent shivers through my spine. I dug my boots into the grass and grasped the trunk of the tree with my free hand.

"Wait. Not yet."

"Don't worry, he's married. Just be glad you changed from that skirt you were wearing earlier. He would be hating life then."

I relaxed my grip. "He's married?" I offered a little smile. He was probably grateful that I'd called the whole thing off. Maybe he'd even thank me. "I'm so happy to hear that." I started toward the pavilion with more confidence. All eyes seemed to land on me. A domino effect. The men pulled a double take. The women scowled. Another wardrobe malfunction. I appeared not to notice. I had more important things to worry about than if my clothes fit in. I caught sight of Brandon. He was standing with his back to us and talking to someone I didn't recognize. I didn't know why I hadn't spotted him before. I would have recognized that stance and the back of his head anywhere, even though the last time I'd seen it was four years ago.

I'd come home for a week right before the wedding. My dress needed some alterations, and my mother wanted to do it herself. I'd gone to the hardware store to run some errands for my father and there in aisle number three, amid dryer ducts and plumbing glue, I heard a familiar laugh. I'd frozen at the sound of his hearty chuckle, his low voice. I wanted to hide and yet wanted to see him all at the same time. Then he was beside me, calling out my name, making a joke that the big college grad had come back to sell dryer ducts. Seeing him again had not been what I expected. I could scarcely take a breath. I became tongue-tied. My legs shook. I'd fiddled with my engagement ring and hid it from view. I was unsure of everything.

Brandon had been on the football team in high school. I was a cheerleader. At first it was just quick glances in my direction as he made his way down the aisle of the bus before a game, despite the coaches' warnings about talking to the cheerleaders. Soon he was sitting near the front of the bus and offering me rides home after the games, calling me every night, showing up at my locker every morning.

For one year we were inseparable. Near the end of the summer he took me on his dirt bike to his favorite swimming hole. A hot spring hidden in a cove. A waterfall spilled over the side of the small canyon wall. I wore a pair of old cutoffs and a tank top, but it felt like nothing as he pulled me into the calm pool and kissed me softly on the lips. His touch had been gentle, his kisses like velvet. It was better than a storybook.

But then I'd gotten a scholarship to Stanford. He asked me not to go. Even took me back to the waterhole and on one knee proposed to me, told me he'd buy his family's farm. We could build a little house and live in the country and have a whole herd of cattle. But as much as I'd loved him, I didn't want that life. I didn't want a farmer husband whose boots were always caked in manure. Who never went anywhere for need of milking or feeding the cows. I had bigger ideas. I wanted to get out of Fremont County. Make something of my life.

Even with all that, I might have said yes if I hadn't already packed for school, but I couldn't let the opportunity slip through my fingers. That was one decision I had never regretted.

I saw him a few times during the next few summers, but things between us had changed. Seeing him that day in the hardware store had left me shaken. So much so that I didn't even tell him I was getting married. After I returned to San Francisco and was reminded of all that Cort was and had to offer, I brushed it off as last-minute jitters.

Walking toward him now those old jitters raged anew in my body. I attempted to squash my nerves. I played it cool, walking alongside Luke like this whole scene was as natural as breathing.

"Brandon!" Luke hollered.

I raised my hand to stop him, thinking it would be better not to startle the poor guy, but it was too late. Brandon spun around and smiled as he spotted Luke. I took a deep breath and smiled as naturally as I could. Ready or not, here I was.

Chapter Six

"Dawson. I thought I smelled something," Brandon teased, as he met Luke and gave him a strong handshake.

"It's just the wind coming off your manure-soaked boots," Luke returned.

He looked like the same old Brandon. Light brown hair, smoldering chocolate eyes, and a killer smile. I waited for him to recognize me.

"Just wanted to introduce an old friend of ours," Luke said, resting his hand against the small of my back. The warmth of his hand gave me the confidence I needed. I pulled my chin up and smiled brightly.

Brandon took a drink of his Coke before turning his eyes in my direction. He stared at me for a moment. Something flashed in his eyes. His stare deepened. I gave a little wave and smiled wider.

He held the can to his mouth. His eyes examined me. I threw my waving hand up to my ponytail and slowly twisted it. He watched me, his eyes turning dark.

"Hey, there, stranger!" I finally blurted when I could no longer stand the silence. I took a couple steps forward.

He lowered his can and swallowed hard. "Marlo. What are you doing here?" There was no smile.

My own ridiculously fake smile slid off my face like melting icing on a lopsided cake I'd once made for Cort's birthday. Before I knew about his preferred bakery for those kinds of things. His response wasn't what I had expected. Where were the hugs, the glad to see you agains I'd gotten from everyone else? Even Kale.

"She's taking care of her dad," Luke interjected when I couldn't get anything to come out of my mouth.

"For a while anyway. Then we'll see what happens," I finally managed.

Brandon's lips spread into a thin line. Not quite a smile, not quite a frown. He set his hands on his waist. "What does that mean? You moved back? You're not in San Fran anymore? Or are you leaving again?"

A lump gathered in my throat. I couldn't speak. My head felt feverish, the back of my neck broke out in beads of sweat. I knew coming here would be a mistake. I rubbed the back of my neck, hoping to ease the sudden ache I felt. "Um, no. I may go back someday. Right now, I don't know what I'm going to do."

His eyes followed my left hand. I knew he was looking at the shiny skin around my ring finger that once held my two carat diamond.

"Where's Kelly tonight?" Luke called out, louder than you'd expect from someone standing so close. It was like he was trying to remind Brandon of his wife.

Brandon crushed the can in his hands and chucked it into a nearby wastebasket.

"She's home with the baby," he said shortly.

"So you're married, *and* you have a baby! That's wonderful!" I smiled, regaining my voice.

"Yep," he agreed shortly.

"Too bad she missed this. I would have loved to meet her."

He stared at me for a minute before turning his attention down to his boots. "Oh yeah, that would have been fun."

"Kelly is always the life of the party," Luke agreed, looking off to one side.

"This having a baby has been tough on her, that's for sure." Brandon turned off to one side like he was looking for someone. I followed his gaze and recognized Kale, my friend from the tire store, talking to a tall blonde I didn't recognize.

"Speaking of, I probably should get headed home. Kelly will want a break."

He finally looked back at me. "Nice to see you again," he said with a short nod. I didn't believe he really meant it.

"Dawson, take it easy." Brandon quickly shook Luke's hand before turning away.

He made his way to where Kale had been standing just a moment before. Now there was only the tall blond woman. Brandon stopped in front of her. She smiled brightly, her eyes fluttering like a caged butterfly. She leaned into him. He touched her arm and spoke into her ear. Her smile faded. She jerked her head back and frowned. Whatever he'd said obviously upset her. His shoulders straightened, his stance when he was upset. I'd seen it before. Right after I'd told him I wouldn't marry him. Again right after I told him about Cort. He turned and walked away. Brandon passed the bar set up at the far end of the pavilion. He swiped a can of beer, popped the top, and took a long drink. Right before he disappeared around the corner, he looked over his shoulder and caught eyes with me. Then he turned away.

I sneaked a look at Luke. He had been watching the same scene. "That didn't play out like I'd imagined at all," I admitted, hoping to break the awkwardness of the meeting.

"Yeah, Brandon seemed kind of upset," Luke admitted, still watching him make his way across the park.

"Oh my gosh! Marlo?"

I turned to see my old friend Darcy standing beside a tall, redheaded man. I couldn't recollect his name. It seemed he wasn't sure about me either.

"Darcy!" I threw my arms around her. I hadn't seen her since my wedding. She looked just the same, though her hair seemed a darker shade of chestnut and hung in curls just past her shoulders. Her face was heart shaped, her lips cherublike. I was sure she hated me after the way I treated her at my wedding, but from her broad smile and grip around my neck it seemed as if she had forgiven me.

She had been my only friend from Idaho to attend our wedding. To be honest, she'd been the only one I'd dared invite. She'd hopped on the plane with my parents, even though I heard later she had spent three months saving just to afford the ticket. I had been glad to see her, but things were different in California. Her strong Eastern Idaho drawl embarrassed me, and I found myself avoiding her. But it wasn't just Darcy; it seemed everyone in my family shamed me to some degree. I recognized Cort's family's recoiling glances when the "hicks from Idaho" showed up, and it was impossible not to feel a part of it. Responsible even. Especially when Melissa's two-year-old Maura reached for a wineglass and had it to her lips when a sixty-ish-year-old woman wearing a powder blue jacket dress caught sight of what was happening and went to grab it from Maura's little hands. Maura turned in surprise and dumped it into the woman's lap. A bloodred stain on the woman's expensive-looking formal. Her mouth opened as she gasped in shock. A small cry echoed through the crowd. Cort's mother quickly guided the stunned woman toward the large house where some housekeeper took her inside to get the stain out.

Melissa, with her arms full of a new baby, had rushed to stop it, but couldn't reach her in time, and Troy, off in a huddle with my parents, who were clearly uncomfortable at their own daughter's wedding, had missed the whole thing. It had been another banner day for the Leavitt family. I'd been sidled up next to Cort, wishing that for once my family could just blend in. I should have told those high brows to take their snobbery and shove it in the ocean, but I'd been too intimidated by their wealth to do anything but duck any time a member of my family or Darcy got too close. They embarrassed me as much as the fact that his parents paid for our wedding. My father had argued hotly in the beginning, contending that he was happy to pay for it, but they insisted, justifying that because it was going to take place on one of their vineyards it would be much easier if they just took care of it all. They finally appeased him with the cost of the flowers. He grumbled about it until he received the bill for the flowers. Then he shut up. The cost of the flowers had been more than my sister's wedding altogether.

Darcy held a hand out, remembering her date. "You remember Jed Cooper? He was a grade older than us."

I smiled and said hello. Now I knew why I couldn't remember his name. We'd come from a class with 150 seniors. You knew everyone, or at least their names. I now recognized his face, but realized I had never spoken to him. By the many unfamiliar faces surrounding us, I had to admit how very little I knew about most of these people. Darcy glanced over my shoulder toward Luke.

"Hey, Luke, how's it going?" She turned her questioning eyes back to me. "So where's Courtney?" she asked, looking around for my "husband." I wished more than anything that I had kept up with her, that I didn't have to explain my life at a party like this.

I ran through the facts. Her face fell.

"I'm so sorry." She seemed genuinely saddened. Another glance over my shoulder at Luke, and then back to me. I only smiled like I had no idea what she was thinking. Luke looked around.

"Anybody need a drink?" he asked, apparently as uncomfortable as I was feeling.

"I'm good, thanks," Darcy answered. I was parched. I thanked him for thinking of me, and he disappeared into the crowd in a hurry.

"I can't believe you're back," she grinned. "It will be just like old times." She grabbed my arm and pulled me close. "You heard Brandon finally got married."

"Yes, isn't that wonderful?" I exclaimed. "I actually saw him tonight."

"Oh, good." She brightened again. "Well, Jed and I are headed to the rodeo. You should come."

"Do they still have rodeos?" I hadn't been to one in years.

She furrowed her brows in mock disgust, "This is St. Anthony we are talking about. There are some things that will never change." She laughed good-naturedly.

"It sounds fun. I'll see if Luke wants to go too."

Again she looked at me with questioning eyes. I ignored her look. I scanned the refreshment table. Luke walked toward us. I had nothing to tell her. Luke was a friend. That was it. I was still trying to understand what went wrong in my marriage, actually, in every relationship I'd ever had. Nothing had ever lasted.

"Come on, Darcy, let's go," Jed said looking at his watch.

"Look for us!" she yelled back as Jed led her toward the parking lot.

Within a few minutes Luke returned, a cold soda in his hand. I thanked him again and took a deep drink. It felt cold and bubbly going down my throat. Then I asked Luke about the rodeo.

He glanced down at his watch. "Sure. We better get going if we want to make the bull riding."

I looked down at my outfit. "Should I change?"

He laughed. "No way, Marlo. I'm having the time of my life watching heads turn."

I shrugged and rolled my eyes. Pretend disgust. A smile crept across my face. Luke gave a little laugh and led me to the parking lot.

Once we reached his motorcycle, he grabbed a flannel long sleeve off the seat and offered it to me along with his helmet. "You okay on a motorcycle?"

I smiled, "Did you see my boots?" I teased as I pulled the helmet on. I took the flannel shirt too. The wind picked up, and I was grateful for the added warmth.

We hopped on and sped down the road and onto the old highway. It wasn't long till I recognized the halo of lights that circled the fairgrounds. My mouth dropped open when Luke turned onto a dirt road and sped across an open field. Instead of a paved parking lot, cars were parked in the fields surrounding the arena and on down the block in any available space, including some front lawns. The rows of cars and trucks were parked in every possible position that proved park-able. Creativity at its height.

"Do they really expect people to do this?" I yelled over the engine.

"Sure, it keeps the weeds down." He laughed. I think he was joking. "But we aren't parking here. We're going to the front."

It had probably always been this way, but I had forgotten, and had certainly not seen anything like it since I moved away, but Luke seemed unconcerned as we bumped along the crazy nonexistent road toward the lit-up grandstand. Up until that point I had been careful not to touch him, but as we jostled up and down I had no choice but to wrap my arms around his waist and hold on tight. He didn't flinch. I hoped he didn't think I was being too forward, but my life depended on it.

He steered up to the gate and parked alongside a long horse trailer where two cowboys were taking a cigarette break. Everything was dirt and rocks—the roads, the walkway behind the stands--the arena itself. The air was blanketed in a fine dust, kicked up from the recent wind and the riders. The rodeo announcer's high-pitched, nasal commentary blasted through overhead speakers. I recognized his voice. He'd been announcing the rodeo for years. It felt like time had stood still. Everything just how I remembered it.

"From Terreton, Idaho, give a St. Anthony hello to Jenny Petersen, next on the barrel racing docket."

Luke jumped off the bike and held a hand out to me. I pulled off the helmet. My hair went flying in a hundred different directions. Static city. I wiped it down with my hands wishing I had some spray or water to settle it a bit. I took off Luke's flannel shirt and handed it to him. I may not have been in California anymore, but I could still care about my fashion sense. We headed toward the arena. The walkway was dimly lit. I caught my foot on a rock and stumbled. Luke grabbed my elbow and helped me regain my balance.

"Are you okay?"

"Didn't see that rock there." I blushed.

The light from the rodeo grounds spilled through the cracks of the stands. Other than one bulb next to the concession stand we were in total darkness. Seemed like a lawsuit waiting to happen. But maybe people in this town didn't sue each other.

"You were always graceful." He smiled as he put the flannel shirt over his dark polo. By the thin smile he was trying to suppress I could see he was teasing me.

"Especially when there are no lights. I'm not a bat, you know."

"Remember when you fell off the homecoming float? You were lucky you didn't kill yourself."

I'd been lying on a piece of plywood while we drove the float back to the farmer's shed. "How do you remember this stuff?" I asked, flabbergasted by his memories of steel. "I'll have you know that I was only doing someone else a favor. I never dreamed that plywood would fly off like it did."

"And take you with it." He smiled and shoved his hands in his pockets.

I always was kind of a klutz, another thing that hadn't ever changed. I glanced toward the concession stand.

"Do you know where the restrooms are?"

He pointed to a row of Porta-Potties off in the distance, nearly encased in darkness.

"Really? Never mind," I said, thinking there was no way on this good green earth I would set foot in one of those things. I could almost smell them from where I stood.

"Are you sure?"

I nodded.

I examined the small line in front of the concession stand. My stomach grumbled again. I could smell that familiar grilling of meat. "Something smells good," I said determined to get myself one of those burgers. We made our way to a concession stand, and I ordered a burger and a bottle of water. Luke ordered the same and together we made our way to the front of the stands and looked for a place to sit.

If the commode accommodations, as my father liked to call them, were a bit disappointing, the grandstands ranked a distant second. To describe the bleachers as weathered would have been an understatement and quite possibly a disservice. If the stands hadn't been packed with fans, I would have felt certain it was dangerous to climb them. But I was determined to be a good sport. Especially after the hard stare I got when I complained that my bottled water had been lukewarm and asked the young girl at the concession stand for a cup of ice, after which she informed me she did not have either thing. I'd taken my warm water and burger and given Luke a knowing glance. He smiled apologetically.

We spotted Darcy and Jed. They were halfway to the top and had draped a plaid blanket across the bleachers.

"I'm so glad you came," Darcy exclaimed as we sat down on top of her blanket. "I saved you a spot. It's a little softer on the rear." She patted the blanket.

The sky let out a low rumble. We all glanced up. The wind had brought some black clouds with it.

"Well, it wouldn't be Pioneer Days without one good downpour," Darcy teased, grinning up at what appeared to be the beginnings of a real doozy of a storm.

I coughed from all the dust. "Is it usually this dusty?" I asked, as something like gravel grinded between my teeth.

"But what's a rodeo if you don't come home with a thin layer of dust over your shoes?"

"Or mud," Luke stated, still watching the churning sky. "It hasn't rained in a month. Probably could use a good soaking." A flash of lightning ripped overhead. A small exclamation went out from the crowd. My hair was static-y. It did that before storms. I remembered that now. I opened the bottle of water and poured a little in my hands to pat down my charged hair.

The rodeo was in full swing. We'd missed the mutton bustin' competition, men's barrel racing, and the cow roping. The announcer called for all kids under twelve to the field. It was time for the fifty-dollar run. Nearly everyone was dressed in Wranglers and button-down plaid shirts. All eyes seemed to stop on me and my sequined shirt and over-the-knee black leather boots. Thankfully, their attention was soon diverted by the roll of thunder coming out of the stands. Not from the storm this time, but from the stampede of anxious kids, all shapes and sizes, girls and boys, bullying toward the field. Luke caught my questioning look and began to explain.

"There's a cow with a fifty-dollar bill attached to it. All the kids chase after it and first to get the money wins."

This game was new to me. Seemed easy enough, but apparently, as Luke put it, "Cows were more agile than they looked."

A shot rang out, and a cow flew out of a chute. Music blared over the speakers. Kids went full throttle, churning their Wrangler-clad legs through the thick dirt. The cow juked like a football receiver. A skinny boy about eight stretched his arms toward the money. The cow spun around and headed in the opposite direction. The eight-year-old went down in a heap of dust. He was nearly overrun by a band of kids skidding across the arena to avoid a collision. Cowboy hats went flying as children pushed to get out of the way.

A little girl about five tripped over her red cowgirl boots and fell facedown in what appeared to be wet dirt from—I could only guess what. The crowd held its breath as one of the clowns pulled the crying little girl out of the mud by her armpits. I cringed. A cheer broke out when she was reunited with her mother.

Along the sidelines the parents hollered—clapping and laughing—

as kids ran, hobbled, walked, or just plain gave up, slapping their cowboy hats against their dusty jeans in disgust while the cow moseyed down the middle of the arena.

A couple young cowboys coming from opposite directions closed in on the animal, the idea of fifty dollars cold cash in their pockets all the motivation they needed. They drew closer to the cow that seemed oblivious to them. The two cowpokes simultaneously stretched their hands out and leaped forward. The cow sidestepped them, and the boys went sailing across the sea of dirt and crashed into each other. At that very moment, a girl around twelve appeared out of nowhere, and in three giant steps, swept to the side of the cow and plucked the money from its secured position on its neck in a very Laura Croft sort of way. The crowd erupted in cheers. Ninety-nine other kids, covered head to foot in dust, stopped running, and upon seeing their hopes for free money evaporate into this girl's thin hands, walked dejectedly back to their seats.

The crowd whooped and hollered their approval. They smiled and laughed like this was the best entertainment they'd seen in years. I was still cringing from the little girl falling in the mud. It was simple. I'd say naïve, but maybe it wasn't that. It reminded me of how I'd felt as a kid. Everyone else—all my friends, that is—had seemed at one with this whole rodeo business, like it was a part of who they were. Like they'd been sprinkled by the dust fairy and set upon a horse the day they were born. I'd never felt that way. Ever. I was an uninvited guest surrounded by things I knew nothing about. Here, ten years later, I was still the stranger. More so, actually. And I envied them in a strangely simple way.

"That's my dream, ya know?" Darcy said in my ear.

I peered at her quizzically.

"You know, to have a kid out there running, cowboy hat and little boots. It's all I want," she sighed.

I smiled and looked back to where the kids where filing through the gates. It was nice. This simple dream. I envied that she knew what she wanted, but I did not share her vision. I didn't want anything to do with dust, manure, or cowboy boots unless they were Lucchese and had been freshly polished.

Darcy nudged my arm. "Would you come with me? I've got to use the bathroom, and it scares me a little to go out there alone. It's so dark."

"No kidding," I agreed. "I nearly tripped over a boulder on the way in. I can't believe how antiquated the facilities are here. Talk about a throwback to our childhood! Nothing has changed. I don't think they've even painted these bleachers since we were kids. I've got to tell you I was so glad you put a blanket down. I was afraid I might get slivers from sitting on the bench."

She looked down at the bleachers. "Yeah, it's pretty lame." She shrugged and looked off to one side. I bit my own lip. I'd done it again. I could tell by the way her shoulders fell, and she struggled to meet my eye I had offended her. But she shouldn't have taken offense. I wasn't talking bad about her. I was simply stating the obvious faults of the fairgrounds.

I grabbed her hand and hollered over my shoulder to a surprised Luke and Jed that we'd be back soon. I hoped I'd find some way to earn her forgiveness.

Chapter Seven

I waited for Darcy a few feet away from the potties. It was the best I could do. Especially when she squealed in disgust once she was behind the closed door. I figured if I was within eyesight, that was all anyone would expect from a friend.

There was movement in a darkened alley between two cinder-block 4-H buildings. I shifted a little hoping to get a better look. Just to make sure the meeting was consensual. I mean, who could resist a dark space in the middle of an exciting rodeo? Certainly not hormone-crazy teenagers. I knew 'cause I'd been one once.

A small beam of light from the arena shifted across the open walkway and into the lone space in the alley. I recognized Kale standing between the two buildings talking to someone. I inched my way a little more to the left, curious to see who he was talking with. I recognized the tall, thin woman from the party. My movement caught his eye. She followed his gaze in my direction. I averted my eye too late. My face warmed. They had caught me spying on them before I realized I was doing it. I wanted to dig myself into a hole, but since I was out in the open, I figured that was out of the question. I waved sheepishly. He ran a hand through his hair and after some hushed words hurried out to meet me.

"Marlo! Nice outfit," he stated with a red face.

I smiled apologetically and pulled my blouse back up on my shoulder. "I didn't mean to spy on you guys. I'm just waiting for my friend to get out of the restroom, and I saw something move in the dark."

He laughed uneasily and led the woman toward me. "No problem. We were just talking. This is Amanda."

I raised my eyebrows. Apparently his relationship with Amanda was not over. I smiled pleasantly and stretched my hand out. She took it, her handshake, weak and uninterested. She looked over my shoulder. A large grin spread across her face.

"Hi, there, Luke," she said sweetly.

"Hey, Amanda." Luke turned to me and said, "I was getting kind of worried," and added softly, "Thought I better come check on you girls."

Just then the door to the Porta-Potty slammed shut and Darcy came bounding out with a mixed look of disgust and relief.

"Well, that was fun," she said with a laugh. Upon making her way into the small shaft of light she recognized Kale and Amanda right away. She smiled warmly at Kale, and then smiled politely at Amanda. "I'd shake hands, but no soap in there," she said with a self-deprecating laugh. Her laughter broke the tension and everyone, especially me, shifted in relief. I was sure my face was still red from being caught spying.

Luke turned to Kale. "Have you seen Brandon?" My ears perked at the mention of Brandon's name. Darcy whispered about the horrible conditions of the bathroom in my ear. I nodded in agreement, but found myself leaning more toward Kale and Luke's conversation.

"Not recently. Why?" Kale said.

"He seemed upset. I just wondered if either of you knew why."

"It's Kelly," the woman named Amanda interjected. "She was mad he went to the party without her. She hates missing anything fun. The baby has been a hole in her shoe as far as a social life goes." She moved between Luke and Kale and put her back to Kale.

"I haven't seen you in ages. You never get out anymore," she whined to Luke, softly hitting his shoulder with her weakly formed fist.

"I've been busy," Luke answered, dipping his hands into his pockets.

"It's not good to be that busy," she said with a small upturn of her mouth. I looked over at Kale. He was watching the rodeo between two large open sections in the stadium. Maybe they weren't together. I didn't get it.

The announcer called for the bull riding to begin. The crowd cheered.

"You ready to get back?" Luke asked, turning away from Amanda.

"Sure." I waved good-bye to Kale and Amanda, and the three of us returned to the stadium.

Once we were settled back in our seats, a large rumble rolled over our heads. The wind blew through my blouse. I shivered. Three seconds later, lightning slashed across the dark sky, turning everything a charged bluish white. The crowd hummed from the explosion, nearly forgetting the bull rider still struggling to hang on to the bucking bull. He quickly lost his balance and jumped from the bull. Large drops of rain pelted against our skin and heads. We looked up into the murky night, hoping the rain would hold out a little longer. The announcer called out the next bull rider. No one paid him any attention as they scrambled for shelter.

"Here," Darcy said grabbing hold of the blanket we were sitting on. "Put this over your heads or you're going to get soaked."

I nodded and pulled the blanket over our heads. Immediately the warmth of Luke's body heat next to mine stopped me from shivering. "Is that better?" Luke asked as he wrapped the wool blanket snugly around us. I gave a small nod. It was strangely intimate, and secretly a little exciting.

The announcer again announced the next rider. Billy Angel from Butte, Montana, riding the notorious "Blue Devil." AC/DC screamed from the squealy speakers. The chute opened. The bull charged out of the gate with hell's fury in his bones. The rider stayed rigid as the bull tipped and jerked violently. His knees squeezed around the bull's shoulders, his gloved hand stretched around the horn. His other hand shot out to his side to steady himself. Clods of dirt flew from the bull's hooves. The rodeo clown jumped to the left, attempting to divert the bull's attention away from the gate. The bull snorted and grunted as it bucked and stomped its hooves in the dirt, nearly flipping the cowboy head over heels and knocking the clown beneath its hooves. The crowd gasped. The cowboy stayed on. The clown scurried to get out of its way.

Monstrous raindrops beat against our blanket, but we remained glued to our seats as the bull hunched its shoulders and bucked its legs, flopping the rider around like a rag doll tied to the animal's back. The buzzer rang. The crowd cheered. The cowboy went to jump off the bull, but his hand got stuck in the rope. The bull kicked and heaved, slamming the rider into the side gate with magnificent force. A dozen cowboys crawled over the fence like army ants to free the rider from the rope. The clown moved into action, tossing a red handkerchief behind him to distract the animal. The bull ran toward the clown, dragging the cowboy behind him. The cowboy fought with his one free hand to rid himself of his glove.

A second clown raced toward the bull. Apparently, confused by the second clown's appearance, the bull hesitated, giving the cowboys enough time to release the rider from the rope. Darcy had her hands clasped in prayer around her mouth. Luke was silent, his eyes intent on the rider. He whistled a sigh of relief, and then burst into applause as the rider hobbled, mostly unharmed, off the field. Winner of the challenge. I sighed in relief, too. It really wasn't that simple, this game, this rodeo, or whatever they called it. The guy could have gotten killed. What would possess a person to want to ride on the back of a raging bull?

I turned to Luke. "Have you ever ridden a bull?"

He shrugged. "A real one or a mechanical one?"

My eyes widened. "Either."

"I've ridden a mechanical one. It's tough, but nowhere near tough like that," he admitted watching the clowns and cowboys steer the bull back into his pen. "Those are some tough dudes out there," he said with a nod of his head.

Thunder boomed. The sky ripped into a dozen jagged bolts of electricity. All heads cranked toward the blackness. The lightning seemed to crack the sky open like weak eggshells, dumping yolk-sized raindrops across the stand. They pelted our blanket and soaked through immediately. I shivered from the wet cold.

"We'd better get going," Luke announced. I'd nearly forgotten he'd brought us on a motorcycle. I handed Darcy her sopping blanket, thanked her, and promised to call soon. On the count of three, we ran for it.

Rain came down in great sheets and soaked my sequined shirt all the way through till I shivered uncontrollably. Luke pulled off his flannel and placed it around my shoulders. He took my hand and led me through the crowd. In a matter of one minute the rain had turned the dirt into mud and the roads into small lakes. Luke helped me onto the motorcycle. I put the helmet on. Luke's shirt was soaked. I leaned in and wrapped my arms around him as he slowly meandered around the puddles, doing his best to avoid splashing people with mud.

We slowly made our way out of the fairgrounds and back into town. We passed the park. Chinese lanterns swayed violently in the wind. People scurried like frantic mice toward the picnic shelter. Another boom of thunder and flash of light ripped through the park and the hundreds of hanging lights went out, leaving the park in total darkness.

"This is crazy!" I yelled over the roar of the rain. After a few more minutes, we reached my house and Luke helped me off the bike.

We dashed to the front door and stopped under the dimly lit porch. Luke's shirt was drenched; his hair dripped. He looked like he'd just taken a shower with his clothes on. He smiled brightly. I laughed. I pulled off the helmet and smiled up at him. He smiled back. We laughed nervously. I felt like I was sixteen again.

I shivered under my dripping blouse and handed him the helmet. Then I took off the flannel shirt. It was soaked all the way through. I attempted to wring it out. He laughed.

"Don't worry about that." He took the shirt and tucked it under his arm. "It was fun," he said, looking at me with eyes of melted chocolate.

"Pays to let some speeders off the hook, right?" I hedged, knocking him on the shoulder.

He laughed. "Just the ones with lots of attitude."

"Or short skirts. I'm not sure which it was with you," I teased.

He shook his head a little and smiled a crooked smile. "Maybe it was a little of both."

We were interrupted by a large clap of thunder that rolled across the river, followed by a strike of lightning that lit up the entire sky.

"Wow!" we said simultaneously.

"I better get going. This storm might be here awhile," Luke announced.

I pursed my lips together. Luke was soaked, and I was freezing. I wasn't sure what to do next. Should I invite him in? Give him a hug and ask him to call? I stood under the porch light waiting for some divine intervention when Luke saved me the trouble.

"I promised Janessa I would help her clean up, and it looks like they've had to end the party early. With no lights she's definitely going to need some help."

We both turned toward the park just across the river. A few headlights shined across the way, adding their light to the sole street lamp on emergency power near the entrance.

"Do you need some more help?" I asked.

"No. You'd freeze in that little sparkly thing," he smiled slyly.

I opened my mouth to argue. I wasn't ready to go in, but maybe he was ready to leave. Maybe I'd worn out my welcome. I pressed my lips together. I certainly couldn't go to sleep. I was still on Pacific time. It felt like 9:30 to me.

A big chill rippled through me. "What happened to the sweltering heat earlier?"

"You know what they say about Idaho's weather: if you don't like it, just wait an hour and it'll change," he winked.

I smiled back at him, remembering the famous saying. It was surreal in a way, like I was talking to someone I'd known for years, yet didn't really know at all. He glanced back at me. I looked away, embarrassed to have been caught staring. Before I could stop myself I reached out and gave him a hug. His arms wrapped around my waist in response. He gave me a tight squeeze. I added a quick, "Thanks for the ride."

"Take care, Marlo," he said. I stood there, an island upon the sea, as he turned down the sidewalk and jumped on his bike in less time than it took for me to get a hold of myself and turn the handle of the door and walk inside.

The rain continued to pound against the roof for two more hours. I'd managed to sneak in the house with little interaction from either of my parents and was glad for it as they were early to bed kind of people and already in their bedroom. I readied myself for bed, and then stared at the ceiling listening to the raindrops. Sleep refused to come. I was jazzed up, thinking about my life, wondering how, at twenty-six, it had landed me right back where I'd started—in my parents' house, in my old bed, in my old town, with my old friends. What happened to that bright dream Stanford had offered?

Brandon had seemed unhappy to see me. I don't know what I had expected, but I had hoped—as someone he once considered marrying—for a little more genuine regard. Did I miss something in our breakup to cause such hate? I went through our breakup in my head, but came up blank. Maybe it hadn't been about me. Maybe he'd been upset that his wife hadn't been there. Maybe he'd had a rough day.

But even as I tried to convince myself otherwise, I knew it had more to do with me than I'd wanted to believe.

And then there was Luke. He'd never been unattractive, but he'd always had a bit of a baby face. A late bloomer, I decided. I was impressed with how genuine he seemed. Like he truly cared about people, the way he checked up on Brandon and offered to help Jenessa with the party cleanup, and the way he had so willingly taken me under his wing.

Darcy. She seemed so happy in spite of the fact she was still holed up in this one-stoplight town. I didn't get it. How could she be happy when she didn't have the things she said she wanted most in life? A family, a husband? Didn't it bother her even a little? She hadn't let off the slightest inclination that she was disappointed with the life she'd been given. I'd traveled all over the world, been married to someone I truly thought I loved, had more money than I'd ever dreamed of, and yet, I'd never felt so at home in my skin as she seemed tonight. I hated and admired her more than I wanted to admit.

I was never going to fall asleep thinking like this. I pulled myself out of bed and quietly made my way downstairs to make myself a cup of hot chocolate.

Chapter Eight

I sat in the sunroom and listened to the sounds of the river roll by. Then I placed my mug of recently emptied hot chocolate down on the rattan table, put on a pair of slippers, and slipped out the back door. The rain had let up. Black clouds parted to reveal bits of a quarter moon. But this storm was not over yet. More dark clouds were crawling from the east. This was only a break.

I stepped onto the wet brick patio and looked up at the soaring black shadows of the sycamore and pine trees that dotted my parents' lush backyard. The yard sat nearly engulfed in darkness. Branches swayed in the wind and gave off the sound of an eerie lullaby. I closed my eyes and inhaled the fragrance of pine needles and wet grass. The small patch of light from the moon reflected off a set of lava stairs made many years ago. The low hum of the river called to me. I took the volcanic steps down to the dock that my father had built when I was a girl.

The dock stood as it always had, a small square of redwood with a long pole off to one side for roping the canoe. The canoe banged rhythmically against the dock. I slid my hand along the wooden canoe. Puddles of water dripped off the sides. I climbed aboard. It groaned from my weight, but held to the pole. I wiped the standing water off the seat and carefully stretched myself out over the two boards.

The smells of the river drifted through my nostrils. I closed my eyes, hoping the gentle movements would calm my soul. My father used to take me out on the river. He taught me how to canoe, always keeping me safely on the side of the sandbar. "Watch out for the current, Marlo. Learn to work with it. You'll never beat the current," he would warn.

I thought about his words. Had I tried to swim against the current? Leaving home, marrying Cort? Had that been the wrong thing to do? I could have accepted my fate of being Brandon's wife instead of fighting it so much. If I'd swum with the current, I would have married Brandon, been that farmer wife, and maybe we would be very happy right now. Instead, I was out of place everywhere I went, never at peace with myself. Brandon seemed unhappy too.

I sat up. To the south the tiny outlines of car headlights driving along the highway lit up the darkness. The wet road splashed against their speeding tires, adding their sounds with that of the rushing river. Who was I anyway? What did I want out of life? I was a car with no headlights, trying to make my way in the dark. Darcy only wanted kids she could take to the rodeo so they could chase after a cow. It seemed too simple, but maybe it wasn't really about that. Maybe it was deeper than the cow. I laughed out loud. I was waxing philosophical about a cow. I stood up. The moon had disappeared behind new clouds. My butt was wet. I dabbed it with my hands and carefully slipped back onto the dock. Straining to see through the darkness, I carefully made my way back up the darkened stairs.

The sleeping house was dark. I wasn't ready to join it. I walked to the edge of the lawn where a row of lilac bushes stood. My hands felt their way around the wet branches looking for the opening that had always served as a secret passageway. I soon found it, though it had nearly grown in altogether. I stepped through and found myself facing an old white building that had once served as a fire station. A streetlight flooded the area with light. I walked along a small gravel road and across a large lawn of grass.

Fallen leaves from the storm swirled like miniature dust bowls down the road. Dark clouds hovered. I stood at the top of the lawn and looked over one of my favorite hangouts as a kid. "The Sand Bar." It had been the local swimming hole for more than sixty years and a place I explored from my childhood up until I left for college.

I stood on the large grassy knoll facing a covered picnic shelter. To the left sat a playground, a rudely made waterslide, and a diving board that stretched over the river. Straight-ahead, just past the grassy area, stood a set of stairs leading to a shallow swimming area roped off from the rest of the river. A retaining wall extended out on either side of the stairs, necessary for the spring and early summer runoffs that threatened to deteriorate the bank each year. Luckily, there was a popular tourist destination just three miles out of town called the Sand Dunes, where they replenished the receding beach with dump truckloads of sand every year.

I walked to the stairs and shed my slippers. Across the river lay the park, where only a few hours before hundreds of people, old and young, had mingled. Now it was shrouded in darkness except for a dim street lamp in one corner. The wind rustled through my hair. Specks of sand stung my eyes. I ground my teeth and felt that same grit from earlier. Did people always have dirt in their mouths around here? I looked up. Another storm was brewing. My eyes watered. I blinked hard to get the sand out of my eyes as I made my way down to the water. The wet sand filtered through my toes. It was moist and coarse, and still warm from the hot afternoon sun. I pulled my sweats up around my knees and walked to the edge of the water. My feet sank down deeper into the wet mud, surrounding my toes like little coffins. Or maybe it was more like cocoons. Then they would emerge as beautiful butterflies. Butterflies didn't have to go with the current. They could go wherever they wanted.

The water splashed against my ankles. The cold water sent a shock up my spine. Warm and cold spots washed across my feet. Goose bumps rose on my skin. A single raindrop splashed against my head. Another slid down my cheek. One by one, droplets of rain fell. *Here comes the storm,* I decided. I shivered and turned to leave, but stopped when I heard what I thought was my name being called.

I glanced up the stairs and saw a dark shape, highlighted by the distant streetlight, standing on top of the retaining wall. I froze in place. A chill ran up my spine.

He shifted his feet, his hands deep in his pockets. *Hardly the stance of a killer,* I thought as I fought for the courage to take a step forward. I could just see the headlines, "Local girl murdered in city park." Things like that didn't happen in towns like this. I shook off the sudden chill I felt and took another step. He turned his head sideways, and I immediately recognized the profile.

Brandon.

A wash of relief fell through me. Something fluttered in my stomach. I quickly made my way up the stairs. He stood with his hands in his pockets, his disheveled hair hanging wet in his face. I moved toward him. The rain dropped with greater force. We simultaneously looked up at the blackness, and then back at each other.

"Looks like it's raining again," I said.

"Looks like it," he returned.

There was more silence. I shifted uncomfortably. "What are you doing here?" I finally asked.

"What, you're the only one that can hang out here at night?"

I stared back at him expectantly.

"I couldn't sleep," he explained.

"That makes two of us."

We stood on the retaining wall ignoring the rain that soaked our clothing, neither saying a word.

He licked his bottom lip. I shivered again. Did he want me to speak? Did he want some sort of apology? So many things I wanted to say earlier now sounded ridiculous in my mind. I kept quiet. The silence was excruciating.

"Divorced, huh?" His voice sliced through me.

"Sort of. Annulment actually." My heart thumped. I opened my mouth to speak, and then closed it again.

"Figures."

My face grew hot. "What does that mean? That I'm incapable of making a marriage work? Thanks." I turned toward the house. I didn't need this. I started to leave.

"That you'd finally come to your senses." I turned back around. He shrugged and looked out toward the water.

I finally came to my senses? He had no idea. I shook my head. "It's kind of complicated."

"Not really. You married some rich guy and thought that everything else would work itself out. But money doesn't fix problems."

My hands balled up. "I never thought it would fix my problems."

He turned to face me, his eyes glaring. "I bet you're sitting pretty now. What did it take to satisfy you? A couple hundred thousand?"

My eyes narrowed. I took a step forward. "For your information, I didn't get a dime from our divorce."

He laughed in contempt. "I thought it was an annulment. Word is you pulled into town in a pretty nice ride. Nice clothes to boot."

Anger burned in my chest. "You shouldn't make assumptions. You have no idea. Why are you acting like this, anyway?"

"Acting like what?"

"Showing up here in the middle of the night. Questioning my motives for marrying Cort. Like I haven't had enough crap to deal with. I married Cort because I loved him. That was why I signed a prenup. His money did not influence my decision to marry him, whatsoever." I started walking away. My blood pressure was boiling. I didn't need to talk to him anymore.

"Sure, it didn't," he chuckled darkly.

"Excuse me?" I demanded, forgetting about blood pressure and walking back to him.

"That is such bull, Marlo. I remember you talking about his fancy car, and how he was buying you all this stuff."

I closed my eyes and took a deep breath. I'd been young and naïve. I'd been showing off, wanting to make Brandon jealous. Why had I done that? My behavior then was humiliating now. Rain pelted against my head and slid down my face. I wiped it away and glared at him. “You’re right. In the beginning it was exciting. But I didn’t marry him for his money. Our marriage was annulled, and I didn’t go after him for anything. Besides, I don’t understand why you want to hurt me. I’ve kind of been going through hell the last few months. We used to be friends. What happened?”

He scowled and looked over my shoulder toward the old building. “I don’t know.”

“Why did you call out to me?” I demanded. “If I annoy you so much, why bother?”

“I don’t know.”

“Do you want to see if I’m miserable? You want me to apologize for something?”

His eyes flashed. I’d hit a nerve.

“Something? You’re kiddin’ me!”

“No, I’m not. Now if you don’t have anything to say I’ll be seeing you.” I didn’t wait to hear anymore. He was being a jerk, and I had a pretty good idea he’d been drinking. I made my way to the picnic shelter. He stomped after me.

“Marlo. How can you act so . . . so . . . clueless?”

Thunder clapped overhead. I jumped around. Brandon stood on one side of the shelter. One hand on his hip. “I waited for you to finish school. For you. To come back to me. I thought this infatuation with Richie Rich would blow over. You didn’t belong with some rich California boy. That’s not who you are. Then one day, I hear through the grapevine that you’re married.”

Lightning flashed again. It lit up his pained face. My heart ached for him. I slowly made my way to him. Water dripped from the tips of his hair and down his face. “Married. Not even a warning. Was that all I meant to you?” He stood so close to me I could feel his breath hot against my skin.

I stared down at my hands unable to face his hurt expression. "I meant to tell you. I just couldn't bring myself to do it. I don't know why."

"Because you knew it was a mistake and you were afraid I'd talk you out of it."

I pressed my lips nervously. I didn't know if he was right, but something in the way he stared through me made me believe he was right. I broke his gaze. It felt like a torch going through my heart.

"That day in the hardware store? You knew then, didn't you, and yet you just smiled and acted like everything was okay."

I flared my arms in defense. "What else could I do? It was too awkward." I wanted to reach out and touch him. Make him understand. "I . . . I could barely breathe when I saw you that day. I doubted everything. Cort, my marriage, saying no to you." I closed the distance between us so I could see his eyes better. "But then I went back to San Francisco and filed it away as last-minute jitters."

He closed his eyes. His mouth opened. His voice quivered.

"If you would have just—" He blinked. Our eyes caught. His eyes glistened. He turned away and wiped the rain away from his mouth with the back of his hand. He looked back at me. Rain or tears dripped down his face.

"You should have talked to me. You could have saved me a lot of years of hurt."

"I did what I thought was best. For me and for you." I stared down at my bare feet. I couldn't meet his eyes. What had I been thinking then? I hadn't felt like I owed him an explanation, or maybe I *was* afraid he would talk me out of it. I had always regretted not telling him myself. The hurt evident in his eyes was crippling.

"Brandon, I'm so sorry."

He waved my words away, then he stepped from the pavilion and walked across the grassy hill, past the playground equipment, and beyond the diving board.

"Brandon, wait!"

He stopped walking and turned back to me. "Was it really that easy? I mean, did you ever think about me?"

I ran after him down the hill. "Of course I thought of you. You were an important part of my life."

"Important enough to tell me face-to-face that you were getting married?"

I stared back at him. This was not the happy-go-lucky Brandon I had known. Had my actions caused this? Or was it just the natural progression of the last four years?

"Brandon," I paused, holding back the emotion rising to the surface. "I'm sorry. I was stupid. I *was* afraid that you might talk me out of it, and I didn't want that to happen, but I *never* meant to hurt you."

"Do you still love him?"

"You can't just turn it off like that."

"You turned it off pretty quick with me." His words were like a slap in the face. A sear of emotion rushed through me.

"That's not fair, Brandon. I went to college. You only came to visit me once. Remember? Spring break. I came home every summer, and every summer it seemed like you had a different girlfriend. We drifted apart."

"I never had a girlfriend. I dated, sure, but I was waiting for you."

Tears burned my eyes. Guilt pushed down on my chest. I sighed to keep my emotions in check. Once I could manage I spoke. "I made a lot of mistakes, but I never set out to hurt you. Besides, you're married now. It worked out for the best, right?"

He let out a small laugh and turned toward the white building now used for storing city vehicles. Beyond the building was a dirt path leading to the river. He made his way down that direction and soon disappeared into the darkness.

"Brandon!" I let out an exasperated sigh and flailed my arms. I knew where he was going. And I knew he expected me to follow him. I glanced up at the dark sky that continued to drop huge raindrops. I growled and dropped my arms to my side and followed him into the darkness.

The building blocked out any light from the far-off lamppost. I groped along the path, my bare feet landing on sharp pebbles and fallen twigs as I searched through the blinding darkness for the path that led to the river. I bit my lip to keep from crying out from the pain. Off to the left were the large lilac bushes that separated the Sand Bar from my parent's property. I fumbled along the gravel trail to the edge of the bank where a looming cement fixture—an old well long abandoned—stood half-buried in the earth while the other side butted against the water. The only way to reach it was by crossing a big black pipe, an old sewer line that extended over a small ten-foot drop too difficult and marshy to walk under.

I knew Brandon would come here. This had been our special place. Sometimes I would sneak out of my house and meet him here. But I was younger then and much more agile. And the moon had been bright, and it was never raining. Now it felt a little bit like suicide.

I caught sight of Brandon. He had slipped across the black pipe and onto the well without any trouble. The cement well was crumbly and broken off in spots. He sat down and dangled his feet over the edge, narrowly missing the swift current below.

The pipe looked slick. I did not trust myself in the rain. I held out my hand to him. "Brandon, I don't want to go out there!" I yelled. "Please come back. We'll talk. Just come away from there."

He turned to face me. The rain slid like beads of oil down his face and over his pressed lips.

"What are we going to talk about?" he shouted over the rain and wind and the hum of the river, his handsome face strained. His jaw clenched. "It's like you said. I'm married. Now you're single. What's there to figure out?"

I shrugged, "Just come back with me. We'll go back to my house. I'll get us some towels. I'll make you some hot chocolate."

"There's nothing more to say." He glared at me. "See you on the other side, Marlo." He waved.

"Brandon, knock it off!" I rushed, but my words went unheard as he slipped silently into the swirling black waters.

Chapter Nine

"Brandon!" I screamed. I ran to the side of the cliff, searching past the fast-moving river for any sign of him. But everything was in shadows. The rain and wind and river rushed in my ears. I hurried back to the pipe. I started to cross and felt my wet, shaking feet slip on the oily pipe, sending me tumbling forward. I grasped onto the edge of the crumbling cement, my legs dangling above the marshy drop. My feet fought for traction, kicking along the side until they found a ledge. I wedged my toes into a hole and pulled myself onto the lip of the well. Carefully, I crawled along the edge and peered over. There was no sign of him.

Damn that Brandon! What was he thinking? I had known too many stories of people swimming in the river during storms like this. Spring and early summer were especially dangerous times as the river rose, its swift current unforgiving, but swimming at night any time was suicide. That couldn't possibly be what he wanted, could it?

I crawled on shaking hands and knees back across the large black pipe, breathing a sigh of relief when my feet touched the earth again, even as the mud squished between my toes. I groped along the path for any sign of familiarity, holding on to the lilac bushes until the small familiar street lamp came into view and I could see the grassy knoll up ahead.

I ran up the slick hill, my feet slipping on the wet blades. My hands flew out to steady myself as I turned toward the sandbar. I called out his name, but my voice was lost in the storm. I called out again as I clambered around the jungle gym and hurried down the stairs to where the sandbar met the river. There was nothing but swirling blackness.

"I told you I'd meet you on the other side," Brandon's voice called from behind.

I spun around. Brandon stood at the top of the hill, his clothes sopping wet.

"Brandon!"

I ran back up the stairs and rushed at him. "Don't ever do that again!" I yelled as I raised my fists to his chest. He grabbed both my wrists to stop me from hitting him.

"You could have gotten yourself killed," I shouted.

"Marlo, don't you know? I'm a damn good swimmer."

"You're drunk," I accused.

He grasped my wrists tightly in his fists. "Maybe. A little."

"Maybe a lot."

The rain slowed. Lightning flashed in the distance. Brandon stood just centimeters from me, his eyes blazing. Neither of us moved. My heart pounded in my chest. Water dripped down my face. A trickle of water slid down his chin. Then another. I wiped the stream of water from his cheek. He loosened his grasp around my wrists and slowly lowered my arms. Then he moved his fingers till he held my hands, loosely, gently, like the lovers we'd been.

I shivered. He pushed my wet hair behind my ear.

"Do you really care what happens to me?" he wondered. The feel of his skin sent a jolt through my body. I closed my eyes. I wanted to wrap my arms around him and hold him, touch him, kiss him. But this was the real world. I dropped my hand and took a step backward, putting distance between us.

"That you might get yourself killed? Yeah, I guess you could say I care." I glanced down at the ground, sure he could see how warm my face had grown. I was still mad at him. I certainly couldn't let him know the effect he was having on me.

He continued to stare at me.

"What about your marriage? Is it really that bad?"

"It's been rough." He laughed self-deprecatingly, "Who am I kidding? I don't know what is going to happen to us. I don't know if we can make it."

"I'm sorry." I apologized, feeling responsible for his unhappy life. Wishing I had handled everything so differently.

"It could have been good, Marlo."

I shrugged away and moved beneath a large tree near the top of the hill. "Maybe," I said.

"Maybe? You don't know? Don't you remember what we had?"

"That was a long time ago. And time has a way of making everything seem better than it really was."

"I know what we had, and it was great. Why did you leave? Why didn't you listen to me?"

"Brandon, I can't change the past."

Brandon joined me under the apple tree. He leaned his head against the trunk and blew all the breath out of him, "What are we supposed to do now?" he looked at me out of the corner of his eye.

"We can be friends. We can always be friends," I promised, taking his arm.

He leaned in. I could feel his lips against my skin.

"Friends? See you in the grocery store, walk the other way? Pretend that it's not you sitting two bleachers away from me at the basketball games? Impossible," he assured me. He traced a finger along my jaw. I closed my eyes. A single tear slid down my cheek. He wiped it away with the tip of his finger.

His touch felt so good that for a moment I forgot where we were. Who we were.

"We could start over and do it right this time. You and me," he said, his voice turning intense.

I shook my head. "You can't do that. You have a child. I can't destroy a family."

His hands cupped my face. He lifted my chin to meet his eye. "You wouldn't be the cause."

I searched his eyes for an answer. For the right answer. "I don't know," I finally managed.

"I could end it right now." He grew excited. "Tonight. Just give me a chance, Marlo. That's all I'm asking." His hands caressed my shoulders and slid up the sides of my neck and into my hair. "We could be happy together. Like we were before." He pulled me in tight against his wet body.

"I don't know," I cried, still not sure. I wrapped my arms around him. We were both shivering. He leaned in close and pressed his lips to my forehead.

I couldn't deny how my body longed for him, craved his soft touches. I hadn't felt this way for so long that I was paralyzed. I closed my eyes and allowed his lips to sweep the top of my skin. I was shaking. From nervousness or cold or both.

"I never stopped loving you, Marlo," he declared.

My eyes flew open; the gravity of his words thrust me back to earth. I pushed him back and stood. I walked several steps away before I turned to face him.

"Brandon, you're still married. You've got to take care of that first. Then we can figure out what's next."

He stood. The spell was broken. His face grew red. "I waited a long time for you to come home." He walked towards the river. He tucked his hands in his pockets. "When I met Kelly, there was something about her that reminded me of you. An independence, like she'd just as soon tell the world to go to hell as serve 'em dinner. Then Kelly got pregnant. We decided to get married and try to be a family. But it's never felt right." He turned to face me. "I just need time to square things away. Okay?"

"Okay," I stuttered, not sure what I was saying. He rushed to me and kissed me quickly on the lips. I smiled sadly. A knot formed in my stomach as I watched him take off running down the road and disappear into the blackness.

I covered my mouth with my hands and stumbled backward. Hot tears stung my eyes. My heart burned. My knees buckled. I shouldn't have said those things. I knew it the minute they escaped from my mouth. There was a hollowness inside me, so cold and lonely. I crumpled back into the tree, wanting its hard, cold bark to comfort me, but it only scraped at my arms and hands as I slid to the ground. I wished that I could start over, fix things with Brandon, find happiness again. Now I had potentially added marriage wrecker to my long résumé of relationship failures. If only I could take it all back; my refusal to Brandon eight years ago, not telling Brandon about the wedding, my entire marriage to Cort. I wanted to start over. Find a way to fix everything.

I lay on the wet grass in a fetal position as the anguish and frustration exploded from my chest.

"Why can't I do anything right?" I sobbed. The sounds were broken into crumbling pieces and carried away by the wind. It was as if a plug had been pulled and I was sitting cold and naked in an empty tub, too discouraged to pick myself off the soggy, wet grass.

Another rumble shook the earth. A flash of light lit across the sky. The hairs on the back of my neck and arms stood on end. My heart quickened. I was a lightning rod. I went to pull myself up. Get myself away from this tree. A warm hand touched my shoulder. I froze. I covered my face, embarrassed to be caught in this position.

"You unhappy," said the old woman from the parade. She was clothed in a bright yellow rain slicker and looked slightly amused.

"I'm okay," I said between sniffles, wiping my nose and tears with my sleeve.

"No, you not okay. You confused."

Her response caught me off guard, and I laughed a little. "You could say that."

"Here." She offered me her hands. I took them, and she pulled me up.

"I know. I see whole thing. But I have a plan for you." She smiled widely, as if she'd just offered me the winning lottery ticket.

"I'm fine. I was just having one of those moments," I said weakly, hoping she wasn't going to try to set me up with someone.

"He say it all your fault. Bah! Not true."

"It is true," I tried to explain. "I've messed everything up. I screwed up my life, and now I've screwed up Brandon's in the process."

"Not true! I show you a thing or two. I can help fix everything."

I raised my eyebrows but said nothing.

"Here." She pulled out a dark brown bottle with a faded tan label that was nearly unreadable. It was topped off with a large cork. The woman popped the cork and handed the bottle to me. "You take. Make you feel better."

I push it away. "No, thank you."

She shoved it back under my nose. "You take; make it all better. It not bad, you see."

She shook it around to expulse some of the aroma. It smelled of black licorice and peppermint candy. Like my Grandpa Marlo used to smell. Certainly harmless.

"No, I really can't."

"You must!" She raised her eyebrows to show how serious she was.

"What's in it?" I asked a little desperately.

"Spices, a little licorice liqueur. Nothing bad for you."

"Really?"

"Try."

What the hell, I certainly could use a drink, I decided as I tipped the bottle and let the liquid slip past my tongue. It gargled and popped like carbonated soda, but did things to my head that only the strongest of liquors could do. I immediately regretted drinking it. I'd heard of those date rape drinks, not that she looked the type, but maybe she had someone waiting in the bushes. My head shimmied. I tried to speak, but the words wouldn't come out right as my tongue flopped like a dead fish in my mouth. I heard her saying something about being all better, and then everything went black.

Chapter Ten

When I awoke the birds were singing. A faint light seeped into the room. I snuggled deeper in bed, wanting to bury myself under the covers. A pair of unfamiliar arms squeezed me tight. I squirmed and stretched contentedly.

And then my eyes flew open.

Two masculine-looking arms were clasped around my waist. Someone was spooning me. Then I remembered the previous night's events. What had that woman done to me? *I've been raped!* I screamed and kicked back at the man with both feet before I struggled out of what I soon realized was a sleeping bag. The man groaned in pain. I leaped to the corner of what appeared to be a tent, then I started to hyperventilate. Things felt a little breezy. I looked down and recognized my own silk Victoria's Secret nightie. It was extremely sheer. I covered my chest with my arms. My face turned warm. The blue nylon walls closed in on me as I huddled in the corner. *I'm going to die! I am going to be one of those women they find gagged and tied, half naked and dead in the bushes. And I'll be wearing my nightie!*

"What was that for?"

I took a quick breath in when I recognized Luke's unshaven face and messy morning hair.

"LUKE!" I shouted.

"You know doing that to a man is kind of a turnoff," he grunted, doubled over, as he held himself. He rubbed his eyes together and yawned. "Did you have a bad dream or something?"

"How did you get this?" I demanded, pointing to my pink nightie before covering my chest again.

"You brought it."

"Oh, I just happened to bring my most sheer pajamas?"

"Yes, you did, and thank you," he grinned.

I threw a pillow at his head. "How did I get here?"

"Ow!" He rubbed his head with his free hand. "I drove you here, remember? In the Explorer."

"You were in cahoots with that old lady!" How could I have been so stupid! I crawled over pillows and bags and blankets to the edge of the tent and searched for the zipper. Luke grabbed my foot and pulled me back toward him. "Are you calling my mom an old lady?" he teased, his face pulled in a mischievous grin. "Now come back to bed."

I screamed and clawed my way back to the door. "I am freaking out right now! Stay away," I demanded, pointing a finger at him.

His smile faded. He cocked his head. "Are you okay?"

Luke climbed out of the sleeping bag we had been sharing. He was only wearing a pair of boxers. My face grew warm. I turned my head away.

"No, I'm not okay!" I didn't even know where to begin. I struggled to breathe. "How did I . . .?" "Did we really . . .?" I couldn't seem to get a complete sentence out, and I certainly couldn't look back at him. "I think I'm having a really crazy dream right now."

"Then why don't you come back under the covers with me and enjoy it," he cajoled, patting the sleeping bag.

"'Cause that would be wrong!" I rubbed my face in my hands and sneaked a peek at his deliciously chiseled abs. My face was on fire. I looked away again. It was tempting. "Wrong," I avowed, wondering what kind of psychedelic dream I was having.

"There isn't another tent for miles. We can howl at the owls all day. Just like we—"

"Stop!" I pressed one hand against my ear. "Don't tell me anymore. Just get dressed and take me home."

With arms strapped across my exposed chest like a straitjacket, I stood up. There was an immense pressure against my bladder.

"I've got to go to the bathroom."

"Here," he said, tossing me a roll of toilet paper. "You'll need this."

I stared down in sheer horror. "Seriously? Like, squatting in the bushes or something?"

He shrugged his shoulders. "Whatever works for you."

I glared in his direction. Not only had I slept with Luke, but I was now discussing bathroom procedures. This was too bizarre. And dumbest of all, he'd fallen for the oldest trick in the book. Except, I really did need a restroom. I'd figure out how to escape after I'd relieved myself. I unzipped the tent and crawled outside.

I took two steps forward. "Ouch!" I yelled hopping on one foot. Jagged rocks and thorns lay scattered all over the ground.

Laughter sounded from inside of the tent. A pair of sneakers whizzed through the opening. I recognized them as my own. Except I hadn't had them last night, either.

"Did you pick these up for me?" I asked, turning them upside down and peeking inside to make sure they were really mine.

Luke appeared in the opening, a crooked grin on his face. Thankfully he'd pulled on a pair of jeans. "You brought them, remember?"

No, I didn't remember, but I kept that to myself. I only glared at him as I shoved them on my feet. Whatever that old woman had given me had worked wonders. I couldn't understand why Luke drugged me; it seemed so unlike him. Even as I tried to make him the bad guy I couldn't believe it. Not because he was a policeman, but because I liked him and I trusted him to, well, not kidnap people.

I walked as far away from the tent as I dared. He was right about no one being around for miles. Our tent was pitched just off the river. We were surrounded by dust, sagebrush, and small olive trees. I picked the biggest bush I could find and squatted behind it to think things through. I had a pair of running shoes on; I could start running. Except I had no idea where we were, and I'd probably end up farther away in the desert, minus food or water, plus I was still in a pair of sheer, silky pajamas. With my luck, some pickup truck full of fishermen would pass me on the road and offer me a ride. What was worse—Luke or a whole gaggle of strange men? I glanced over my shoulder. Luke was nowhere to be found. My bladder pulsed. I really did have to go. I stared at the bush I was hiding behind. It looked thick enough to hide me, but I had to be sure. I couldn't stand the thought of mooning my bare behind in the open.

I walked back around to the other side and peered through the openings in the branches. It was pretty tight, but if someone really wanted to sneak a peek and stood right about here, they'd probably get an eyeful. I looked over my shoulder at the tent. The zipper was still closed. Apparently Luke wasn't very excited about watching me. At least he wasn't a total pervert.

I made my way back to the other side of the bush and squatted for real.

"Ouch!" I hollered. Something stabbed at my bare behind. I glanced down to see a prickly weed. I shifted to one side, this time careful to steer clear of the pokey weeds. I was actually pretty good at this squatting thing. My dad could fish for hours without hardly breathing, let alone having to "go." Over the years, my sister and I had learned how to pee in the woods with the best of them. You name it, we had used it or tried it. But I hadn't had to do this in at least fifteen years and had hoped to never do it again if it could be helped. But the way my kidneys were pounding, I knew I couldn't wait. I spread my feet as far as I could, squatted, and then closed my eyes thinking about the angry words I would use against this Luke guy in court. When I got back to the tent he was dressed head to foot in fishing garb.

"You're going to need these," he announced, handing over a pair of tall green wading boots.

I stared at the waders.

Memories of poles tangled among the thorns along the banks of the rivers filled my head. Now I knew I was in a nightmare.

"Stop!" I yelled.

His face fell. He let his arms drop. He stared at me, his eyes trying to read mine.

"I need to know what happened last night!"

"What we did in the tent or something else?" He seemed confused, but how could he be more confused than I was?

"All of it. Did you find me at the Sand Bar? Were you with that old woman or what? And how much of it was I aware of?" I asked, eyes squinting as a pink blush dusted my cheeks.

"It was that uneventful? You didn't seem to think so last night."

"I think I'm going to be sick."

"Harsh words, Marlo. And what old woman? Do you have a fever?"

I placed my hand on my forehead to see for myself, but all seemed fine. "I don't know. But I don't understand any of this. The tent, us together . . ."

Luke stared gravely at me. "What is this all about?"

"All about? Are you for real? You should be ashamed of yourself. Drugging me and leading me out here in the middle of nowhere. What are you going to do to me now? Tie me up and leave me for dead?"

"Is this about the fishing thing? 'Cause I told you, you didn't have to come. I'm fine fishing by myself."

"This is insane! How can you stand here so calm like that?"

His face reddened. "What do you want me to do? Throw a tantrum like you're doing? I'm the one that doesn't get it, Marlo. Last night you seemed happy enough, now you're accusing me of kidnapping you. If you don't want to go fishing, fine! Stay here." He took a deep breath, looked into the early-morning white sky, and then directly at me, and waited.

"Are you trying to tell me that I consented?"

Luke groaned in disgust. Without another word he laid his pole and basket against a folding chair and turned toward the tent. I watched as he rolled the sleeping bags up with quick, angry precision and threw them in the back of a blue Explorer parked off to the other side of the tent. In a matter of minutes, he had the whole thing dismantled. He shoved the tent and a black duffle bag in the back of the truck, slammed the door, and then stopped just inches from where I was standing. If he had drugged me, he certainly wasn't acting like it; in fact, he was acting like I was equally responsible for getting us into this mess.

"I haven't asked you to go fishing all summer. You can come with me, or you can stay here and wait. Either way, I'll be an hour or two." He grabbed his pole and basket without meeting my eye and turned to leave.

I watched as he disappeared through the brush that led to the river and fought the ridiculous notion that I was being a brat. *Kidnappers are often very manipulative,* I reminded myself. Didn't the victims sometimes fall in love with their captors, like Patty Hearst? I had to stay focused and get myself out of there, no matter how cute he might have looked in his fishing gear.

Once he was out of sight I rushed to the car and lifted the hatch. I grabbed the black bag Luke had thrown in the car and unzipped it. Our clothing lay neatly folded side by side. I couldn't believe the attention to detail. My underwear, makeup, all my own. There was no way he'd made a special trip to Victoria's Secret or Sephora's. Like there was even anything like that in a hundred-mile radius. It really looked like we were together. My head pounded. I dug through his clothes, looking for some kind of clue that he had drugged me, and found nothing but a small medicine bag with his toiletries inside. There was nothing unusual in it.

I frowned. When you drug and kidnap someone you don't leave them alone to go fishing. At least not before you've chained them up, or gagged and tied them. I knew a lot about this sort of thing because during all those nights I spent waiting for Cort to come home, I had watched hours of those cold case crime shows on cable. I got to where I could see the signs even before they pointed them out, shouting to the TV that it was that distraught-looking husband who murdered his wife and left her for dead at the bottom of the stairs. One went so far as to dip her cold dead hand in blood and write the name of her recent boyfriend on the wall. Pretty convincing except for one significant detail. She was left-handed, and it had been written with her right hand. It was always the husband, boyfriend, or jilted lover. But Luke hardly qualified as any of those things. We'd dated a little in high school, but I didn't think either one of us was heartbroken when we called it quits.

I caught sight of the car keys hanging in the ignition. He left the keys? Nothing added up. No shovel, no duct tape, or rope. What kind of low-budget kidnapper was he? He was either innocent or the world's worst kidnapper. I leaned toward the first idea. I shut the hatch, opened the driver-side door, and hopped inside.

The car was already warm from the morning sun. A sack of pistachios sat opened on the passenger's seat. I took a handful, but spit them out. Maybe this was part of his ploy: lace my favorite nuts with some kind of sleeping drug so he could have his way with me . . . again, apparently. I went to start the car and noticed a pocketknife hanging on the keychain. At least I knew I could stab him if worse came to worst. I turned the key. A CD was playing. It was Florence and the Machine, my favorite band. I shut the engine off. Things were really weird around here.

I leaned across the console and opened the glove box. I didn't know what I was looking for: duct tape, rope, the things usually found at crime scenes, but there wasn't anything like it. Only a black maintenance book with pink copies of oil change receipts or car tune-ups folded inside.

My hands froze as I touched something hard and cold. I shoved my hand in and pulled it out. Tucked in the back was a handgun still in its holster. The sudden fear that he might have drugged me returned. I quickly pulled my hand away. I shoved the maintenance book on top of the gun. A picture fell onto the floor. It was a small 2x2 photo, water spotted and fading, of me and Luke arm in arm in what looked like a tropical paradise: Hawaii maybe, or the Caribbean. When did we go anywhere like that together? I thought back to our senior trip to Mazatlan. I think he'd been there, but we weren't dating then. In fact, I'd been with Brandon most of the time. Where did this picture come from? Something was not right with any of this. I had to find that lady and find out what had happened. And I had to do it before Luke returned. I shoved everything back in and slammed the glove box shut.

Filled with new determination I turned the key over and nervously steered the car up the hill to the dirt road that led to a paved road. Behind me the Teton Mountains soared into the morning sky. That was east, that much I knew. I turned left and prayed that I hadn't totally forgotten my bearings as I traveled south toward St. Anthony.

Chapter Eleven

It didn't take me long to recognize the surroundings as being close to Chester Dam. But remembering how to get to town was a completely different thing as the long, empty road turned south, and then east. It wove around for another mile before I found myself going in the right direction again.

All the way back to town I thought about Luke in his boxers. If this really was a dream, I'd blown it. No one can be held responsible for their dreams, right? And if I found myself in the arms of a handsome former boyfriend, well, it couldn't be helped. No harm in a little promiscuity during the sleeping hours.

All the same, it didn't feel like a dream.

I screamed through town toward the Sand Bar where I'd last seen the old lady. I parked Luke's Explorer along the street and crossed the grass, shielding my eyes from the early-morning sun as I scanned the park. It was deserted. Too early for beachgoers.

"I thought that looked like Luke's truck," my mother called from across the street. I turned to find her standing on the curb, mail in one hand, and the other shielding her eyes like me.

I stared at her. It seemed like I hadn't seen her in years. She looked different somehow. Older, sadder. A few more bags under her eyes.

I hurried across the street. "Mom, are you okay?"

"Oh sure . . . I'm doing fine. Did you two have a nice time?"

Her words caught me off guard. I stammered a little. "How did you know?"

"Well, I may seem to be going senile, but I'm not there yet." She glanced down at my outfit. I followed her gaze.

"A little see-through, isn't it, dear? I know you two wanted a chance to be together, but did you need to come home and advertise it?" She winked. She looked over my shoulder. "Where's Luke? Didn't he get the day off? Anniversary and all."

"Anniversary?" My mother was in on it too? My head felt like it was filled with helium, ready to lift me over the water and out into the great wide yonder of the sky, never to be seen again.

"Are you okay, honey?" she asked, popping the balloon and sending me crashing to the earth.

My eyes filled with tears of frustration. Why was I the only one that did not know what was going on? All I could think about was that little old lady. She had pulled some kind of prank.

"Mom, have you seen an old lady, like five feet tall, salt-and-pepper hair, maybe Hawaiian, hanging around here?"

"Like that woman?" she asked, pointing across the street where the same old woman was standing under the same tree from the previous night.

"Yes!"

I ran toward the old woman.

"Hey!" I yelled, pointing a finger at her. "What did you do to me?"

She stood with arms folded. The rain slicker was gone. A different, but similar muumuu on her slender frame. Her smile fell flat. "You have fun?"

"Fun? Are you sick? You don't drug people. It's against the law. What did you do?" I insisted.

"I make it all better. Do you like?"

"Are you crazy? It doesn't work that way! I don't just wake up in bed with someone I hardly know!"

"You shout. I not deaf." She covered her ears and scowled.

I straightened up and took a deep breath. "Sorry, but I'm a little worked up right now."

"I give you a little glimpse. Not forever."

"A glimpse?" I scowled trying to understand. "Like it's just pretend?"

She nodded her head and put her hand on her hip. "You eat sucker, right?"

I stared back at her, totally blank.

She motioned with her hand, like sticking a sucker in her mouth.

"Oh, yeah, I did," I remembered, scratching my head in confusion.

"Sucker shows what your heart like. I not choose; you choose. Now you like!"

"No."—Though it was tempting to set all morals aside and head back toward the campsite in search of Luke. "Besides, I didn't choose him. If I were really going to choose I'd pick Cort or Brandon. Not Luke!"

"But Luke is good, huh?" she hedged with a wink.

Her lightheartedness took me by surprise. She was right. Luke was good. More than good, and if I hadn't thought that I had been drugged and kidnapped by him I could have really enjoyed that fantasy. I shook my head. I was getting way offtrack.

"What about Cort?"

"It can't be Cort. I sorry. Hearts have to match. His heart not match."

"Well . . . what about Brandon? Surly his heart would . . . match?" I could hardly say the words. This whole matchy business felt silly. "Just tell me what was in that drink. What have you done to me?"

She looked over both shoulders to see if anyone was watching and pulled me behind the trunk of the tree.

"I give you a short glimpse of how it can be," she explained.

"Okay, if I were to believe you, which I'm not sure I do, I would still say that Luke is not my destiny. Brandon is."

"Who say?"

"Brandon."

"Pfttt," she spat through her lips. "Only Brandon?"

"No . . . me too. I at least owe him a chance." I straightened and looked her in the eye but could not meet her glance for long. *I owed him, right? It was the least I could do,* I thought to myself.

She crossed her skinny arms and sighed. "Okay, fine. You have Brandon." She pulled out the same elixir bottle from a hidden pocket in her wide dress and popped the cork. Immediately the scent of peppermint and black licorice filled the air.

"Here? Now?"

The old woman seemed surprised. "Why not?"

"Well . . . what about Luke? I left him stranded," I explained, looking back at the SUV.

"Doesn't matter. All just a glimpse anyway. Now drink."

I turned around. My mother was no longer watching from the mailbox. In fact, no one seemed aware we were even there. I shrugged. What did I have to lose? I tipped my head back and drained the bottle.

It began its numbing effects immediately, but this time I didn't fight the paralysis that was swallowing me up into its blurry existence. I embraced it.

Chapter Twelve

When I woke I was lying on a bed surrounded by a pile of unfolded clean clothes, a half-folded shirt clutched in my hands. I wiped a string of drool from my cheek and opened my eyes. The room was hot—stifling, actually. The generic brown-paneled walls bored into my eyes with their ugliness. Beads of sweat gathered on the back of my neck. One droplet broke from the others and trickled down my back. There was a clock on the wall that seemed to have melted, the hands between the eleven and the twelve dripping like a Salvador Dali painting. The air conditioner must have broken. I sat up. The shades were down, casting an amber hue over the bedroom I was in like a hot blanket.

I wiped my hand across my forehead and caught little droplets of sweat in between my fingers. A nasty-looking nineteen sixties nightstand sat in a corner. I pulled the laundry off me and wiped the sweat off the back of my neck. I glanced down and noticed my blouse had an unknown stain that mirrored the state of Texas. I recognized it as a tee I'd had from Stanford. At least I had changed out of the silky pajamas. I stood. My legs felt shaky.

I walked out of the bedroom and into a living room. A small moan escaped my lips. The room was a closet, or at least might as well have been. My hand-loomed rug from Chinatown lay across a badly scuffed wood floor. A small original oil of Central Park I'd purchased from a street vender on one of Cort's and my trips to New York hung from the shabby dull wall. I rubbed my head to make sense of this crazy acid trip I was on.

I went back to the bedroom to change into something clean and preferably pressed. I rummaged through the tiny closet and found that nearly everything I owned had some sort of ameba-like stain on it. What kind of life had I thrown myself into this time? I moved to the window and immediately recognized Bridge Street. The famous one-stoplight street in St. Anthony. I had passed these little tiny Depression-era houses a hundred times and had never dreamed I might live in one someday.

There was a hard line to this house and the ones I could see out the window. Hard as in worn down and unkempt. Down pillows and Egyptian 400-count cotton sheets that mimicked the feel of silk were replaced with polyurethane fill and 200-count barely there sheets. Before marrying Cort, this kind of house wouldn't have bothered me, but I'd been removed from bare white walls and flat panel doors for so long I'd almost forgotten people really lived like this. I could only hope that life with Brandon more than made up for our lacking in chintz pillows and cashmere sweaters.

I moved to the kitchen and winced. I knew it wasn't going to be the row house with its gourmet commercial range, but this was substandard at any rate. It was not a kitchen, but a butler's pantry; one wall of eggshell-colored cabinets, an almond fridge, and a rack full of drying dishes beside the sink. Something inside me panicked. No dishwasher? Was this the old woman's idea of a joke? I rolled my eyes and turned back toward the living room where I scanned the pressboard bookshelf for photos. There were only two. One of Brandon and me together that by the suit Brandon sported and the white dress I wore appeared to be our wedding. Brandon's face was smashed against mine in a kiss while I stared off in the distance, a faint smile upon my face. And another of a little boy. A baby boy.

I heard crying behind a closed door.

My heart dropped. I froze in place.

Oh no. "Not a baby. Please, don't throw a baby on me," I begged out loud as I slowly made my way to the whimpering sounds.

I stood in front of the door—afraid to turn the handle. The

whimpering stopped. I had nothing against kids, but having one thrown on me full time, well, I wasn't sure I was ready for that.

A screen door clattered noisily from the kitchen. I dropped my hand from the doorknob and slowly backed away from the door. I rounded the corner and found myself face-to-face with Brandon. He looked much the same as he had the night before, if it really had been just one night ago, except his face was a little fuller. His eyes were still a deep chocolate color. He was still incredibly handsome.

"I'm starving," he hollered. "What you got in the pot?"

I sputtered for words. My face turned red. I struggled to keep from laughing at this ridiculous scene. I was really going to play house? Pretend to be married to Brandon? See what life would have been like if I had married Brandon just like the woman said? Okay. I wasn't much for acting, but I could try.

"I didn't realize it was lunchtime already," I finally answered, searching for the stage that I appeared to be on.

His face fell. "I only have forty-five minutes to eat. What am I supposed to have?"

My smile quickly faded. How did I tell him that I had just been thrust into this life only minutes before and had no idea what was in the fridge for him to eat? Let alone in the pantry, if there even was such a thing.

"Why don't we see what there is," I replied, spotting a loaf of bread on the cramped counter. "How about a sandwich?"

He stared dumbfounded at me. "A sandwich? I'm starving." He peered into the freezer and pulled out a frozen pizza. "This will have to do, I guess."

"Oh, Brandon, it's like eighty degrees in here. I'll make you a nice sandwich." But as I opened the fridge and searched through the drawers I could only find one small bag of lunch meat, nearly gone.

"Wow, looks like someone needs to go to the grocery store," he announced, glancing over my shoulder.

He was right.

"I'll go this afternoon," I said, wondering how long this glimpse would last. Would I be gone in an hour? A day? A week? I turned away from Brandon. I felt like an idiot. I should have asked her more questions instead of just diving into it.

When I turned back around Brandon had the pizza out of the box; the oven already preheating.

"Really?"

"What else am I going to eat?" he pouted.

I opened a drawer to find a pen and paper. "I'm not really hungry, so after I make a list I'll go to the grocery store."

"Whatever."

"Are you mad?"

"Nope. Just wonder why I wasted my time coming home for lunch."

"Anything you want in particular?"

"Meat. And maybe a little of you."

"I meant at the grocery store."

He shrugged. "Whatever." He cocked his head and listened. "Hey, is that Dylan?"

I stopped writing and listened. The whimpering had returned.

"I swear you'd leave him in there 'til he could call his own taxi." He stormed out of the room.

I stood frozen in place.

I was a mom. I was a mom?

Oh laws, how was I going to fake this one? I really hadn't spent much time with little kids. I was the youngest in my family and when it came to babysitting I had gotten out of most jobs. I knew there was something wrong with my DNA, but I just had no interest in other people's babies, honestly, not even my sister's. And now I had my own, and I wasn't prepared. Most people had nine months to come to terms. I had about seven seconds to suck it up.

I was expecting a little baby, like in the picture, but when Brandon returned with a kid sitting on his hip, I felt my knees begin to weaken. He looked more like a toddler. A cute toddler, but a toddler nonetheless. His eyes were bright aqua like the beaches in Cancun. His hair was curly brown and looked soft as lamb's wool. He leaned his body toward me, his arms extended.

"Does he want me to hold him?" I wondered aloud.

"He's just about to jump out of my arms. I guess you might take that as a yes."

Hesitantly I lifted my hands and made the exchange. I held the little guy awkwardly on one hip. Dylan, still sleepy from his nap, inched his hand down the front of my blouse.

"Whoa there, little buddy," I laughed, trying to pull his chubby little arm out of my shirt. He shook his head no, threw his head down on my shoulder, and shoved his hand back down my shirt.

"Come on, give the kid a break. You know that helps him calm down," Brandon said, looking hungrily to where his son's hand swam freely beneath my shirt.

"I'm not sure this is a good thing to teach him," I stated matter-of-factly as I yanked his hand out more forcefully.

"He's just going to cry," Brandon explained. Sure enough, little Dylan started to whimper, and then began to cry as I held his hand away from my chest.

Barely two and he was already vying for a feel.

My blood pressure was rising. Dylan's crying was stressing me out, and Brandon seemed completely unwilling to help as he plopped himself down at the little farm table under the small kitchen window. I let go of Dylan's hand. Quick as a snake under grass he slithered his little mitt down my shirt again. This time I left it alone.

"So what do I do about the grocery store?"

Brandon lifted his head from the dirt bike magazine he'd opened and stared at me.

"You go?" he guessed, thinking it was some kind of lame trivia game.

"But what about Dylan?"

"Take him. I don't know. What do you usually do?" Brandon was losing his patience. I bit my lip realizing I was coming off as a complete ditz.

"I mean, should I drive or walk?" I persisted.

Brandon closed his eyes, and then sighed. "I don't care. You walk everywhere. I don't know why we bothered getting your damned car fixed anyways."

My car! It was fixed! Thank heaven. "So I guess Dylan and I are off to the grocery store then," I announced, feeling better about having an excuse to cut loose.

The buzzer for the pizza went off. My stomach grumbled noisily. Dylan was now sucking on his thumb.

"Do you think he's hungry?"

"Jeez, Marlo. What do I look like? How 'bout you ask him. Dylan, are you hungry?"

Dylan nodded yes.

He could understand? I know, I was acting like an idiot. I just felt frozen, like I didn't know my lines in this stupid play. I looked over at the pizza. What was I supposed to feed him? I couldn't ask Brandon. He already thought I'd lost my mind.

The timer was still beeping. I noticed Brandon hadn't moved from his spot. *Time for me to suck it up.* I sat Dylan on one hip and pulled the pizza out of the hot oven. The oven easily added ten degrees to the already scorching room. I snagged a small piece for Dylan and cut it up into bite-sized pieces, dropping the pizza and Dylan into the high-chair next to the farm table. He had a few chompers in his mouth, so I figured he could handle it. If not, I'd eat it myself. He grabbed a small piece with his fingers and stuffed it in his mouth. At least he seemed to know what he was doing.

I was sweating like mad. I needed some air. With Brandon ignoring me and Dylan busy eating, I escaped out the screen door to check on my car.

I was met by a large Dodge truck sitting in the tiny driveway. I sighed. I was glad Brandon didn't expect me to drive to the store in that monster. Tucked behind the house was a small garage. *My car must be in there,* I thought with relief. I opened the side door and poked my head in. I frowned. My Mercedes wasn't sitting in the driveway. Only a small white Escort sat in the dingy shed.

A sick feeling churned in my stomach. I shut the door and made my way back up the steps. The screen door slapped noisily against the doorjamb. Brandon was sitting at the small drop leaf table, eating the last piece of pizza.

"So my car is in the garage?" I asked with great trepidation.

"Should be."

"The white Escort?" I swallowed hard.

"That'd be the one," he said slowly, watching me suspiciously.

Of course. It all made sense. This was a glimpse; therefore, there was no Mercedes because there was never a Cort. The only problem was I still remembered Cort. I still could feel the purr of my Mercedes. How could I get an honest glimpse when all I saw were the things I no longer had?

"Right. I just had this dream about having a Mercedes. I guess I haven't fully woken up yet." I laughed. Sort of.

"We traded it for the truck, remember? And you promised you didn't care." For the first time that day Brandon really looked at me.

"Wait, so I did have a Mercedes, but now I don't?"

"Marlo, I know you miss your car. I know you're embarrassed to drive the Escort, but I don't understand why you're giving me grief about it now. Kelly never minded it."

"Kelly? The Escort is Kelly's car?" My stomach did a funny loopty-loop. This wasn't sounding like the glimpse I had hoped for.

"*Was* Kelly's car. What is going on with you today?"

"I don't know. I think it's the heat. Is the air conditioner broken?"

"Ya mean that one?" He pointed to an oscillating fan sitting unplugged on top of the fridge.

I closed my eyes and took a deep breath. Something foul rose in my throat. "I'll be back," I said weakly, picking Dylan up and carrying him outside.

Brandon's enormous pickup, courtesy of my beloved Mercedes, was like a giant elephant in the tandem driveway. My hands shook, and Dylan grew heavy in my arms. A few minutes ago I believed I was seeing life from eyes that had never known San Francisco or Cort, or any of the things that came with it. I was willing to play along, even though I knew from the minute I spotted brown paneled walls that this life was not going to be easy, but this was just plain wrong. I couldn't play "glimpse" with a man who was married to someone else in real life. This wasn't fun or interesting. I had to stop this from happening. I had to get Brandon back with Kelly.

I spun around and stomped back to the kitchen.

Brandon had just finished washing his plate. I made a mental note that while he couldn't be bothered to make his lunch, he did seem to help out. A little. He looked over in surprise.

"What now?"

"I just need to talk to you about Kelly." Dylan started to fuss in my arms. My back burned from his weight. I shifted him against my hip. He was like holding a sack of alive rocks. It relieved the pressure. Now I knew why women held kids on their hip. He was still fussing, so I started to rock him back and forth. He settled down for a moment.

"I don't want to talk about Kelly again. I've got to get to work." He grabbed his keys from the counter and headed for the door. He clasped the doorknob in his hands and turned to face me. "There was nothing I could do. You believe me, right?"

Nothing he could do? What did that mean? Had she left him? Or was he only saying that he couldn't help the way he felt about me? Dylan started fussing more. I stopped rocking in place and looked at the little boy in my arms. I examined his curly hair, his bright blue eyes. No one in my family, not even Melissa's kids, looked like Dylan. I turned to Brandon, took in his chocolate brown eyes, his straight hair. I could see a hint of Brandon in Dylan's features but nothing of mine.

Because he wasn't mine. He was Kelly's baby.

Chapter Thirteen

"So Dylan, he's Kelly's?"

Brandon dropped his keys and stared at me. "What the hell are you getting at?" His face burned red. I held Dylan tighter. Dylan hollered and squirmed in my weakening arms.

"I'm sorry. I just wanted to get the facts straight."

I was certain he thought I'd gone crazy. "Sorry," I repeated, hoping to dispel the situation. I glanced out the window and stared at what had become of my beautiful car. Why had I allowed him to trade the car in for that monster truck? Okay, I knew he lived in St. Anthony and that a Mercedes was probably more ostentatious than he would have been comfortable with, but why couldn't we have agreed on a family car? Something that was practical for all three of us? It seemed to me that the Marlo in this glimpse was as big of a pushover as the Marlo in real life. And this Marlo was sick of it.

"Look, I'm sorry. I fell asleep and had a really weird dream. It's probably just the heat. Dylan and I will go to the store now," I said, grabbing my Prada bag off the hook on the back of the door, hurrying out the door, running away from Brandon's anger. Brandon stood in the doorway and watched me. I refused to meet his eye.

I spotted a stroller on the side of the house, sun bleached but in decent shape despite that. I strapped Dylan in. There was no way I was taking Kelly's car anywhere. What if she saw me? What if I were mistaken for her? Dylan smiled and kicked his legs. He knew what a stroller meant. I would walk from now on, though it seemed evident from the dust on the car that I'd made that decision long ago.

By the time I reached the supermarket I had sweat marks under my armpits and drops trickling down between my breasts, leaving a small circle in the middle of my shirt. *Midday in July is probably not the best time to take long, vigorous walks,* I realized. Dylan loved the walk though. He kicked his feet and jabbered the whole way, pointing out anything that proved of interest: birds, airplane, leaves on the trees. He noticed everything, though most of the time I had no idea what he was saying.

While Dylan jabbered, I tried to find out where in time I was. Dylan was obviously no newborn, but when Amanda and Brandon talked about Kelly and the baby that night at the park, it seemed like Dylan had just been born.

The longer I walked in the heat, the more upset I became with that old woman. This wasn't what I had agreed to at all. I had wanted a do-over. She had tricked me again. This was not a glimpse of the life I could have had if I hadn't left for Stanford, if I hadn't married Cort, but was only a continuation of the life I had chosen. The more I thought about Kelly and Brandon splitting up and me—taking care of her child, driving her car—the angrier I became. How had I let this happen?

I parked the stroller just outside of the grocery store and pulled a sweating Dylan out of his sticky seat. He lay his head down on my shoulder and slid his paws down my blouse again. Inside, the grocery store was nice and cool. I sighed, relieved to feel modern conveniences again. I placed Dylan in the cart, carefully untangled the belt that had been weaved in and out of the metal bars, and then tied in some elaborate knot by someone too old to be sitting there in the first place, and made my way down the fruit and vegetable aisle. I grabbed some fresh basil and tomatoes.

Before I'd figured out that this was not exactly a do-over I had wanted to make something nice for Brandon, a specialty dish that Cort had taught me called cioppino; a soup that dated back to the early days of the Gold Rush, or so the story went. It was said that the fishermen used to gather after the day's work was done and throw different pieces of fish and seafood into a communal pot for supper. They would call out to each other in broken English "chip in," "hey you, chip in," hence the word cioppino. It was impossible to know if this story was real, but I liked it, so I took it as fact.

I grabbed an onion, some celery, and then headed to the meat department. I picked up two packages of lunch meat, and then headed towards a worker who informed me that the only crab and halibut they had was in the freezer section. When I mentioned mussels and prawns, the man stared me down.

"What kind of soup you making?"

I tried to explain it to him, but he looked like I was pulling his leg.

With a crinkled up nose he added, "Why don't you just stick some trout or salmon in there. I also have shrimp. But that other crap . . ." he made a funny face. "You might have to go to the Mexican store to find any of that stuff."

"Do Mexicans eat more seafood?"

"Hell, they eat all kinds of weird stuff. You never know what they might have in their freezers." My eyes bulged out of my head. Apparently the political correctness that I was used to hadn't reached St. Anthony.

I thanked him and ordered a pound of shrimp. Luckily, I found a couple small bags of halibut and crab in the freezer section. It wouldn't taste like it came from Farallon's, or any of the other five-star restaurants in San Fran, but Brandon would be none the wiser.

After I played this little game of house, I was definitely going to find the old woman and wring her neck. Then I would demand she get me out of this glimpse. Dylan leaned his body toward the candy aisle. Great. A screaming toddler in a grocery store. That was all I needed. What was I supposed to do? Tell him he can't have any candy? I patted his arm and reminded him that we'd get him some cheese sticks in just a minute, but he only screamed louder, demanding he wanted a "cuk, cuk." I could feel my blood pressure rising. I imagined that old woman was having quite a laugh right about now, watching me struggle with a little person who had more will in his tiny legs than I had in my whole body.

"I think he wants a cookie," a familiar voice whispered in my ear. My face flushed. I turned to see Luke standing, head to foot in fishing gear, a grin on his face. He was wearing the same fishing garb that he'd been wearing when I left him stranded out at the dam. Crazy thing was, he didn't even look mad.

I stood staring at Luke for what felt like an eternity.

How could I explain why I'd left him stranded? How would I explain this little boy in my shopping cart? I wanted to hide. It didn't help that I was having flashes of his disheveled nakedness in the tent. I bit my lip and pretended to adjust Dylan's belt buckle some more.

"I figured as much," I finally answered.

"So why not get him one?"

"Because I shouldn't give in to his tantrums," I explained, digging deep into a past child development class I'd taken ages ago.

He nodded in agreement. "Watch this. Hey, Dylan, check this out." He pulled a quarter from his pocket and held it out for Dylan. Dylan stopped fussing and kicking and stared at the quarter. Luke hung his keychain in front of Dylan. I recognized the pocketknife. Dylan stared at the shiny contraption. "See, it's all about distraction." He pushed the cart. "Now we'll slowly walk over to the cracker section. You do let him have crackers, right?" he asked without looking back at me.

"Of course," I glared at him, but he didn't even notice. He was playing with me again. This guy was always playing with me.

"Dylan, want some animal crackers?"

Dylan squealed in delight. Luke grabbed a box of crackers. "Kay, let's go pay for them, and then you can have them." He pushed the cart toward the checkout.

Dylan clapped. I stared in amazement. "How do you know how to do that?"

"Lots of nieces and nephews." He stood up straight and offered me back my cart. "So, I haven't seen you for a while. Everything going okay?"

I slowly pushed the cart down the lane and said apologetically, "I am so sorry about this morning." I shook my head and stared down at my feet.

"What?"

"What?" I answered back, realizing he didn't seem to know what I was talking about.

He stopped walking. He looked at me with a concerned face. "Did you say something happened this morning?"

I paused, falling into his deep brown eyes. Eyes that held no evidence of my abandoning him. It had been just a glimpse. It hadn't really happened, just like this wasn't really happening, which was confusing, because Dylan's little happy kicks against my leg felt very, very real.

"Oh, I . . . no, I was just thinking it's been so long since I've seen you too. How are you?"

He nodded his head. "Doing good," he said, slapping me on the shoulder. We started walking again. "Things are good, though? With you and Brandon?"

"Sure. Good." My face burned when I met his eye. Luke helped me unload my cart of the few groceries I'd gathered. How could I explain the truth? He must have thought me such a terrible person to have taken Dylan away from his mother, to have taken Brandon away from Kelly.

I checked out, and then helped Dylan open his animal crackers while Luke finished checking himself out.

"Let me help you with those bags." He looked around the sparsely filled parking lot. "Where did you park?"

"I didn't park; I walked."

"In this heat? Why don't you let me take you home?"

The thought of Luke taking me home felt too weird, especially after this morning. Especially weird that he didn't seem to remember it at all. "Thanks, but it really isn't necessary," I said, waving him off.

"I insist, and anyways, we've got a lot to catch up on," he said as he took my bags from my hands.

I sat Dylan in the stroller and followed him out of the store.

"Whatcha making?" he asked, taking a sneak peek.

"A tomato-based soup called cioppino. Lots of seafood."

"I bet it would go good with the rainbow trout I just caught."

"You've been fishing?"

He looked down his body, waving at his waders. "You could say that."

"Near Chester Dam?"

His eyes lit up. "Yeah, that's right. The backwaters, by Seeley's place. Had a heck of a morning. Caught two rainbow trout and two cutthroats. Frying them up tonight."

This was too weird. "Sounds . . . delicious."

He stopped for a moment. "You should come over." He glanced down at Dylan and corrected. "You and Brandon and Dylan, I mean. I haven't seen Brandon in ages. Might be good to catch up with the guy."

"That sounds great. What about you? Are you dating anyone?"

"What?"

Oh, I'd done it again. He must be married, and I'm supposed to know that. "Who, what is . . ." I didn't know how to phrase it.

"I've started seeing Amanda. I thought you knew that."

"Amanda? Like Kale's friend, Amanda?"

"Kale's friend? They dated like three years ago, and I'd hardly call them friends now."

"She's very pretty." It was all I could say as I hadn't been that impressed with anything else about her. "I'll call Brandon about tonight."

He led me to his Explorer. I wondered if the gun was still hidden in the glove box. Or if there was still a picture of me and him in there. I stared at the glove box. It took all of my self-control to keep from cracking it open and having a gander.

Just then, Luke slapped his hand against his forehead. "What was I thinking? I don't have a car seat for Dylan. I'm really sorry, Marlo, making you wait and all."

"Oh. That's fine. I forgot too," I answered honestly.

I was the worst mom in the world. If only I could explain that I was actually new at this.

"You guys still live in Brandon's Grandma's house, right?"

"His grandma's house?" I repeated.

"Yeah, don't you remember his grandma Clark?"

I had totally forgotten. In fact, I'd actually stopped by once with Brandon, but it had been dark and I had been too preoccupied with Brandon to pay much attention to her house. It had smelled of moth balls and old dust and now, lucky me, it was all mine. "Oh, yeah, of course I remember Grandma Clark." I needed to just get home so I could stop screwing up everything.

"Talk to Brandon and have him call me. Tonight's as good as any seeing as I've got this fresh fish here." He smiled and my mind flashed to that moment when he was sitting up in nothing but a pair of boxers. I squeezed my eyes shut trying to rid myself of the mental picture.

"I'll talk to him," I agreed, waving Luke off as I turned and slowly pushed the stroller down the street.

Chapter Fourteen

I unloaded the groceries onto the table and poked my head in each cupboard looking for places to put stuff. There was a small gap beside the fridge where I hung the bags on a hook. Dylan toddled off to his room in search of something.

The phone on the wall rang. It was my mother. The sound of her voice was like a cool glass of water on a hot day.

"Mom, I saw Luke today."

"Oh," she sounded grave, "was it okay?"

"He's dating a girl named Amanda."

"Well, glad he got over you."

"Got over me?"

"Well, you know he had a crush on you when you first came back."

"You mean by pulling me over and scaring me to death? Definitely a childish crush."

"You were speeding."

I sighed. "I've been thinking about Kelly. About little Dylan and how she should be raising her son and not me. I don't think I'm a very fit mother." Dylan had returned to the kitchen with a small Spider-Man figure. He held it out to show me. I smiled and nodded. He toddled off toward his bedroom again.

"I know it's hard, honey, but you're doing a fine job. Don't get discouraged."

"No, really. I think Kelly should have Dylan. I feel terrible."

"We all do, honey. It was such a tragic accident. And it was so brave of you to run to Brandon's side like you did. We all think so. Including Luke."

I couldn't hear my mother's voice anymore. My hands grew weak. The phone fell loose against my ear as I wrapped my head around my mother's words. Kelly had been in a tragic accident. I had rushed to Brandon's side. I had been brave.

Wait . . . that meant that Kelly was dead.

The phone beeped in my ear. The caller ID showed it was Brandon. I murmured an apology to my mom and clicked over.

"Hello?"

"Hey. I just wanted to apologize for getting all over your case. It's been a rough week."

My lips went to form words, but I couldn't get them out. How could I ask Brandon what happened to Kelly without sounding more bonkers than I already did?

"Luke has invited us to dinner tonight." It was the only thing I could think of.

"Luke Dawson? He just called out of the blue and invited us to dinner? At his house? What is he trying to pull?"

"I don't think he's trying to pull anything," I said with a hint of sarcasm. "I saw him at the grocery store. He asked how you were and thought it would be good to get together. I thought you two were friends."

"Yeah, we *were* until he thought I had something to do with Kelly's death, and then he tried to change your mind about marrying me. I'd rather castrate a bull than have dinner with him."

"Luke was involved with investigating Kelly's death?" I asked, ignoring the castrating comment.

"Well, he's not a detective, but he's still on the force. How could you forget? It was a nightmare and a bunch of bull," his voice sounded brittle and edgy. I definitely hit a sore spot.

"But the investigation is over, right?" I hoped.

"Sure, but it doesn't stop people from talking."

I bit my lip and tapped my fingers nervously on the table. I wanted to ask him what happened, but knew it would sound crazy.

"Maybe it's better we don't see him then, if it's too uncomfortable," I agreed.

"Wait. I don't want him thinking I'm hiding from him. Call him. Tell him we'll be there."

So much for castrating the bull.

We hung up. My bags of groceries sat untouched. I had no desire to cook or do anything besides find out what happened to Kelly, but how could I go around asking questions about things I should have already known?

I looked Luke up in the phonebook. He seemed surprised when I told him that Brandon and I would be happy to come.

"There were so many questions surrounding Kelly's death. I guess after two years we all have to move on," Luke said.

"Right," I agreed. My hands started to shake.

"I didn't think about it, but last night was the anniversary of her death."

"Last night? Um . . . what's the date today?" I asked, moving over to a calendar that hung beside the fridge.

"Twenty-sixth. You don't get out much anymore, do ya?"

"I guess not," I agreed, seeing that the calendar said June and there was no way this hot weather was happening in June. Not in Southeastern Idaho, anyway.

I flipped the calendar forward to July. "We're in July, right?"

He laughed, thinking I was making a joke. I laughed right along with him. It did sound ridiculous. The date was July twenty-sixth, two years since I had returned home. A pit grew in my stomach. Brandon's wife had been alive that night—last night—at the Sand Bar. I remembered our conversation about starting over. Brandon had mentioned leaving Kelly. Brandon said there had been an investigation. That some thought he was responsible. Had Brandon killed his wife? Something mimicking bile rose in my throat. I pushed it back down. I said good-bye to Luke, promising to bring my cioppino soup with me when we came over.

I attempted to chop basil while I replayed the conversation I'd had with Brandon last night. Was it possible that I hadn't made myself clear that I didn't want him to really leave his wife? It had been a lapse of judgment on my part and because of that, maybe he decided to kill her. I shuddered at the idea. Of course he wouldn't do that. Brandon was a good guy. He wouldn't do something so irrational. I was instantly ashamed of myself for even thinking it.

Dylan started crying in his bedroom. I dropped the knife and hurried to his little bedroom. It was awash in a yellow glow from the late-afternoon sunlight. The walls were painted in large green and yellow pastel stripes. Little elephant and giraffe motifs lumbered across the walls toward matching café curtains and an identical comforter in the crib. This room had been decorated by a woman's hand. Probably Kelly's hand. Dylan screamed out in pain, his hand stuck in the doorway of a little barn. I knelt beside him and tried to pull his hand out. I couldn't figure out what was keeping his hand in there until I noticed a small boot sticking out of his fist. The action figure was too tall to come out of the door. He refused to let go or bend the hero down to escape. He was totally trapped and growing more frantic by the second.

"Ya gotta let go of Spider-Man, buddy," I coerced. He cried even louder at the thought of leaving his superhero behind. I reached in and wriggled the too-tall Spidy out the front door. Dylan's tearstained face looked up at me in simultaneous frustration and gratitude. He lifted his chubby hands and murmured through wet tears, "Houd you."

"What?"

He pulled himself up and flung his arms toward me and repeated, "Houd you."

"Okay, sure." I picked him up and laid him against my chest.

"Bankee."

"Bankee?"

"Bankee," he agreed, burrowing down into my neck again. I walked over to the crib and peeked over the railing, still not sure what bankee meant, but when I caught sight of the ragged Winnie the Pooh blanket I understood immediately and grabbed it.

He snagged a strand of my hair with one hand and started twirling it in his chubby hands while nuzzling his face deep into my neck. I rocked him in the rocking chair while he sniffed and hiccupped and lulled himself to sleep.

While Dylan took a late-afternoon nap I threw the ingredients together for the soup. I wasn't sure why I kept playing along with this glimpse, except I didn't know what else to do. Between chopping onions and shelling shrimp I dreamed up concoctions of how Kelly might have died. My imagination was a horror movie playground. I hoped it had been a legitimate accident, but the fact there had been an investigation left most common accidents off the list of potential ways she could have died.

I put the soup on the stove to simmer, cleaned the kitchen, and returned to the living room, where I scanned the single bookshelf for anything involving Kelly. There wasn't anything. Not a picture. Not a scrapbook. I moved to the bedroom and ransacked Brandon's drawers and peeked under the bed. The floor was covered with a thin layer of dust. There was no sign of Kelly in the entire house. It was like she had never existed. It was worse than an annulment. At least with the annulment I still had some things to remind me of my life with Cort. This felt like Brandon had erased any connection to Kelly, his only reminder his little boy. And that car. I wondered if Dylan looked like Kelly. I wondered if that was why Brandon had become so angry when I mentioned Dylan being Kelly's child. I leaned over and poked my head under his side of the bed and slid my hand under his mattress.

"What's going on?" Brandon asked from behind me.

I yanked my hand out of the mattress and held out a sock. "Just looking for the match," I said, feeling ashamed for not trusting him.

He raised his eyebrows, and then tapped the doorjamb with the palm of his hand.

"What time is this shindig?" he asked with a frown.

"Six o'clock."

He sighed, and then scratched his head. "I'm gonna take a shower first."

I took a look at him. He was covered in dirt. His pants looked stiff from being wet, and then having dried in the sun. Thankfully he'd removed his boots.

"Good idea," I agreed. "I'll get Dylan."

We walked carefully around each other as we prepared to leave. I kept Dylan near me at all times. Every time Brandon walked in a room I jumped. Brandon didn't seem like a killer, but there were too many unanswered questions. When it was time to go we all loaded up in the truck—Dylan in between us and the soup on my lap—bouncing our way down Bridge Street in the giant truck.

"You're biting your nails again," Brandon reminded me, still not looking at me, as a toothpick dangled out of his mouth. I stopped mid-bite. It was like Cort all over again. This was so déjà-vu-y it was scary. Brandon stretched his hands in front of the steering wheel and popped all his knuckles. The hairs on the back of my neck sprang to life. I kept my thoughts to myself and tucked my hand under the warm pan.

"Where does Luke live anyway?" I asked.

He slammed on the brakes. Hot soup splashed over the sides and onto my lap. "What do you mean you don't know where Luke lives? Are you playing some kind of game with me?" He glared at me.

My eyes grew wide. The hot liquid searing my skin was nothing compared to the look Brandon gave me. I stammered for an answer. "No, you just misunderstood my question," I tried, hoping to cover my stupidity. "I meant, does he still live in the same place?"

"Here," he muttered, leaning under the seat and pulling out a roll of industrial-strength paper towels.

"Thanks," I said as I wiped up red soup off my black Capri pants. At least my pants only looked damp.

"You trying to tell me that you don't keep track of him? You don't just happen to go to the grocery store the same time he does?"

"It was a total coincidence, Brandon."

His blazing eyes narrowed in on me. I caught my breath and grasped the edge of the seat. He looked handsome, but his eyes were ablaze and I thought for the first time that it might be possible that Brandon was capable of murder.

"I'm sorry. I don't want to fight." I conceded.

Brandon turned left past the Del Rio Bridge where the osprey nest lay, and steered the truck toward the white ranch house nestled against the river. I opened my mouth in surprise, and then promptly shut it. I was supposed to know where Luke lived already.

"Whatever happened to the lady that used to own this house?" I asked nonchalantly.

"Moved in with her daughter. She was Luke's aunt, I think," Brandon said shortly. I hoped I wasn't supposed to already know that too.

We wound our way down the private lane and eventually parked in the wide drive. We sat there staring at the beautiful white brick home for a moment.

Brandon muttered, "I just want to know how a guy like him can afford a house like this on his cop's salary."

"If it was his aunt's, maybe she gave him a good deal."

Brandon made a sound in his throat, opened his door, pulled out the now mangled toothpick he'd been gnawing on, and chucked it into the grass. He lifted Dylan out of his car seat and together, we made our way to the front door.

"Let's get this over with," he grumbled.

From the looks of things we seemed like a real family. Soup in my hands, child in Daddy's arms. But I was sure my knees would collapse any minute as they'd turned into wet noodles ever since I'd learned of

Kelly's death. Brandon leaned across me and rang the front doorbell. I cringed at his touch. It chimed for several seconds before the door opened.

Luke, donning a red Tabasco apron, and standing with a tray of raw fish in his hands, stood in the doorway. His face was tan and gleaming; his eyes sparkled. He felt like a breath of fresh air. I put on a fake smile and hoped my newfound worries wouldn't be too obvious.

"Hey, guys, glad you could make it. Amanda is running late, but she'll be here soon," he explained.

Brandon met my eye with a look of confusion. I could only stare back, my eyes wide. I had no idea what he was mad about now.

"He sure is getting big," Luke smiled while ruffling Dylan's locks.

"That's what they do," Brandon muttered.

When Luke turned away I gave Brandon a stern look. He shrugged innocently as he followed Luke through the door. We walked directly to the back and out two large glass doors that led to an expansive deck. Luke set his tray down on a wrought iron table, and then took my soup out of my hands and set it down next to the tray.

"This looks delicious."

"Thanks," I said, avoiding Brandon's stare.

The yard stretched north and south along the cascading riverbank. The freshly cut green grass added a sweet aroma against the smoking barbeque coming from his grill. Grass. That was something I missed in San Francisco. Except for Cort's parents' estate, our barbeques were usually set on stone, cement, or wooden decks, and there was seldom enough grass to lie on, let alone play a game of football on, like you could here. I glanced past the broad yard and discovered a long wooden dock extending into the river. I remembered when Melissa and I used to sneak through this yard to float our tubes down the river to our house, which by inner tube was only a leisurely half-hour ride, an easy one to pull off on a lazy summer afternoon.

"I've always loved this place, Luke," I sighed.

"Well, I haven't done much since I moved in, but I hope to eventually."

We made our way down the deck stairs to a large patio. Dylan rushed out of Brandon's arms and toddled away down a slight embankment before tripping in the thick grass and rolling down a small hill. I rushed to help him up, but he was already going again, probably excited to have someplace to run. Our yard was little more than a postage stamp. Luke took us for a walk, showing us where he'd like to build a tree hut one day and a bigger shop for himself. He led us to a small pond surrounded by cattails and day lilies. A canoe sat tied to a small dock.

"Do you fish in this?" Brandon asked.

Luke shrugged his shoulders. "To be honest, I haven't even taken the canoe out. Guess I should sometime, huh?" He looked down at his feet, embarrassed, though I couldn't imagine why.

"I'm going to go start that fish. I'll be right back," Luke announced.

I turned to follow him, but Brandon grabbed my arm. "Why are you acting like this is all such a big surprise?" he hissed when Luke was out of earshot. "I know all about that night he tried to stop you from marrying me, so you don't have to play stupid with me."

His face was red. His jaw clenched. I blinked hard. Luke disappeared around the corner. My heart pounded. Adrenaline shot through my insides.

"Let go of my arm." I panted, like all the air was gone out of me. My hands shook. I squinted and refused to look away. He dropped his hand and straightened up. He peered over my shoulder and scowled.

"Oh great. Here comes hell on wheels." he said in a low voice.

I turned to see what he was looking at. A yellow Volkswagen Bug came careening around the corner at a breakneck pace and pulled our attention away from each other.

Amanda.

Chapter Fifteen

Brandon's fists curled at his sides. The car stopped inches behind the truck, the fender nearly kissed his bumper. Amanda was all leg as she stepped from her Volkswagen Bug: red high-heeled sandals, short shorts, and a blouse so low I could see to her navel. And Luke gave me grief for my off-the-shoulder sequined top.

"Hey, Brandon." She smacked florescent green gum between her front two teeth. I waited for a bubble, but it didn't come.

"Amanda," he answered shortly, glaring at her, and then turning away.

"Hi, Amanda, it's been awhile, but I'm Marlo," I said, offering my hand.

She glared down at my outstretched hand with a look that could kill a tiger.

"I know who you are," she spat.

"I'm sorry. I just thought maybe it'd been awhile?"

"I don't care if it's been ten years. I'd know the little whore that stole my best friend's husband anywhere, now, wouldn't I?"

My face burned red at the accusation. I felt three feet tall.

"Amanda! Get a grip," Brandon blurted. He glanced down at her legs. "Where'd you get those shorts anyway? Stole them from your five-year-old niece?"

"Funny, Brandon," she huffed. "But I'll have you know these are all the rage. Haven't you seen Paris Hilton lately?" She pulled a cigarette from a small handbag and lit it, took two short puffs, and then attempted to hold it sweetly in her nicotine-stained fingers. "I guess you wouldn't know since the last thing you'd want is to show your wife's legs off."

"It's not legs I'm concerned about exposing."

She blew the smoke into the air and gave a strange clownlike smile, reminiscent of the Cheshire cat in *Alice in Wonderland*.

I glanced down at my soup-stained capris. *I have nice legs!* I wanted to argue. Amanda turned around looking for Luke. My eyes widened. Her backside was hanging out of her shorts. Now I saw what Brandon was talking about. I quickly averted my eyes.

She waved to Luke and turned back around. "Kelly, on the other hand, now there was a set of nice legs for ya."

"Amanda, I swear I could punch you in the face sometimes," Brandon hissed through tight, thin lips.

"I'm so scared," she admitted calmly. He looked over her shoulder and refused to meet her eye.

All I could think about during this strange conversation, besides the fact that her bright green gum had come dangerously close to falling out several times, was the fact that Luke was dating this person. Luke, whom I admired and cared about, was dating *this* fine specimen? How could this happen?

"You made it!" Luke called from the front door.

She stomped the cigarette out, spit the gum into the freshly mowed green grass, and before you could blink, had a new piece of gum shoved into her red-lipped mouth. "I'm starving, honey," she said sweetly, wrapping her arms around Luke's neck and kissing him on the lips. I cringed and looked the other way when I spotted her tongue literally lick his lip. Luke's face went red. He pulled back and gave a flabbergasted laugh. I felt sick to my stomach. Dylan wriggled out of Brandon's arms and started running down the slope toward the backyard.

"I'll get him!" I yelled as I pushed by them.

Brandon didn't follow, and I was glad. Glad to escape all of them, even if it was to chase after a two year old through the grass in my high heels. Dylan was getting fussy, probably from hunger. I opened my Prada bag. It was stained with some type of oil or grease marks and was littered with crumbs. I swept through the toys and extra diapers for something he could eat and found a small Tupperware bowl of cheerios. I popped the lid and handed it to Dylan. He took it in his chubby hands and plopped down in the grass and stuffed them, one by one, into his mouth as fast as he could.

"Dink, dink," he called to me.

"Dink? What is dink?" I couldn't be sure, but I thought he might be thirsty. I scooped him into my arms and ventured inside to find a drink. From this door I found myself in the basement. I recognized Luke's hushed voice coming from the top of the stairs. I stopped at the bottom and listened.

"That was completely inappropriate!" he declared. "I mean, what came over you?"

"It's been a long time since we've been together, and I missed you . . . And let's just say . . . I kind of owed him one."

He cleared his throat. "Listen, try to be nice, Amanda. It's been two years; we've all got to move on."

"Are you sure *you've* moved on?"

"Yeah, I have," he stated matter-of-factly. There were footsteps across the floor, and then the sliding glass door opened and shut.

I started up the stairs. I didn't want them to know I'd overheard. When I reached the top I caught my breath in surprise. Luke stood in the hall. Dylan immediately cried out and wriggled out of my arms.

"I think he wants you," I said with a laugh.

"Hi, there, little guy," Luke said, taking Dylan in his arms. "Listen, about what happened back there," he glanced over at the door. "I don't know what came over Amanda. She isn't usually like that," he apologized.

I gave a polite smile. "She seemed very happy to see you."

Dylan sat contentedly in Luke's arms. I walked over and petted his soft mane of brown curls. "This little guy didn't even get scared when you picked him up." He blinked his blue-as-the-sea eyes at me.

"I think he remembers me. I had him that first night, remember? Brandon's parents were still in Parker, and Kelly's parents were in Pocatello. Brandon was pretty messed up that night. Remember?"

"Not really. I've kind of blocked the whole thing out of my head," I said, hoping he would want to jar my memory.

He nodded. "I just hope you don't still blame yourself."

Blame myself? Does he know about Brandon and me and the talk we had that night? I opened my mouth to ask what he meant when we were interrupted.

"Hey, there." Amanda stood in the doorway, hands on hips. "No offense, but hanging out with Brandon is as much fun as watching milk curdle, so, if you don't mind?" she sang in a sweet singsong voice.

"Sorry," Luke apologized. I took Dylan out of his arms. Luke hustled out to save her any further misery. I rolled my eyes after them. How could someone as nice as Luke date someone as awful as Amanda?

When we returned to the patio, Dylan threw an all-out tantrum. I'd forgotten to get him that drink. And when I attempted to appease him with the Cheerios, he flipped around on his head, dumped the Cheerios out, and tossed the Tupperware bowl, which hit Amanda in the face. Brandon picked Dylan up and took him back inside to get that drink. Amanda rubbed her head and moaned.

"I'm so sorry, Amanda," I said.

Dinnertime wasn't any better. Brandon looked ready to jump out of his skin every time Amanda opened her mouth, and I was coming apart over Dylan's whining, Brandon's indifference, Amanda's flapjaw, and Luke's total lack of good judgment.

I was certain I had really missed the mark on this guy after Amanda took one look at my soup and eeked, "Does it have clams? I'm allergic to clams."

"No clams." I gritted my teeth imagining how nice it would feel to dump the whole big bowl of soup over her head.

"Let's eat!" Luke announced, smiling broadly as he held a plate of grilled trout in front of him.

One thing was true. Luke cooked a mean fish. But he had lousy taste in women. And my soup, despite using frozen ingredients, was a hit with everyone but Amanda. Brandon, however, was about as much fun as an IRS audit. Whatever was going on between Brandon and Amanda caused such a cold chill that even on a hot July night I couldn't seem to get warm. Maybe it was because of the coolness in the air, but I grew impatient with sweet Amanda. For an hour I listened to that overripe peach with the daddy longlegs complain about everything under the lemon pie sun. *The sun was right in her eyes, and could she trade places with Luke?* Putting Luke as far away from me as possible, and when she bit into the trout she caught a bone and complained about how she could have choked, *and was he trying to freaking kill her?* I had just rolled my eyes, secretly hoping he would succeed, and the sooner the better. Then Dylan started whining.

Amanda asked repeatedly, "Why is Dylan whining so much?"

"Maybe he's just following your example, Amanda," I said under my breath as I pulled my much-needed Dr Pepper up to my lips.

"Maybe you could take the little fart for a walk."

The back hairs on my neck bristled. *Breathe,* I reminded myself.

For the life of me I could not understand what Luke saw in her, or what any guy would see in her. Any jealousy I might have felt for her long legs flew out the window when she compared her job in the bakery department at the grocery store to Brandon's job milking cows. "I'm covered head to foot in flour and powdered sugar every day! Roll me in a little oil and fry me up in a pan," she giggled. Her laugh grated on me like a high-pitched scream.

I rolled my eyes. Brandon just looked out past the trees toward the setting sun. Luke chuckled and patted her bare thigh. "Kind of makes me a little hungry for something sweet. Did ya bring us anything from the bakery?" He rubbed her leg with his strong hand. I glared at him. He looked over at me and caught my stare. His hand jerked from her leg. I turned away, pretending not to see. Why was I glaring? I had no right. Brandon continued to stare over his shoulder like he expected someone to come out of the bushes and rescue him.

"You okay?" I asked, leaning in to him.

"Five more minutes with Miss Donut Hole is all I've got left in me," he sighed.

I laughed a little. "Okay. We'll go." Five more minutes and I still didn't know anything about Kelly's death. Five more minutes and I'd be alone with Brandon again. I frowned.

"You two ready for some lemon meringue pie?" Amanda interrupted. "I brought it straight from the bakery." My eyes swept the patio for Luke. Amanda followed my look. "Luke's gone to get the pie from my car." Her eyes narrowed. "Honey, would you mind running inside and getting some plates and forks?"

I stiffened. I'd never been a fan of girls my own age calling me honey or sweetheart or any other term of endearment. It made me suspicious of their motives, and Amanda's behavior was off the charts in the suspicion category.

"Sure. I'd be happy to. Brandon, you want to come with me?"

"Brandon wants to visit with me a minute. It's been a long time, and we have lots to catch up on." She smiled with her perfect teeth.

Brandon stared down at his phone, texting someone.

"Maybe you could take that li'l stinker with you. Looks like he could use a walk."

Again with the flatulence comparison! I bit my lip and picked Dylan up. Instead of walking through the back door, I walked around the side of the house. If I'd hoped to learn something about Kelly, I'd have to get Luke alone. I could ask him what happened.

Luke was stretched across the front seat of Amanda's Bug, reaching for the pie. Dylan wriggled out of my arms and ran toward a soccer ball that was lying in the grass.

Luke crawled out of the car with the pie in his hands.

"I don't think he likes Amanda very much," I announced. Surprised by my voice Luke shot up, barely keeping the pie upright in its box.

I suppressed a giggle. Luke smiled. "I didn't know you were there."

"Sorry," I said.

Dylan kicked the ball. It rolled and stopped at Luke's foot. Luke dribbled the ball with his foot, reminding me of how well he'd played soccer in high school. He kicked the ball past Dylan. Dylan didn't mind. He turned and hobbled his way toward the ball.

"What were you saying about Amanda?"

I bit my lip deciding whether to be completely honest about Miss Amanda Wilkins.

"She's a bit of a wench, isn't she?" I stated bluntly.

"Kind of harsh, isn't it?"

"Luke, she's kind of a jerk." How could he not see this? I had to save this man from making a bad decision. Dylan had the ball. He dropped it in front of Luke. Luke dribbled the ball between his feet, and then kicked it off into the grass. Dylan went chasing after it again.

"Yeah, well, the good thing is I'm only dating her." He shut the car door with his foot and walked down the hill toward the backyard.

"You can't even begin to compare that whack job to Brandon."

He turned and feigned a crooked smile, but his eyes were dark. "Are you jealous?"

I looked off into the distance. Was I jealous? Of course not. Then why was my chest burning? "Just observant."

"When I want your observation, I'll let you know," he said, taking the pie and walking toward the backyard once again.

"Luke!" I called.

"What?" He turned around. All joking was gone from his face. I'd definitely hit a raw nerve.

I wanted to ask him what had happened to Kelly. How she had died, but his angry eyes dissuaded me. I asked the only thing I could think of. "Amanda sent me for plates . . . for the pie. Could you show me where to find some?"

He stared back at me. My cheeks grew warm. I didn't want Luke to stay mad. I smiled a half smile.

"Please?"

I saw him take a deep breath. In three swift steps, he was across the driveway and headed up the front stairs.

I ran to catch up.

Chapter Sixteen

I couldn't sleep. The room felt like an airtight death chamber. I lay on the bed with my thin nightgown pulled up around my knees and the covers pushed down around my feet as the room slowly cooked us to a nice medium well.

I didn't dare move, afraid Brandon would wake. All the way home from Luke's house Brandon had been silent; a ticking time bomb. Something had upset him, and I got the feeling it wasn't me, or at least not just me. He seemed preoccupied. After we'd gotten home I managed to stay out of his way. As I put an exhausted Dylan to bed, the side door slammed, and his truck roared to life. I expected he'd gone to a bar, but within ten minutes he was home again. I didn't dare ask where he'd gone. Instead, I puttered around the kitchen until the house settled down around me and I knew he was asleep. Then I sneaked into bed, hoping to keep from waking him. But now I couldn't sleep. I'd opened the window, but there was no relief in this stifling can of sardines. I glanced over at Brandon who was quietly snoring. Had it only been one night ago that he'd gushed his loving devotion for me? One night and two years.

I ran over the few facts I knew. Brandon had been unhappy in his marriage. He had implied he was willing to leave Kelly for me. I had barely discouraged that plan. Surely whatever happened to Kelly wasn't related to that conversation I'd had with him. But why had Luke asked me in passing if I still felt responsible? I hadn't asked him what that meant, but somehow I feared the worst. I'd only wanted a do-it-over—go back, change the past—but she hadn't changed the past at all. And now Kelly was dead, and I had a sickening premonition that the man lying next to me was somehow responsible.

I needed to know the truth.

I crawled out of bed and felt around for a pair of jeans and T-shirt I'd left lying on a small side chair. I slipped them on and searched around in the dark for a pair of slip-on shoes. I found them at the end of the bed and carefully closed the bedroom door behind me.

The old floorboards creaked the hallelujah chorus all the way to the kitchen. I stopped half hidden by the kitchen wall waiting for any sounds from the bedroom. All remained quiet; the only sound, the tick tock of an old clock upon the wall.

The truck keys dangled from a nail by the door. How inconspicuous was that truck going to be in the dead of night? Our neighbors and everyone in the upper valley would hear that monster start up. I groaned. And with our driveway being tandem, Kelly's little Escort was trapped in the garage. I left his keys on the hook and made my way out the side door. The warm night was bright, lit up by street lamps. I'd just have to walk.

Even for July, the air felt unusually muggy. I crossed an empty Bridge Street, my heart pounding as I made my way toward the old Yellowstone highway. The moon's silvery light spilled onto the pavement ahead of me and led me toward the large metal bridge. I glanced down at the river. The moon was bright against the moving waters. What had become of Kelly? I squeezed my eyes shut and pushed out the grotesque images that splashed across my mind. Brandon wasn't capable of doing something horrible, was he? I didn't know. After all, I had proven to be a lousy judge of character in the past.

A large swooshing sound whooshed above me. I ducked as a dark shadow passed overhead. The large creature rattled the bridge as it gently landed on the top of the metal overhang and disappeared in the huge osprey nest. It was only the osprey that called the metal bridge its home. I had enough adrenaline to get me the rest of the way thanks to the large bird. My steps turned into a jog toward the lone streetlight that marked the private drive.

I turned left and headed up the lane to Luke's house. As I ran, gravel crunched behind me. I stopped running and listened. There were definitely footsteps belonging to someone else. My pulse went into overdrive. My ears pricked at the crunching footsteps. My heart thumped wildly in my ears. Someone was behind me. What was I thinking—walking alone in the dark in the middle of the night? Bad things still happened in towns of 3,000 people. I was always so naïve, thinking nothing bad would ever happen to me. I glanced up the lane. A porch light flickered ahead. If I could just get to the door I would be safe.

If I couldn't make it I had to be prepared for the next option. Plan B: Attack. What I needed was the element of surprise. If I spun around and planted one of my karate chops to his groin maybe I'd catch whoever it was off guard. I closed my eyes, willing myself to turn. I pulled my arms up around my waist, my hands forming into fists. *I can do this,* I tried convincing myself. It I spun around, leg extending, I would aim for a possible groin. It felt like slow motion. I hadn't taken self-defense classes since college.

I was awkward and slow, and my kick was horribly mistimed. A hand rose out of the blackness and grabbed my foot. My hands waved wildly in the darkness as I hopped around on one foot. I let out a small scream, expecting to come face-to-face with someone who might want to hurt me. Instead, I found Luke holding my foot in one hand, a slight smirk across his moonlit face.

"Easy now!" he warned.

"Luke!" I exclaimed, still hopping on one foot.

He dropped my foot. "Was the fish that bad?" he teased, his eyes growing wide in amusement.

"I . . ." I swallowed hard. I needed to catch my breath. "I was hoping to ask you some questions."

He scratched his neck. "At one in the morning?"

I turned it back on him. "What were you doing out here at one in the morning? Why didn't you just open your front door to me?"

"I wasn't sneaking. I was just getting home myself."

I tried not to be revolted at the thought of where he might have been returning from.

"I couldn't sleep so I went running," he explained, pointing to his running shorts and T-shirt. Sweat rolled down his temple.

"And Amanda?"

"Went home."

At least there was no Amanda in the picture. One point for Luke.

"I'm sweaty and need a drink. Do you want to come in?"

He led me inside the dark house and clicked on a small table lamp. The entry came alive in a soft yellow wash of light. I glanced around. The situation earlier had been so awkward, what with Amanda's French kissing and Brandon's sulkiness, that I had hardly had the time to admire Luke's big house. It was all wrong. Too country, mauve and flowery, and the heavy swag drapes screamed 1990. *Definitely not your typical bachelor's pad*. I felt sort of sorry for Luke living in this big house all by himself. Sitting on his aunt's country sofa, drinking from one of her teacups.

"Life sure does throw some curveballs, doesn't it?" he explained from behind. I turned to him, thinking of what compliment I could offer. He smiled sheepishly and handed me a tall glass of ice water.

I blushed. He'd caught me staring at the feminine décor.

"I'll drink to that." I took the glass and took a deep drink. The cold water soothed my burning throat. "This is nice, though. Not exactly you, but still nice."

He laughed out loud.

"No, really, it has a lot of potential."

He emptied his glass and set it down on the coffee table. The condensation dripped down the side and puddled around the edge of the glass.

"Have a seat," he said, pointing to the fluffy sofa that looked thick enough to sleep on. I sat. The cushions were made of down. It reminded me of my sofa in San Francisco. Luke sat across from me. He wiped a towel over his face. "This always happens after I take a big drink after a run. Watch," He pointed to his forehead. I watched as beads of sweat filled every pore. He wiped his forehead again.

"Cool," I answered, too distracted with the real reason I was there to be really impressed. I clasped my drink tightly in my hands and sat it in my lap. Then I sat back in the sofa. It was too deep, so I slid to the edge of the seat.

"Amanda. Amanda was weird tonight. I've never seen her act so on edge, so over the top. I swear she isn't usually so hell-bent on making everyone miserable." He bent down and pulled off his running shoes. He chuckled and wiped his forehead with a sock.

"I don't remember her. Did she grow up here?" I asked.

He peeled the other sock off his foot. They were long and thin. *Runners' feet,* I thought. I took a long drink and held the glass against my face, pretending to cool myself from the run.

I shifted in the sofa, unable to find a comfortable spot. All I could see was Luke in his boxer shorts again. It was like my brain was one of those tilt-a-whirls turning midair. You'd think I'd never seen a man half-dressed like that before. I glanced over at Luke who was sitting with his elbow up on the back of the sofa, a thumbnail in his mouth.

"She was Kelly's roommate. Moved here about three years ago."

I nodded slowly. I'd forgotten we were talking about Amanda. I twisted my mouth thinking that one over. No wonder she didn't like me. I was glad he brought up Kelly's name. It would make it easier to ask about her death. But how to do it without sounding crazy? I shifted on the couch again. I needed a place to put my drink.

I noticed a box of coasters. I placed one under his glass and one under mine. He picked up a wooden cork coaster out of the little box on the coffee table and twisted it around in his hand.

"I always wondered what this was for," he said before breaking into a large grin. His smile was so nice. It reminded me of Cort's. The thought hurt my heart a little.

"Sorry. It's just a habit. All I see are future water rings."

"My aunt would appreciate that."

"Where is your aunt anyway?"

"She moved in with one of her daughters in Arizona. She still visits occasionally. We have sort of a lease-to-own deal. She left her furniture, and I haven't cared enough to change it."

He set the coaster back in the container. "What were we talking about?" he asked, settling back, his arms spread along the edge of the couch.

"I actually wanted to ask you about Kelly's death." I fiddled with the bottom of my jean hem. "Brandon is still really upset about it all. I just wondered what you thought about it?"

"I thought what everybody thought. Why would a woman with so much to look forward to jump in the river and commit suicide."

I froze. Kelly had drowned in the river.

"Lucky for Brandon he had you as his alibi."

I was Brandon's alibi? Did Luke believe that or did he think I was lying for Brandon? I stared at him for a moment hoping to read him. His face remained stoic. I had no idea what he thought about it.

"Of course," I answered as if someone had poked me full of holes.

I gripped my hands over my knee. "But the police thought Brandon had something to do with it?" I could barely get the words out.

"Brandon threatens divorce because you're back in the picture—it seemed suspicious."

My heart nearly stopped. He did know. "Who told you that?"

"Amanda told the police that Kelly told her just before Kelly left their house with Brandon. One hour later she was in the river."

"Did Brandon corroborate her story?" I asked, my eyes wide.

"Yes and no. He said they were fighting, but when I asked if he threatened to leave Kelly he adamantly denied it. I don't think Brandon and Amanda like each other very much now. They seemed to be in some deep discussion tonight, though."

"When was that?"

"When we came back with the pie. Didn't you see them? They looked ready for a fist fight."

He leaned forward and rested his elbows on his knees. "Probably just a police thing, but I notice people's body language. We interrupted something kind of intense." He settled back against the cushion and rested his foot on his knee.

The hairs on the back of my neck bristled again. "She was being a jerk all night. He was probably telling her to grow up." Brandon had a lot of unattractive qualities, but at least he was man enough to put that girl in her place.

"I told you, she was just really uncomfortable. She's not usually like that."

I suppressed an eye roll. I hardly doubted she was ever anything but a wench. But I didn't want to talk about Amanda anymore. I hunched forward, my hands clasped tightly. Then taking a deep breath, I mimicked Luke's relaxed stance, settling back into the cushion. I wanted to change the subject.

"So a lease to own?"

"My aunt doesn't want the house to leave the family, but her kids are all grown and moved away. Honestly, I probably couldn't afford this house, but she made me a deal I couldn't refuse. At the time I thought I might be sharing the house with someone, so I took her up on the offer. Course that didn't work out, but it's a hell of a piece of property, so I'll hang on to it."

"What happened? I mean you were going to share the house with someone?" A flash of jealousy burst through me at the thought of Amanda living with Luke.

Luke stared at me, a look of hurt and confusion flashed briefly across his face. I cringed. One of those things I should have known. It must have been me. Did I say no to him just to say yes to Brandon? Did I repeat things with Cort all over again? "Oh. Right."

"Ah, yeah," he said, absently staring out the large picture window toward the silvery moon reflecting off the river.

"It's late, and I should go." I stood to leave. "Thanks for the drink and the talk."

He stood and walked over to me. "Why the questions, Marlo? You were there for all of it. Are you okay?" he leaned in close. His warm eyes melted me. I could almost feel his arms wrapped around me.

"I'm fine," I answered with a quick shake of my head. "I was confused about what the official record was."

"So you're good then? You got the answer you were looking for?"

"Yeah, mostly. Thanks." I attempted a smile. "I'll see you later."

He grabbed the edge of my sleeve. "You don't think I'm going to let you walk home alone, do you?"

"I'm fine. I've put you out enough."

"Come on. I'll give you a ride."

"Really? Are you sure?" Brandon would be furious, but he would never know.

"I insist." He replaced his shoes and led me through the kitchen and out to the garage. I made my way to the now-familiar Explorer.

"Let's take the bike. Nothing like a midnight ride on a warm night," Luke taunted good-naturedly.

"Brandon is not going to like this, you know."

"I guess we could always call him to pick you up." He smiled. He had a point.

I took the outstretched helmet. Luke gave me a crooked grin. I ignored it. I knew I was in trouble. No need for him to gloat. I was a horrible pretend wife. On the other hand, if Brandon killed his wife, then maybe I didn't owe him my loyalty, and maybe it didn't matter what I did. Maybe having feelings for Luke wasn't necessarily wrong, just mistimed. But even that seemed like a stretch. It was bad timing, for sure. I'd find that old woman and demand she get me out of this glimpse. My life depended on it.

Chapter Seventeen

We turned down Bridge Street. I could see the house. My stomach sank. Brandon's truck was gone. I loosened my grip. I swore under my breath. I thought I heard Luke do the same. He turned down Fourth North, and then veered left and parked on the side of the red Presbyterian church.

"Brandon's truck is gone."

"Yeah, I saw that," he answered back.

I squeezed my eyes shut. I was in for it now. How could I explain to Brandon or even Luke that I hadn't really done anything wrong? That I needed to know what had really happened to Kelly the night she died. I pulled off the helmet and jumped off his bike. "I'm sorry, Luke. I didn't mean to get you in trouble."

"I'm not in trouble." He turned to me, his face serious. "But you are."

"Thanks for the reminder." I handed him the helmet.

"You gonna walk from here?" he asked. I stared at his face, his clear eyes. I hardly knew him, but I wanted to jump back on the bike and have him take me far away from here. I couldn't speak, for fear I would tell him as much. I nodded.

A truck veered around the corner. We jumped at the noise. Headlights blinded us. I squinted and shielded my face. The truck screeched to a stop. It's door opened, then slammed shut. Brandon rushed at Luke.

Oh laws! Where was that old lady?

Luke jumped off his bike and held up his hands in defense. "Brandon, don't jump to conclusions."

"I don't have to. The facts are right here in front of me!" he yelled. He bounded forward and gave Luke a shove. Luke caught his balance just as Brandon swung his fist. It connected with Luke's jaw, knocking Luke backward into the grass in front of the Sunday School schedule sign.

Luke nursed his jaw with his hand. "You idiot!" he spat as he picked himself off the ground. Too fast for Brandon to react, Luke grabbed Brandon's arms and flipped him on his stomach. Brandon grunted aloud, exhaling all his air. Luke sat on Brandon's butt and yanked his elbows further back. Brandon grunted again.

"You gonna' hit me again?" Luke challenged.

Brandon gasped in pain.

"Next time, get your facts straight before you start whaling on somebody or you're gonna land yourself in jail!" Luke released his grip on Brandon's elbows and stood up. He wiped at his jaw, nodded to me, and without another word, hopped on his bike. I stood and watched him start up his bike. The sound of his engine echoed long after he was out of sight.

I turned to Brandon. Brandon crawled over and sat down on the steps of the church.

"Brandon," I began, "I know you're not going to believe this, but there isn't anything going on between me and Luke."

"Right. Because it's normal for a married woman to go joyriding with a single man in the middle of the night."

I shook my head. "I know. It looks bad. I just needed to . . . wait, where's Dylan?"

"He's asleep in his crib. I locked the door. I was only planning on being out for a few minutes. I rode by your mom's place and the Sand Bar. I circled the neighborhood a couple times. I thought maybe you'd left me." Brandon's face grew contorted.

It reminded me of the day I walked in on Cort and his lover. Cort had tried to explain that it hadn't meant anything—that things had just gotten out of control. But it didn't matter how it had happened. The fact was it did happen. That horrible day had only been the beginning. The more I dug, the more I found. Cheri wasn't the first woman he'd had over to our place. Cort tried to explain it was no big deal. That I was the woman he had married, and these other women were just distractions. This was what men did. His father had done it, and his mother had always looked the other way. But I hadn't been raised that way, and I couldn't look the other way. Now here I stood, causing pain for someone else. Real or not, it didn't matter. I was still responsible.

I sat down on the steps next to him. "Things have been tough for us. I needed some answers."

"That only Luke could give you? What did he say? That you should have listened to him and never married me?"

"Not at all. I just feel like everything has been backward and inside out."

"What, because of Kelly?"

Kelly was only the beginning. "I don't know," I said more to myself than to him. I fiddled with what must have been my wedding ring. From the street lamp I could just make it out. It was a third the size of the wedding ring I'd been given by Cort.

Brandon's wife had drowned. Something was missing from that police investigation. I needed to find out how she drowned. What really happened that night?

And there was the other unavoidable question that I couldn't ask myself, let alone Brandon.

He was capable of hitting someone. Was he also capable of murder?

I awoke the next morning to the sound of Brandon's truck pulling out of the driveway. I peeked out the window and watched him roar down the road. I sighed. What I did was thoughtless and stupid and I didn't want to have to face him...yet. I fell back on the bed. Brandon's pillow was missing. He'd slept on the couch. Shouldn't I have been the one on that forsaken couch instead of Brandon? Yes, he'd punched Luke, but he was only doing it out of love for me. What was I doing? Did I care about what happened to Brandon? To Dylan?

It was already warm in the bedroom. The hideous shades couldn't keep the brilliant sun from seeping around the cracks. I pulled myself off the bed and avoided the guilty face in the mirror. I didn't want to think about Brandon or Luke. I didn't want to remember the way it felt to wrap my arms around Luke's waist as he sped down the highway or how I had wished he would just keep on driving. Or how Brandon had looked at me with such hurt.

I tiptoed out of the bedroom and stood by Dylan's door. All was quiet so I quickly showered. Still in my towel, I rummaged through the closet for something to wear. There were a lot of my favorites missing, like those wedge shoes that I picked up on a trip to Beverly Hills or my favorite jeans. Finally, I found a skirt and matching sleeveless hoodie in a bag near the back. Several other favorite outfits were also folded up in the black garbage bag. Was future me saving them for special occasions?

There was still no sound from Dylan's room. I didn't know much about children, but I did know they were usually, as my father always phrased it, "Up with the sun." I opened his door and peeked in. The crib was empty. He wasn't capable of climbing out of his crib, was he? He was certainly big enough, but did he have the coordination or know-how? And if he had climbed out, where was he now? Fear shot through my toes at the possibilities.

I rushed to the living room hoping to find him in front of the one-eyed babysitter, but he wasn't there either. I moved to the kitchen. A note sat under a magnet on the fridge. I recognized Brandon's hurried handwriting. I ripped it off and read it.

"Took Dylan to Grandma's. Be back around five to pick you up."

I relaxed. He'd taken Dylan. I didn't know if that meant my mom, or his mom, or Kelly's mom, but what I did know was I needed to get out of this life as fast as I could, and this seemed the perfect opportunity to find the old lady and plead with her to get me out of this mess.

I grabbed my Gucci bag from the bag in my closet (one that I obviously didn't use very often because it was still clean and crumb free) and headed out. I lifted the garage door. A thick layer of dust covered the car and everything else in the hot garage. The car door croaked. It seemed like everything around here squeaked, croaked, or creaked. I gave the key a turn. It sputtered and choked like an old pipe smoker, then shuddered twice and died. I turned the key again and pumped more gas. It finally coughed to life. *The car might be Kelly's, and it might barely run, but it had to be faster than walking,* I decided.

I put it in reverse. I hadn't driven a manual in years. It's like riding a bike. I backed it on to the road and put it in first gear. Clutch out, gas in, I reminded myself from my days of driving a manual. I tapped on the gas and released the clutch. It jerked to a stop. *Maybe it's been longer than I thought.* I glanced in my rearview mirror. Four or five cars were stopped in the road waiting for me. I waved them forward. The cars carefully made their way around my stalled Escort. I kept my face down, though I was sure they probably all knew who I was. I looked up and waved as the last car passed. It was Mrs. Johnson, my seventh-grade math teacher. She smiled and waved back. Once they were all passed, I pushed the clutch in, turned the key, and gave it some gas. It started up. I breathed a sigh of relief. Now for the next part. I slowly released the clutch. It bounded forward. I gave it some gas. It reared forward, but didn't choke and die. Yes! Careful not to stall the car again, I maneuvered my way down Bridge Street. I dragged Bridge for ten minutes hoping to run into the old woman. Ten minutes will get you from one end to the other twice. There was an unwritten rule about dragging Bridge Street. Once was necessary, twice was expected, but the third branded you a loser.

But to my dismay there was no sign of the witch lady on my third trip down. I veered left at the light and made my way to my parents' house. I walked over to the Sand Bar. There were a few teenagers loitering about, but no sign of the lady who had turned my life from bad to worse. After some time standing around waiting, I finally gave up and made my way back to my parents'.

The house seemed draped in darkness. I called out, but got no answer. Everything seemed buttoned up tight. They were not home. I could always tell. Our house turned into a cold, dark crypt when everyone was gone. I made my way to the kitchen. The kitchen hadn't changed at all. The same lace curtains hung in the window. The same beige vinyl covered the floors. The brown oak cabinets I nearly burnt up when I left the plastic bowl on the hot stove plate were still there. The painting of the man praying on the wall unmoved. My mother used to tell us about the man in the photo, how 'he was a reminder that though we didn't have a lot of worldly riches, we were rich if we had a thankful heart.' I wondered now if I still had a thankful heart. After last night, and the previous six months before it, I doubted it. A bowl of shiny red apples lay in the center of Mom's oak pedestal table. I grabbed one and took a big bite. If this glimpse wasn't real, it was the best hoax I'd ever seen the way the apple crunched and the sticky, sweet juices ran down my lip. The taste would convince the biggest cynic.

I moved to the living room. The shades were down. Pulled shades usually meant my parents were out of town. *That could be a good thing*, I thought as I peered out the window. I could just make out the top of the retaining wall. Maybe I could hide here until the old woman came back. I took another generous bite, savoring the juices as I moved to the fireplace mantel. The pictures on the mantel had changed. There was one of my dad and one of me around ten holding up a large rainbow trout while my dad smiled proudly beside me. One of Melissa and my parents on her wedding day, and another of my parents on a trip to Shanghai four years before—a gift from Cort and me. There were no pictures of Cort and me, and only one snapshot of me and Brandon. I wasn't smiling. Neither was Brandon. *Why did we get married?* I wondered. Was it only because of Dylan? Had I made a conscious choice to marry someone, not out of love, but out of duty? And duty to whom?

I wasn't sure Brandon loved me either. So why had he blamed me for ruining his life? Maybe no matter what I did, I couldn't make things better. Maybe Brandon thought it would, maybe I thought it would, but we sure seemed a pathetically miserable couple together. Were we always?

The front screen door clanked open and shut. I spun around. Melissa stood in the doorway. She looked different, more angular, and not chubby like I last saw her at the family party. She crossed her arms.

"Hello," she said coldly.

Oh, please, don't tell me I'm still in a fight with my sister. "Hey, Mel," I said, pretending not to notice her icy stare. "Where's Mom and Dad?"

All the skin around her mouth wrinkled, like she was trying to hold something back. "*He* is not our dad!" she corrected through clenched teeth.

"What?"

"Have you been drinking again?"

My eyes flew wide. "Of course not! It's ten in the morning."

"That's never stopped you before."

I scowled at her.

"What does that mean?"

She set her thin hands on her hips, "You know."

"No, I don't."

"Let's just say the first question answers the second."

I could only stare at her. She was talking in riddles. So my sister thought I was a drunk. What did I do now?

"Mel, are you mad at me?"

"No," she blinked nervously.

"I just talked to Mom yesterday; she didn't say she was going anywhere."

"She's gone to Jackson with that band teacher," Melissa explained with a sour face. "She didn't want to bother you, so she asked if I wouldn't mind watering her plants while she was away. Not that I don't live three miles out of town and *you* are only a few blocks away, but we mustn't overwhelm you now." Her voice rang high, imitating her mother's.

I stared at her. She glared back. No one spoke. Was she still mad about dad's heart attack? That was two years ago. Why was she still bitter? She acted as if I were a bedbug she'd just found in her clean sheets.

"But where is . . ." My mouth went dry. Her words finally caught up with me. Band teacher? I turned my head back to the mantel. A large picture of my dad stood in the center of the mantel. Something he would have never allowed. I scanned the room. His favorite recliner was missing too. The room began to spin. The truth finally hit me square in the forehead.

Dad was dead.

Nausea rose again. I tried to swallow it back down as it forced its way up my throat. "What happened, Mel? You've got to tell me." Sweat beaded on my forehead. I had an instant fever.

"You *have* been drinking again." She rolled her eyes and sidestepped around me to the kitchen. I turned and followed her. A water pitcher sat in the sink. She filled it up and began dousing the plants with drink. I bit the inside of my cheek to stop from screaming at her.

"Melissa, really, I just need to hear it from you."

Melissa sighed. "I don't know why I bother." She sidled around me again and headed for the sunroom.

"Please!" I begged, afraid she wouldn't explain it.

"It's because of you he had another heart attack in the first place. You were totally freaked out trying to care for Dylan. You started drinking. Dad came over to give you a break. And then he—" Her voice broke, unable to continue. The bile forced itself up my throat. I covered my mouth and ran from the room.

I threw up in the toilet. Sweat crawled down my temples. Melissa was nowhere to be found when I left the bathroom. I crawled up the stairs to my parents'—my mom's now—room. The very idea, alternate or not, that my dad was gone was beyond devastating. And it was my fault. Really my fault.

I felt so unaware, like I'd missed the whole thing. The last time I'd talked to him I'd been acting like a spoiled teenager instead of an adult daughter. My head was a pent-up steamer, an instant sauna. I lay prostrate on my parents' bed and allowed my grief to flow like a gushing wound from my broken soul. Every lost opportunity weighed down on me, every missed chance to tell him I loved him tore at my heart. For nearly ten years I had pushed myself away from those I had truly cared about. Especially my father.

The last time I saw him I was angry that he thought I was weak. I wanted him to be proud of me. To know I could manage the storms of life. My father was a simple man who never asked for anything. He had accepted my choice to marry a city boy and had put on a brave face at the wedding, even though he thought he was losing his little girl forever. But I had felt embarrassed of his old-fashioned clothing and colloquialisms. I had ignored my family for so long. I'd almost shut them out of my life. Not once in four years did I invite my parents to visit. And when I came to Idaho, I came by myself, not wanting to remind Courtney of my "humble beginnings." And now my father was gone, and all I wanted was to wrap my arms around him and tell him how he had been the greatest father a daughter could have ever wished for. But it was too late. And it was all my fault.

I made my way to their bathroom and examined myself in the mirror. Puffy eyes; head pounding. I opened a cabinet and rummaged for medicine. An old bottle of aspirin sat on a high shelf, probably my dad's from his first heart attack. I swallowed two dry. They scraped all the way down my throat.

I ventured back down the stairs. The pitcher was in the sink again. The room dark. I glanced out the window. Melissa's car was gone. Melissa gone and still angry, my dad dead. Brandon hurt. I collapsed into the chair at the kitchen table and buried my face in my hands. I had to get a grip. The idea of a glimpse had been fine when I was sneaking around with Luke, but now, having my father gone, it felt painfully real. Besides, how did I know this wasn't the way life would be from now on? Maybe I would never see that old woman again. I'd stay married to Brandon, raise Dylan as my own, and spend the rest of my life wishing I had taken better care of my family.

My phone rang in my bag.

"Where are you, cupcake?" I recognized Darcy's voice on the other line.

"Darcy! How are you?"

"I'd be doing a lot better if I wasn't trying to keep your sorry butt from being fired!"

"Am I late?"

"Just a half hour is all, but Brenda is none too happy." I was getting quicker, or at least better, at guessing.

"Listen, slick, you better be sick or otherwise detained."

"I was sick, or at least I felt sick."

"Felt means you're better, so get your derrière over here. Lunch rush is just about to begin, and I'm telling you, I can't hold back the gates of hell much longer."

Lunch rush? I was a waitress? I rolled my eyes and threw my phone back in my purse. Could this get any worse? Oh, mercy. I needed to wake up from this glimpse, this nightmare, this . . . whatever it was. I took a deep breath. This was all a dream. I would find the old woman and fix everything. After work. I grabbed another apple and hurried out the door.

Chapter Eighteen

"What has gotten into you?" Brenda growled as she dragged me to the kitchen where the hot ovens were now recooking the order I had dropped and spilled all over the floor. So far everything had gone wrong. The first was the fact I didn't even know I had a job. I should have clued in when Brandon took Dylan to Grandma's. Then there was the fact that I didn't know what restaurant I worked at, and though there were only two to choose from, I wasn't positive it was either one of them. I'd rushed back home and dug through the tiny closet and found a black pencil skirt and button-down blouse with my name tag hanging over the pocket. Underneath it read "JoAnna's Kitchen." I breathed a sigh of relief. One more mystery solved.

I changed and hurried back to the Escort. I started the car; it chugged, but never turned over. I tried again and again, each time wearing the battery down a little more. I gave up. I slammed the door, pulled my Gucci bag over my shoulder, and hoofed it the five blocks to the restaurant.

But walking to the restaurant had only been the tip of my troubles. Brenda a spiky haired woman with bleached tips and an unusually deep tan, informed me this was my first official warning for being late. Great, I'm getting future Marlo fired. Just add it to the heap.

Darcy was taking orders, her curly chestnut hair pulled back in a low ponytail. She hadn't changed much. She gave me a worried glance, and then turned back to her customers.

To punish me, Brenda gave me three of the fussiest tables. I didn't know anything. A lady asked about the special of the day. I had to run back past the sign in the front to see what it was. Then she asked what kind of house dressing we had. I hurried over to Darcy who was busing a table. She looked at me funny, but said it was raspberry vinaigrette. I wanted to explain that it was my first day, but nobody would have believed me. Besides, people—especially the paying customer type—don't want excuses; they just want their food, and the sooner the better. I understood this, because I'd been a paying customer a lot longer than I'd been a waitress. I lifted my chin. I could do this gig. I'd gone to Stanford on a scholarship. I could certainly handle the simple job of being a waitress. It wasn't like it was rocket science. Keep their glasses filled, ask how they enjoyed their food, and turn the table quick.

But it didn't work out that way. The food grew cold, the people were hungry, and I was too slow. And then things went from bad to

"I'm pretty sure this is pergatory," when Brenda threw a tray full of steaming food in my arms while yelling, "Go, go, go." I'd spun around and smacked into Darcy who was just coming into the kitchen with her own tray of dirty dishes. Roast beef, buns, pickles, French fries, and shakes went crashing to the floor, breaking the plates and spilling the shakes to create one nasty-looking Jackson Pollock piece.

I bent over to mop up the gooey, bleeding mess. I wanted to yell back at Brenda to cut me some slack. Instead, I bit the inside of my cheek and started wiping it up.

"Are you okay?" Darcy asked as we wiped up the mushy mixture.

"I'm fine. I just have a really horrible headache. This waitress thing is just not my cup of tea. I'm better than this, and I don't know what I'm doing working in a place like this," I said more to myself than to Darcy. Darcy stopped working. I glanced up. There was hurt in her eyes. "I'm sorry," I said, avoiding her eyes.

As the day wore on, I felt more compelled to explain myself to Darcy, but I didn't have a chance until the lull of four o'clock rolled around. We were wrapping silverware into napkins.

"So how is life?" I floated, to see if she'd forgiven me enough to bite.

"It's okay."

She wasn't biting. Or maybe she was as exhausted as I was. Try something else. "Love life?"

"Mark never called after we went out, so I figured that was a no."

No more Jed Cooper. Now it was Mark. Or not Mark. I made a mental note. I tried to think of what I could ask her that wouldn't sound like I'd ignored her for the last two years.

"Look, Darcy, I just wanted to apologize . . ." But Darcy was no longer listening. She'd gone rigid. She sucked in her breath. I glanced over to where she was looking. Luke, dressed in his uniform, those *Top Gun* sunglasses on his face, and looking better than ever, had walked through the door. He was followed by two other patrol officers.

I resisted the urge to duck and hide under the counter only because he probably already knew I worked there. He pulled off his sunglasses, nodded at the two of us, and turned down toward a booth. I could see the small scrape on his chin. My heart fluttered nervously. I pressed my lips together. I needed fresh lipstick, or at least gloss. I tucked a loose hair behind my ear.

Darcy grabbed menus and headed toward their booth. Luke sat across from us. My hands shook, and I dropped a fork. I could no longer perform the simple task of rolling the utensils into a napkin and taping it shut. I wanted to go to him. To see if he was all right and apologize again, but I couldn't get my feet to move, and now my skin was all prickly hot. What was it that got me all goose fleshy and nervous whenever he was around?

Darcy visited with them. She seemed so relaxed, like this job was not humiliating to her. She was probably friends with these men, knew their names, their wives' names—if they had them—and knew some of their stories. *This is not my place; this is not my life*. I could not pretend to enjoy this job or to love this simple town.

I really missed life in San Francisco, which was weird, because I'd never felt like I fit in there either. But I was different now. And this simple café life wasn't me anymore, either. While I didn't miss everything—the girls with their shopping obsessions, their unhealthy fascination with celebrities—there were many things I longed for: the smell and sounds of the ocean, the nearly constant light breeze just off the bay, the diversity of the people, the food, the beautiful surroundings, the white buildings dusting the hill like a light sprinkling of snow over an old Tuscan city. I missed my row house; a gift from Cort's parents with its expansive layout and shabby chic furniture. Maybe if I hadn't experienced all of that I wouldn't ache for it so much, or feel so picked on now. But I couldn't be simple like Darcy. That was why she moved about so freely; she didn't know any better. In some ways I envied her.

Darcy laughed at something Luke said. They all seemed to light up as she responded with something equally witty. I could see how attractive that quiet confidence was. Confidence was definitely something I lacked. A wave of hot jealousy rippled through me. I had a degree. I should be doing more than waitressing at the local diner for minimum wage. And, of course, I was a green-eyed monster to Darcy's simplicity.

Darcy came back all smiles and pulled me to the back kitchen.

"Do I have anything in my teeth? Did you see him smile at me?"

"You look great. Here, let me help you." I loaded a piece of rhubarb pie on a plate. Darcy filled their cups of coffee.

"He's looking over here," Darcy squealed under her breath.

I glanced out to the booth. Luke watched us with weary eyes. When he realized we were both watching him, he turned his gaze toward the window.

I caught my breath. "Luke?" I gasped in shock.

She nodded excitedly and picked up the tray. "Thanks for your help."

Darcy liked Luke.

"You like Luke?" Jealousy surged through my veins.

"You didn't know?" She stopped in the doorway, her eyes questioning me.

Did I know? No. Was I jealous? Absolutely. "I didn't think he'd be your type. I thought you'd go for someone more like . . ." I scanned the restaurant for a replacement.

"Him," I said, pointing to a man with shaggy hair poking out of his Farmers Insurance hat, simple T-shirt, Wrangler jeans, and Roper boots, taking a big bite of a cheeseburger.

"Billy Jones?" she gasped under her breath.

My eyebrows raised as I recognized a former classmate. "That's Billy Jones?" Billy hadn't been much to look at in his youth. To be equally truthful, he still wasn't.

"Why would you say that?" she asked.

I shrugged. "I don't know. He just looks simpler, like someone you'd like; you know, the rodeo and all."

She stared back at me, her forehead wrinkled, her eyes confused. "Simple? Like simpleminded?"

"Luke is a pretty complicated guy. I'm just not sure if you're up to that."

"Complicated? You mean because I never went to college and only work as a waitress, I can't possibly be attracted to the likes of Luke Dawson? Or I'm not good enough for him?"

I shook my head and stammered for the right words. "No, of course not. I just thought maybe you'd want somebody different. Not in a bad way."

"Billy Jones is your idea of different?" she questioned. "So because I don't mind working here I should lower my standards in guys?"

I reached for her arm. "I didn't mean it like that."

She pulled her arm away, nearly spilling the tray of coffee mugs. "You complain about how much you hate this job and how embarrassed you are to work here. Don't you know how that makes me feel? Do you really think I'm stupid just because I didn't go to some big fancy university? You went to college and look where it got you! I had to cover for you twice today. First when you were late, and second when you placed an entire order at the wrong table! You couldn't even remember the house dressing! So sorry that this simpleminded girl has her eyes on someone way out of her league, but at least I get the orders right." She stomped out of the kitchen.

I watched her go, my own hands shaking with frustration. Darcy passed out the cups to the men. Luke thanked her. Color crept behind her ears. I spun on my heels and disappeared to the kitchen toward the walk-in freezer. Darcy and Luke. They'd be perfect together. I smacked my hand against the steel door. My palm stung. I grimaced and shook my hand out. How could I have said those things? Why did I think Darcy wasn't good enough for Luke? Luke was handsome, single, nice, certainly a rarity in these parts. She was a living, breathing woman with hormones. Of course she would have noticed him. Of course she was in love with him. He was probably the dream of every eligible girl in town, and apparently in my case, the dream of a few ineligibles as well. The very vivid, very real memory of Luke and I cuddling in a tent made it very difficult for me to be happy for Darcy. And now I had probably lost a friend forever. How would I ever crawl out of this grave I'd dug for myself? Darcy deserved better.

I dabbed at my moist eye. I had to apologize to her. I had to set things right. I returned to the front counter just as Brandon walked in with little Dylan on his hip. He stopped when he saw Luke. Luke noticed Brandon. I watched them size each other up. Brandon quickly recovered. He turned and made his way to the counter.

"Let's go," he said shortly.

The clock showed it was just after five. That's right! Brandon had said he'd pick me up at five. I was done for the day. Done forever if I could only find that old woman.

"How did you know I'd need a ride?"

"You never drive the Escort. I always pick you up."

"Right." I scanned the room for Darcy, but she was nowhere to be found. I hoped I hadn't ruined our friendship. "I'll be right back."

I dropped my dirty apron in a bin near the back door. On the way out I checked the schedule. I didn't have to work until Thursday, which was two days away. I breathed a sigh of relief. I'd be long gone by then. I dragged my very sore feet (these wedges were supercute but so not appropriate for a waitress) toward the entry, still looking for Darcy. A cute high school-aged girl was refilling the salt and pepper shakers. She was apparently my replacement. I went to her.

"Have you seen Darcy?" I asked.

"She went to the bathroom a few minutes ago," she answered without looking up at me. Brandon was still waiting for me at the door. I glanced over at Luke who was in deep conversation with the other two men at his table. A wave of shame fell over me. I asked Brandon to hold on a minute and hurried to the bathroom. The door was locked. I knocked.

"Darcy?"

There was a small "What?" through the closed door.

"I'm sorry I hurt your feelings. Luke is a great guy. You can like whoever you want. Don't be mad, okay? I think I'm coming down with something, and I've just had a really rough couple days, okay?"

There was a moment of silence, and then finally a sniffle and an "Okay" through the door.

"Call me," I begged before I turned and walked to the front door. I took Dylan from Brandon and set him on my hip. When Brandon turned toward the door I sneaked a glance Luke's way. He was watching, his eyes narrowing, something like apprehension across his face. I quickly turned away.

We drove down Bridge Street with Dylan between us in his car seat. I had gone from misfit city girl to misfit country girl. All that was missing was the dog pacing in the back of the truck and the shotguns hanging in the window.

We stopped at the light. It was red. It was always red. Didn't matter what direction I was coming from, that thing turned red as soon as I pulled up. Not another car going left or right. *It's an engineering marvel.* Even as I thought these words I recognized how cynical I had become. I hadn't always been like this. Then I met Cort, and I discovered that life sucked sometimes. But I was tired of waiting for "life" to set things right. Who was going to make me happy? Nobody, that's who.

I had to make my life my own. I had to stop letting everyone else make life's choices for me. What was this glimpse for anyway? This alternate reality felt like I'd put myself away. Folded my dreams up nice and neat and stuffed them in an old trunk, padlocked tight, like all those outfits in the black bags in the closet.

Was I here to fulfill some destiny? Solve some mystery and then I could go home without the old woman's help? Who had I seen? Luke? Darcy? Maybe I was supposed to get them together. A tightness grew in my chest that I recognized as jealousy. I didn't want to consider that. Maybe help Brandon? Take care of Dylan? But was there a way to do that without living this horrible life?

I watched the empty buildings, for rent signs, broken blinds hanging in the apartment over the drugstore pass by, looking for a clue. An old woman hobbled down the blazing sidewalk. It took me a second to register who she was.

"Pull over, now!" I yelled. I unclipped my seat belt and unlocked my door.

Brandon jerked the truck to the curb. Before there was time for an explanation or for the truck to come to a complete stop, I'd swung the door open and jumped out, stumbling down the street, my feet slipping in the wedges.

"Hey," I called out. The woman continued walking. I reached out and spun the old woman around. "Where have you been?" I yelled. "I thought I was getting a do-over! This is no do-over, and I want out!"

Her eyes went wide as pepperonis. Perhaps she was afraid I might strangle her. I certainly felt capable of it just then. "No do-over! Nobody get do-over, only glimpse," she barked sharply.

"Fine. I got a glimpse, now get me out of here."

Her squinting eyes were surrounded by deep wrinkled lines like the lines I used to draw around circles to make a sun in grade school. She examined me, her thin mouth set in a pucker.

"No," she answered simply.

"No?"

"No. The dog who travels will find bone. You must find bone."

"What?" I grabbed her arm and refused to let go. "What bone? Just tell me so I can get out of this life and back to my old, less complicated one ASAP."

She shook off my hand. "When you ready, I take you back, but you not ready," she said with a huff. She spun back around and began walking. I wasn't finished.

I reached out to spin the old lady back around, but she beat me to it. With a glare she threatened, "You may never be ready. I just keep you here for good."

My hand froze in midair.

"Okay . . . please don't do that. I've just got to know that when you think I'm ready you'll take me back." A black crow cawed over my head. I swatted it away.

"Marlo!"

I glanced over my shoulder. Brandon waved one arm impatiently out of his open window. I turned back to the woman. I heard Brandon sigh in exasperation.

"At least tell me where I can find you."

She waved her arms. "Oh no. I not have you knocking down my door all hours of night."

"But what if I need you? What if my life depends on it?"

She stared back at me, her dark eyes turning into tiny pins. She glanced over my shoulder toward the truck. "Please?" I pleaded in desperation.

"Fine. Grey Opera Apartments. But only if you must!" she yelled, before turning away and hobbling down the bright sidewalk.

When I returned to the truck I saw that Dylan had fallen asleep in his car seat. Brandon glared at me. I sighed and climbed inside. Assuming a bone was a destiny or a riddle, I was stuck here a little longer to solve something. I wasn't sure what the old lady thought I should learn from the experience, but if it meant being a good wife to Brandon, then I would do it. It wouldn't last forever, and then I'd be back to real time. Back home with my father and mother.

Knowing that there was an end to this glimpse gave me new determination to do it and do it well, whatever *it* was.

Chapter Nineteen

I couldn't sleep. Again. Frankly, I couldn't stand being in the same bed as Brandon. I could barely stand being in the same room as him. I had cared very much for him in high school, but that was a long time ago and I had changed. He had changed. There didn't seem to be much we had in common, no evidence of shared hobbies or interests. And as far as feeling romantic toward him? I prayed I wouldn't have to get frisky with the guy.

So far I'd been lucky. He hadn't even so much as touched me with his foot in the lumpy double bed, but still I was afraid he would wake up and start something—because even with things cool between us I knew from experience that being in a fight rarely slowed a man down, and I didn't want to fight—and the other option, well, I didn't know how much was expected of me in a glimpse, but I was pretty sure I couldn't pull it off.

I waited until his breathing slowed to that steady, unconscious pattern that announced he was asleep, and then slipped out of the bedroom, through the darkness, to the kitchen. The moon was a bulb of light spilling across the table. I grabbed a loose piece of paper from a small pile on the counter, then I sat at the table.

I needed to make a list. There was something about numbering and prioritizing that always calmed me down and gave me clearer focus. And that was what I needed more than anything right now. Focus. This was not going to be any regular to-do list. If I were to understand the purpose of this glimpse, I needed to understand where I was needed. I wrote down the names of the people I had interacted with. Brandon, Dylan, Luke, Melissa, Darcy. Mom. I wrote my dad's name down too.

I'd figure out a way to save him when I returned to the present. Maybe if I understood what happened, then I could prevent it.

I chewed on my pencil as I deliberated. Prevention. I liked the idea. I wrote Kelly's name next to my dad's. By uncovering what happened the night she died I could go back and prevent any of it from happening. If I wasn't taking care of Dylan, then Dad couldn't come help me and have that second fatal heart attack.

In order to know what happened to Kelly, I was going to have to ask Brandon. He knew what happened the night of her death. I drew a star next to his name. So far, I hadn't given much effort to this whole marriage thing. Being thrown into a marriage had not been a good way to start the relationship. I needed to draw from my high school memories, remember the good times we'd had. I traced the star with my pen. From now on, I would work harder to support him. Maybe that could grow to love. At least it would feel like we were a team. Then maybe he'd talk to me.

I stared at little Dylan's name. He was equivocally tied to Brandon and Kelly. Taking care of Brandon and Dylan equaled saving Kelly. He was a cute little boy, but often his eyes seemed too old and sad. I would play the part of mother. Then maybe that old woman would send me back, and I'd find a way to save his real mother.

I made little checks by Brandon and Dylan and Kelly's names. That was project number one. Save their family. I put another check next to my mom and dad's names. I had to save Kelly in order to save my dad. They were all tied together.

I glanced over the other names. Luke, Darcy, and Melissa. I was torn. I didn't want to put Luke and Darcy together. I wasn't that selfless. I wanted to save Luke for myself, but if that wasn't my purpose, then I needed to let go of that desire. Darcy was a real friend, and I had been horrible to her. How had I allowed myself to think she was any less deserving than me?

Then there was Amanda. Could I do anything for her? Maybe I

could hook her up with Kale again. I wrote their names at the bottom of my list.

Melissa's name was next. I had no idea what I could do to save my relationship with Melissa. I wasn't sure where it had gone wrong. Perhaps she was angry about losing our dad and my apparent role in his death. I loved my sister. She was the only one I had, and I didn't like the idea of her being angry with me. I had to find a way to win her back.

I knew what I had to do. Now I just had to get started. I'd play the wife and doting mother, even if it killed me. Maybe if I believed I was steering this ship I'd enjoy the ride more. I folded the paper in half and placed it in my bag that hung on the back of the door.

I stared at the closed bedroom door. I couldn't go back in that sauna. I returned to the living room. An afghan I recognized as one of my grandmother's lay on the top of the sofa. I pulled it off. It exposed a small rip in the sofa's flowery fabric. Now I understood why I had it sprawled across the back. I took a deep breath. I would practice having a thankful heart by not minding the hole in the sofa. At least I had a well stitched memento of my grandmother's love to hide the tear.

I lay down and pulled the soft blanket up around my shoulders. The sofa clinked from a broken spring as I shifted. I practiced being thankful for springs, broken or otherwise, and before long, fell into a deep sleep.

When I awoke the room was awash in a soft grey light. A dark shadow loomed across from me. I raised my head off the pillow. My eyes adjusted to the light. It was Brandon. He sat in the small tan armchair. I think he was waiting for me to wake up.

I pulled myself up on my elbow. "What time is it?"

"Five in the morning, but don't get up," he explained. "I need to talk to you for a minute."

I sat upright and tucked me knees into my arms. The room was finally cool. I pulled the afghan around my shoulders.

"How long is this going to go on?" he asked.

"Which part?"

"All of it. I'm sick of it, Mar. You haven't let me touch you in what . . . a month? I can't live like this." He sighed and leaned forward on his elbows. His jaw flexed. He stared at me with his deep eyes. "I need time to think. I'll be back tomorrow night."

He shifted in his seat. He was dressed in hiking boots, cargo shorts, and a long sleeve flannel.

"Where are you going?"

"Yellowstone." Brandon stood from the chair. "I suggest you do some serious thinking. I know I will be."

I was tempted to stop him. Tell him that I had decided to try harder, but for some reason I just sat there and said nothing. He pulled the sheer curtain open with the back of his hand. Grey light seeped through the small opening.

He stared out the window and said, "My mom will watch Dylan when you have to work tomorrow." He bent over and picked up the pack. He heaved it across his shoulder, and then briefly met my eyes. They glistened in the grey morning light. I remembered the time I'd forgotten we had a date. He had prepared a special dinner for me, but I went to a movie instead. Brandon had waited for an hour. He'd had it set up overlooking the river, candlelight and all. He'd been crushed that I'd forgotten, and I had felt awful. But the past was the past, and I couldn't change any of it, apparently, despite the old woman's special drink. He took a deep breath and then, as if filled with a new determination, straightened his shoulders. He swiftly crossed the room and disappeared through the kitchen. The screen door clanked noisily.

Three hours later, dressed in a ratty T-shirt and pair of sweats, I sat in the middle of a heaping pile of stuff I'd dumped onto the bedroom floor. I'd raked through every drawer and tore into shelves for something with Kelly's name on it, or anything that might have had something to do with her. I peeked under the bed, but came up empty. It was as if she had never existed, in this house anyway.

I kept asking myself what I was looking for. I didn't know exactly. Something that would explain what had happened to Kelly. Maybe a journal. I wasn't surprised when I didn't find one. I'd been a religious journal keeper up until late in my marriage. Then when things got ugly, I didn't want to write or acknowledge things were bad. Still, I wished Brandon had written something down about Kelly, or me, or even Dylan.

Dylan sat on the couch and watched cartoons. Every once in a while the sound of his laugh made its way to the bedroom. I was surprised that he understood what he was watching, but I was glad he was entertained because I'd torn our bedroom apart and couldn't afford to have him wreck what I'd already destroyed. I didn't find anything of value. The only thing I did discover was that Brandon never threw away a single receipt, or gum wrapper, or anything.

The house was turning into an oven again. The clock read late morning. It was almost noon, and I had yet to discover anything about Kelly. I changed into a pair of shorts and a loose blouse and went to get Dylan dressed. His diaper was a sagging disgrace, but all the same was amazing, because it was down to his knees and still holding it all in. The Hoover Dam couldn't have done much better.

Once Dylan was bathed and fed, and we'd cleaned up, we escaped the heat of the house for outside. Of course, outside wasn't much of an escape, but occasionally the wind blew and cooled us off. Dylan seemed thrilled to be out of the house. I glanced around the small backyard. There wasn't much to it: a small square patch of bumpy yellowing grass and a clothesline held up by two rusted steel poles, black from years of weather. The grass was burnt. A hose attached to a spigot slithered across the grass. A fountain sprinkler was attached to the end; I was probably supposed to be watering the lawn. A bee buzzed by my ear. I ducked and swooshed it away.

"Ouch!" I yelled out. There was a stinging pain on my neck. I scooped Dylan up and ran to the house.

In the bathroom, I could see the beginnings of a red welt on the side of my neck. A thin sharp stinger stood embedded in my skin as if marking me with its miniscule, yet unarguable, potency. I hadn't been stung by a bee in years. I tried to think of what my mom had done when I'd been stung as a little girl. Was it a paste with baking soda? I couldn't remember now. I rummaged through my makeup bag, lamenting that all my good makeup had been replaced with grocery store stuff more appropriate for teenage girls. Poison burned like fire in the welt. My heartbeat pulsed.

I took a pair of tweezers and pulled out the stinger. The fire in my neck continued to wage. I searched the medicine cabinet for something to take the edge off the burn, but only found a small bottle of Neosporin. Dylan stood by the door chanting "side, side." Apparently he wanted to go back out.

"Okay, we will," I promised. I made a bag of ice, stuck it against my neck, and followed Dylan back outside.

Outside had only grown hotter. There was no shade, and I had no idea what to do with Dylan besides take him for another blistering, scorching walk. Did he have toys to play with? Maybe a trike or something? I glanced at the small garage. If there were toys they were probably in there. The garage door made a loud clanking noise as I hoisted it up. The yellow light from the midday sun uncovered a cloud of dust hovering thick in the air. The garage that was more like a shed was cluttered with typical shed items: an old lawn mower, a dusty, never used ten-speed with a flat tire, some old farm tools hanging from rusty nails, a metal toolbox that by the ring of rust outlining it, had probably been sitting in the same spot for a decade. In one corner was a bright yellow and red Big Wheel. Dylan hobbled over, plunked down on it, and scooted himself out of the garage.

A large green army locker sat under the old wooden worktable. It wasn't covered in dust.

"Stay right here, Dylan," I told him as I made my way to it.

It could have been Brandon's grandfather's were it not for a shiny new lock. I tried to lift it, but it was too heavy, like weights were inside. I dragged it out of its hiding place with one hand. It scraped like fingernails on a chalkboard against the cement floor.

I could hear Dylan riding around on his Big Wheel on the driveway.

"Stay close by, Dylan," I called out. I couldn't keep on eye on him from here. I'd have to somehow carry this thing outside. I dropped the ice on top of the locker and carefully carried it out of the garage and over to the side steps. I let it down with a grunt. I sat my bag of ice down beside me and squinted at the small lock. It needed a key. After my earlier ransacking of the house, I had a pretty good idea where the key might be.

I hurried back to the bedroom, slid a drawer open, and waded through Brandon's socks and underwear like I had an hour before. A small key that looked to be about the right size lay under a pile of tube socks. I snatched it up and hurried back outside. I jiggled the lock with the key, but it didn't open. I took the key out and examined its edges. It looked to be a perfect fit. I tried it again, but it still did not flip the lock open.

"What are we going to do now, Dylan?" There was no response. I glanced over my shoulder toward the garage. Dylan and his Big Wheel were gone. I'd been so deep in thought I'd forgotten to keep an eye on him. I strained to hear the crunch-crunch of big plastic wheels on cement but heard only a car pass by. I called out his name. No answer. A sick feeling curdled inside me. I stood and walked toward the street. No sign of Dylan or his trike. I dropped the key into my pocket and ran to the front yard. I looked right. No Dylan. I looked left and let out a gasp. Dylan and his Big Wheel were halfway down the block. A policeman was pulled over and leaning out of his hastily parked patrol car. I closed my eyes in embarrassment as I recognized the sunglasses.

"Hey!" I yelled, waving my hand high over my head. Luke nodded and jumped out of his patrol car.

"Lose a little boy?" he called back with a smirk.

"I just turned away for a minute. I didn't know he was so fast on that thing." I wiped my hands nervously on my shorts. "I'm glad you were here."

"So am I."

I ran down the old sidewalk, avoiding the places where the cement was breaking up from the roots of the tall cottonwoods. I stood beside Dylan who was examining an anthill growing out of a crack in the sidewalk. Luke walked around.

"You on duty right now?" I asked, out of breath.

"Just finishing up, actually." He stretched his arms. "Two days straight. I'm tired. I'm thinking about going fishing."

"Sounds . . . tiring," I smiled.

He shook his head. "Invigorating. Relaxing, yes. Tiring, no." He looked back toward the house. "What are you guys doing?"

"I was trying to open an old locker, actually. That's what I was doing when Dylan got away from me."

"Do you need help?"

I smiled shyly. "Can you take off a lock?"

A smile spread across his face. "Give me a minute," he said as he got back in his patrol car.

"Come on, Dylan," I said as I turned his trike around. He gave no resistance, as if this happened all the time. By the time we got back to the house, Luke had pulled up along the curb and crossed the lawn. He carried a tool that looked like an eagle's beak.

"You have a lock that needs opened?" he teased.

"It's over here." I led him down the narrow strip of driveway. He leaned over and clipped the lock off the latch.

"That was easy."

"What's inside?" he asked.

"I don't know. Maybe nothing," I admitted. With a deep breath I raised the lid.

Chapter Twenty

The locker was filled with books; college textbooks mainly, plus a few paperback romance novels. A grocery sack of photos in cheap gold and black frames lay scattered to the other side. A silk fuchsia scarf was rolled up in a ball and stuffed in the corner. I picked up a frame. It was of Kelly and Brandon on their wedding day. Brandon looked happy, really happy, and very handsome in his suit and tie. Kelly was stunning in a spaghetti strap gown. She had a very pretty waiflike face, bleached blond hair cut in a wedge, and penetrating green eyes. From the photo she looked tiny, a very petite 5'2" maybe. They seemed happy and very much in love, nothing resembling the unhappy couple Brandon had described. Nothing like the few pictures of the two of us together. There was another photo of Brandon and Kelly on the beach appearing tan and relaxed, probably in Southern California. Maybe on their honeymoon.

I picked up a small 4x6 snapshot of Kelly holding a newborn that I was sure was Dylan. She looked tired, her smile not all the way to her eyes, her overly bleached blond hair disheveled. My heart ached for her. For all of them. This was Dylan's mommy. And she was gone, and somehow I had to bring her back. Tears pricked my eyes. I pinched the bridge of my nose to stop it. I felt Luke's eyes watching me. I turned to him. I didn't know what to say.

"Does Brandon talk about her much?" he asked.

I stared at the two of them looking happily off into the sunset. "I don't think so."

"I mean to you?"

I shook my head. Maybe he did at one time, but he hadn't in the few days I'd been here. And judging by this locker with all her things locked away, we hadn't ever talked about her.

Luke sat back and rested his elbows on the steps. "You know, just between you and me, something about it never sat well with me."

My head shot up. "Really? What part?" My heart pounded in my chest. Luke was giving me the opening I needed to learn about what happened that night. Maybe there was still a chance to get out of here today.

"I don't know. I guess I just think Brandon is lucky he had you for an alibi, even if it did raise eyebrows."

"Why do you say that?" I said with a steady voice.

"Kelly and Brandon had been fighting. She had a new baby that she loved. Why would she commit suicide? And with Brandon right there with her, a lot of people believed he pushed her into the river."

My heart sunk like gravel in quicksand. "Pushed her? Like murder?" My throat grew too tight to swallow.

"I know I'm just speculating. You saw the reports. It just seems like there are a few holes."

"It's been awhile, and I can't remember the details. Can you explain it to me?"

He shrugged. "I don't mean to bring this all back. But after you asked me about it the other night, I went to work and pulled out the report. I could make a copy and you could read through the sheets if you'd like. Maybe it would set the events fresh in your mind again. Maybe you would remember something new."

"Maybe," I lied, knowing full well that I wouldn't remember any of it. I swallowed hard, trying to appear calm while my insides flopped around sickly.

I looked back at the locker and picked up the fuchsia scarf. It was a gorgeous vivid fabric that fluttered like liquid silk in the light wind. I glanced back at the photo of Brandon and Kelly on the beach. The scarf fluttered around her neck in the picture. It set off her bright eyes and nearly white hair. She was very intriguing looking. I held it up to my face, expecting to smell her perfume, but it only smelled of old books and dust. I suddenly felt like I had no right to be rummaging through her things. I went to put it back. As I did, my hand touched a red leather-bound book small enough to fit in the palm of my hand. I picked it up. It was about the size of a diary. I was too curious not to open it. A woman's handwriting filled the pages. I shut the book.

"Is that her journal?" Luke asked.

"Looks like it."

"Can I see it?" he asked, hand outstretched.

I didn't want to share it with Luke, but I had no choice. I'd seen all those TV shows. If Kelly had been murdered, wasn't this evidence? I handed it over to him. He flipped through a few pages, his mouth set.

Dylan toddled up to us and pulled the book out of Luke's hand. "Kook, kook," he said, pointing to the book as he backed himself into Luke and lifted his arms.

I chuckled. "I think he wants you to read to him." I took the opportunity to pull the book from his hands.

"Can I get you a drink, Luke?"

"Dink, dink!" Dylan yelled, jumping out of Luke's lap.

Luke stared at the book held tightly in the palm of my hands. He stood up.

I glanced down at Dylan, and then back at Luke. "I've got to get him some lunch. Can I get you something to drink?" I asked again.

"Do you have a Diet?" he asked, still staring at the book.

"It's all we drink around here. Come on."

I set the journal back in the chest and picked up Dylan, who immediately buried his head into the nape of my neck and twisted my hair in his fingers.

Once we were inside I sat Dylan down in his high chair and asked, "What would you like for lunch, bud?"

"Sanich?" he said, his eyes lighting up.

"Peanut butter and jelly?"

He nodded excitedly. Thank goodness kids were pretty predictable. A PB&J was an easy guess.

I pulled a soda from the fridge and popped the top. The sound of the carbonation made my mouth water. I grabbed another.

"Where do you keep your glasses?" Luke asked, glancing around nervously.

"They're . . ." I had to remember myself. "They're in the second cupboard over from the sink," I hoped.

Luke moved from the door to the cupboard. He grabbed two glasses and set them on the counter. While he poured, I put a sandwich together for Dylan.

"Squares or triangles?" I asked.

"Scares!" Dylan called out. I tried not to smile. I'd seen this very scene on a commercial once. It felt surreal to be living it. I cut the bread crossways once, and then again in the opposite direction and set the plate in front of him. I ignored the heat of Luke's watchful eye as I made the sandwich. Our eyes met. He took a quick drink and looked away. I ignored how handsome and important he looked in a uniform, and how the gun on his holster made me slightly nervous.

Dylan grabbed his little squares of sandwich and took a big bite. He smiled up at me, and then took another bite. His foot banged happily against his chair.

"You want a sandwich? Maybe one with meat?" I asked Luke.

He held a hand up to stop me. "No, thanks. This is all I need." Luke held both glasses of bubbly soda. I shrugged and led him to the living room.

"Have a seat."

He handed me a soda, and then sat on a side chair. I sat stiffly on the sofa. The broken spring creaked and dug into my backside. I shifted off the painful spring. I looked around the tiny room, the sofa with a slash in it, the mismatched chairs, and felt my face grow warm. I took a deep drink. *Thankful heart. Thankful heart,* I reminded myself. To most people, this was acceptable. The way you started out when you were first married. And it would have been fine with me too if I hadn't experienced the other side. Luke was from here. This was how all newlyweds started out. I glanced over at him. He appeared quite at home sitting opposite me, one ankle up on his knee.

"Do you mind if I ask what you were hoping to find in that locker?"

"I don't know. I thought it was strange that I couldn't find anything that had belonged to Kelly around here." I waved my hand over the blank walls and bookshelf. "Dylan is her son. He should have some reminder of his mother."

"Maybe Brandon thought it would make you uncomfortable."

Why hadn't I thought of that? It seemed reasonable. Luke took a deep drink, and then set it on his knee.

"Seems like you're doing better with Dylan," he said.

"It does?" My eyebrows went up in surprise.

"I just remember that night I ran into you at the park and you were really struggling. He was so young, and you were thrown into motherhood all of the sudden. It was really brave of you . . . to fill Kelly's shoes." He took another deep drink and finished off his soda.

I shifted in my seat. Calling me brave was stretching it. "I wouldn't say I've filled her shoes. I'm a sorry excuse for a substitute."

He gave a tired smile. "Don't be so hard on yourself."

A small scab lay on Luke's chin. I hadn't noticed it before. "Luke, I'm sorry about the other night." I took another drink, and then set my glass down on the floor. "It was selfish of me to get you mixed up in my problems."

He waved a hand in front of his chin. "Not a problem. I need a good fight every once in a while. Besides, I hear chicks dig scars." He set his own glass on the small side table.

"Luke . . . can I ask you something?"

"Sure." He sat back in his chair.

"What was Kelly like?" I asked, picking at the cotton fibers on the afghan.

He shrugged his shoulders. "Kelly, was . . . different."

"What do you mean by different?"

"I don't know . . . she was kind of like a drug for guys. They were attracted to her, and she flirted a lot. Even after they got married. Probably why Brandon is so jumpy with you. Brandon got in more than one fight over guys flirting with Kelly. I had to bust up a couple of 'em. Might be another reason we aren't the best of friends right now." He looked out the window. "Speaking of—Brandon gonna be okay if he comes home and finds me here?" His head cocked to one side, a little smile crossed his face.

"Probably would punch you in the face again," I admitted with a little laugh. I grabbed my glass and took another drink, and then held it tightly between my fingers. "To be honest, things aren't good between us. He's gone hiking up into Yellowstone," I said, scratching my neck nervously and wiping the sweat away with my hand. "I guess that's why I wanted to find out what I could about Kelly, about her accident."

"I shouldn't accuse Brandon of any wrongdoing. I hope you didn't get the wrong idea." He stood and grabbed his empty glass. "Thanks for the drink. Is there anything else I can do? Any other locks you need opened?"

I smiled. "No. I'm fine. Thanks for keeping Dylan safe."

"That's my job."

Dylan sat in his high chair rubbing his eyes. His messy hands had smeared peanut butter and jelly sandwich all over his face.

"I know a boy who needs his face washed and a nap." I scooped Dylan into my arms. "I'll be right back."

I carried Dylan to the bathroom and washed his face and hands with a warm washcloth, and then put him down for a nap. He snuggled, his blanket in his arms, and turned on his side. I couldn't believe how easy he was. I heard nap time was murder for most mothers. Maybe this parenting gig wasn't such a big deal.

I found Luke washing out his glass. I glanced over at where Dylan had eaten his lunch. His high chair was cleared and wiped down. Dylan's plate was drying by the side of the sink.

"Leave no trace," he said with a hint of humor behind his serious eyes.

I bit my lip and rubbed the sweat off the back of my neck again. "You're pretty fast. I could hire you."

"I don't think Brandon would approve."

Brandon. He was right. And I had promised myself I'd be a better wife. This didn't look like I was really trying very hard. "Sometimes I forget I'm married. If you can believe that."

Luke turned to me, a look of worry on his face. "You didn't have to marry Brandon, Marlo. Kelly's death wasn't your fault."

Was that why I had married Brandon? Guilt? Maybe.

"Well, Dylan needed a mother." I straightened. "And you know what? I really like the little tyke." It was the first time I'd really considered it, but it was the truth. I kind of liked being his mother.

"Don't forget that Brandon needs a wife too."

"I know." His words stung as much as my bee sting.

"I better get going. The fish are calling my name."

I followed him out the door. We stopped in our tracks at the sight of a pair of familiar legs holding a butt high in the air as she rifled through the open locker.

The screen door slammed. She shot up, her big eyes flashing in surprise.

"Amanda?" Luke asked.

She glowered. "Hi, there, Luke."

Chapter Twenty-one

Amanda dropped a picture frame and a few books back into the locker.

"I thought that looked like your car, Luke. You making a domestic argument call?" she laughed.

"I'm a state trooper. I don't generally deal with domestic calls."

"Where's Brandon? I need to talk to him anyway." She stepped away from the locker. Her body rocked from each step. If I didn't know better I'd swear she'd been drinking.

"He went hiking in Yellowstone. He'll be back tomorrow," I answered.

Her forehead creased. She squinted at Luke, and then back to me.

"Is that a hickey?" she asked, pointing to my neck.

I touched the welt that was still pulsing. "It's a bee sting," I explained, my face flushing red.

"You made a police call for a bee sting?" Her face twisted in disgust.

"Amanda," Luke warned.

"No! He helped me find Dylan," I explained.

"You lost Dylan! Why didn't you call me? I knew you couldn't handle him." Amanda took a step toward me. Something fell out of her shirt and dropped to the ground. It was the red book. The journal.

"What are you doing with this?" I bent over and picked it up.

"Give that to me," she demanded, her eyes glued to the book. "You do not have any right to read her private thoughts. Brandon is an idiot. Neither of you deserves this book."

"Amanda, you can't just take her journal," Luke said. "Brandon was listed as Kelly's next of kin. The journal belongs to him now."

She stumbled toward me. "That doesn't mean it belongs to her!" She slashed her hands in the air reaching for the book. I took an involuntary step backward, hit the cement stairs, and tripped into a small cluster of bushes.

A huge fat snake, not an Idaho local, shot out of the bushes and slithered over my foot. I froze in place, too frightened to scream. Too scared to move. Amanda let out a blood-letting scream. My hands flew up, searching for something to grab so I could pull myself up. I still had the book in my fist. The only thing I could do without letting go was just roll out. So I did. I flung myself out of the bushes and rolled over on my hands. Quickly, I scrambled to my feet and spun around, running straight into Amanda who was still screaming hysterically and turning in circles. The force knocked us both down again. The snake disappeared into the bushes. The book slipped from my hand. Amanda stopped screaming. She caught sight of the book and snatched it up.

She jumped to her feet.

"Give me the book!" I said hotly. I stood and held out a hand.

She grinned and said sweetly as she walked backward down the driveway, "You might want to do something about that snake. Probably courtesy of Mr. Golborne."

"Amanda, you can't take that book," Luke called. He didn't seem nearly as angry as he should. He almost had a look of enjoyment on his face.

"I'm not giving this book back," she yelled, taking careful steps backward. I spied the snake slithering across the driveway again.

"Amanda, don't," I yelled.

She laughed in her throat and stuffed the book deep into her oversized rainbow-striped handbag. "Tell Brandon to call me the minute he gets home."

She took another step backward. Her feet tripped over the

enormous boa constrictor. She screamed and fell backward, landing on the cement. The snake glided easily around her head and disappeared under the house again. Amanda screamed. I rushed to her side. Luke followed behind me. She thrashed her arms and legs in the air and cried what I'd guess were real tears.

I reached out to help her up. She swatted my hand away.

"Luke! Luke!" she cried. I turned to Luke. His hand covered his mouth. He was laughing.

"Hey," I reminded him, "a little help would be nice."

"Sorry," he laughed, "but you two are classic."

I suppressed my own laugh. "Shut up and help me here."

Luke helped Amanda to her feet. She nearly melted in his arms. I looked away. I'd forgotten for a moment that they were dating. The idea left me feeling slightly nauseous.

"It went under the house!" Amanda cried, pointing her long-nailed fingers toward a small hole near the front of the house.

Luke stifled a grin. "Sounds like Mr. Golborne lost one of his little reptile friends."

"Little? Are you nuts? It was probably six feet long and three feet thick. It could have killed me. I don't know why it didn't," Amanda lamented.

"Me neither," I wondered aloud.

"I'll go talk to Mr. Golborne," Luke promised, rubbing her back with his hand. He disappeared around the corner to Mr. Golborne's house. Amanda moved to the curb and sat down. I didn't want to be alone with her.

"I'll be back," I yelled and ran after Luke.

Luke stood at Mr. Golborne's front door. Mr. Golborne answered. He wore a stained undershirt and sagging slacks held up by suspenders. Luke explained the situation and offered to call the city pound to help catch the snake. Mr. Golborne scratched his grey, scruffy chin.

"If I know where the snake is hiding I can catch him pretty quick."

I shuddered to think of what types of slithery reptiles lay hidden inside his house. Or Brandon's.

Mr. Golborne disappeared inside the house to get his "kit."

When we returned a few minutes later, Amanda was standing on the top step with her hands on her hips.

Luke calmly walked to her side. He looked up at her. I glared at her. She shifted her feet and rubbed her cherry red lips together. "What?" she asked innocently.

"You need to give the book back to Marlo," Luke calmly stated.

"Kelly was my friend. Just 'cause she married Brandon doesn't mean she gets Kelly's things."

Luke sighed and turned his head back to his patrol car. "Tell ya what. I'm headed out on the river in a bit. Why don't you come with me?"

"What's the catch?"

"You give the journal back to Marlo until we can talk to Brandon. It really isn't your property, Amanda."

"Brandon does owe me. He'll have to give it to me."

Luke shrugged, "Maybe."

She glared at me, and then spat a quiet, "Fine!" as she gingerly made her way down the steps. She pulled the book out of her purse, pushed it in my hands, and then ran to Luke's car, never looking back until she was safely locked away in the passenger's seat.

Mr. Golborne appeared around the corner with a cage containing two plump-looking mice.

"I designed this myself, see? And it works like a charm." He turned the wiry contraption around to show us how he installed an opening for the snake to enter, but also kept the mice from escaping.

"I'll have the old sneak back in his proper cage by nightfall," he boasted, a fresh cigarette dangling from his lips.

Luke turned to me, his eyes full of concern. "You gonna be all right?"

I nodded. "I'm sure Mr. Golborne will take care of everything," I said.

His head tilted to one side, looking at my neck. "You sure it's not a hickey?"

My hand traced the red welt. "Funny," I simply stated.

He laughed. "Tough luck today."

"Tell me about it."

"Luke! Come on!" Amanda yelled from his lowered window. Luke glanced over his shoulder and then back at me. His lips were tight, his eyebrows creased.

"Gotta get out on the river before it gets any later. I'll check in tomorrow, okay?"

"Sure." I watched him climb into the driver's seat and disappear down the road with Amanda at his side.

June 3 . . .

He called again. Why can't he leave me alone? I'm going to have to change my cell number. Brandon heard it buzz. He looked over at me, but he didn't ask who it was.

June 10 . . .

Took Dylan to the store for the first time. Everyone stopped to admire his beautiful blue eyes, but all I could muster was a slight smile. I feel empty. Drained. Sad. I don't know what to do. I can't explain it to Brandon. I feel so alone.

June 17 . . .

Better day today. I took a shower before noon. Dylan slept for three hours this morning. No one's called. I'm glad. Maybe he is finally getting the message.

June 28 . . .

Brandon and I got in a fight. Why does he have to be like this? Leave it alone. Just leave it alone. But he won't. Can I blame him? Dylan cried for three hours. So did I.

July 1 . . .

Everything seems to have settled down. I'm glad. I'm sick of the drama. Brandon seems better. Over it. Whatever he thinks IT is. Dylan is sleeping better. Slept four hours last night before waking. I've quit nursing. I hated it. Being chained down every couple hours was making me crazy, not to mention how raw my nipples were. It's not right. The car is starting to act funny. I don't want to have to take it in. Overall, doing better.

July 20 . . .

I am shaking. What am I going to do? I can't look at Brandon. He looks mad enough to kill me. Amanda tells me to relax; that this will all blow over. She said she'd talk to Brandon, but I don't like the way she looks at him. Sometimes I think about running away from all this. I hear tickets to Vegas are cheap, but what would I do with Dylan? I'm trapped.

July 24 . . .

He called. I wanted to be mad at him, but it felt so good to hear his voice. Sometimes I wonder how I got myself in this mess, and then I remember the feel of his touch, the sound of his voice as it vibrates through his chest. I just want to go away, but Brandon watches me like a hawk. I have to tell the truth. First thing when Brandon comes home. Maybe. Dylan smiled at me today. I swear it. He understands this hell I'm living. It's all going to be okay. I just have to do it.

There were no other entries. The last one was the night before her death. Murder or suicide, who knew? I closed the small red journal and slid it in front of me. I looked out the kitchen window. A car slowly passed. Dylan was still napping, and I'd been able to read most of the journal. In the beginning, Kelly spoke of starting over with Brandon. She was pregnant, and she seemed convinced that she loved Brandon and spoke continually of not wanting to hurt him, but as time went on there was definitely evidence that something troubled Kelly. Something she only hinted about. Never anything more than "him."

Plus, Kelly had sounded depressed. I wondered if Brandon had recognized any of the signs of postpartum depression. It reminded me of Melissa after the birth of her second child. She'd come home to live with mom and dad for a few days until they could get her to a doctor who helped her. But what about Kelly? Did anyone see the signs? Did Brandon know she wanted to leave him? Did Brandon read any of this? Was he aware of her struggles? Though it didn't clearly define that she was having her own problems, the journal didn't exonerate him from guilt either. I didn't blame him for locking the journal up in the trunk. And now Luke knew a journal existed, and he'd have to read it.

My phone rang. It was Darcy.

"I don't know if you remember, but I was going to watch Dylan this afternoon for you, and you were going to pay me with one of your outfits. I have a date tonight, and I was hoping to wear that little miniskirt number of yours. Is that still going to work?"

So was that where all my clothes were going? I remembered finding my miniskirt outfit folded neatly in a bag.

"I actually forgot about it, but that would be great. I have to warn you that I recently wore that outfit and it needs to be washed. And Darcy, again, I am so sorry about yesterday."

"It's already forgotten. And don't worry about washing it. It will give me something to do since you don't have cable. Girl, when are you going to get cable, just for your babysitters' sakes?" she laughed loudly into the phone.

"Did I tell you where I was going, by chance?"

"No, but even if you don't have anything going on, I'd still like to babysit Dylan. He is such a sweetie, and I'd really like to have that outfit."

I really liked that outfit too. Why was I giving away my clothes? Had things gotten that bad that I had to sell my clothes to pay for babysitting? Or was Brandon too cheap to give me the money? Darcy agreed to be here in half an hour. I glanced at my watch. It was almost 2:30.

Darcy had sounded like her old self again. I was relieved. I opened the fridge. A few condiments, a half-gallon of milk, and some leftover soup sat in the near-empty fridge; the bulb in the back stared back at me. I had no idea what our financial situation was. Were we poor? Could I go to the store again? I closed the fridge door, moved back to my purse, and rifled through the baby toys and small cardboard books, looking for a checkbook. All I found was a couple dollar bills, a check card, and a driver's license picture that did nothing to help my ego. I searched every drawer in the kitchen and finally found the checkbook, but discovered neither Brandon nor I had been balancing it. That was either really good or really bad news. Maybe I'd stop by the bank and check out our balance while Darcy watched Dylan. But what if it was really low? How would I face the teller if she informed me I had seventy-five dollars in my account? Or worse, that it was overdrawn? With Cort, I hadn't needed to be very careful, but I knew—seeing our living conditions—that money was probably a bigger concern for Brandon and me.

There was a knock on the door. It was Darcy. I called for her to come in. I threw her "payment" into the washer. The small laundry room just off the kitchen was an addition. A "lean-to." Big enough for a washer and dryer, but not much else, including me.

She let herself in. "Why is Mr. Golborne sitting in a lawn chair in your driveway?"

I smiled wide, wanting to tell her about the adventurous morning I'd had.

"Let's just say that I might have one of his snakes loose under my house."

She pulled a sour face. "I thought he got rid of those things years ago."

"So did I." I cleared my throat. "Darcy, I'm glad you aren't still mad at me. I didn't mean to hurt you."

"I'm not mad. I was a little hurt, but we've been friends too long for me to stay mad at you. Besides, it's thanks to you that I have a date tonight. So thanks."

Darcy flittered like a ballet dancer across the kitchen floor. "So . . . aren't you going to ask me who I'm going out with?"

I could see by her freshly made-up face that I probably did not want to hear. She failed to notice my reserve and went on anyway. "I just went up to him at the restaurant and asked if he wanted to do something sometime. Crazy, I know, but he was so cool about it."

"Luke?" I asked, shuffling the stack of loose papers around like I was organizing them.

"Of course, Luke!" She flopped down on the kitchen chair and tapped her nails against the table. I smiled and shoved my discontent down into the corners of my shoes, hoping I could stomp out the jealousy.

"He is such a gentleman. Most guys I end up dating are jerks, you know? But Luke . . . he's different."

"Yeah, I know."

I grabbed a rag from the sink and wiped the already clean counters, remembering how Luke had cleaned my kitchen for me. He was pretty amazing.

"Is Amanda okay with all this?"

She rolled her eyes. "Amanda is a fickle fanny. She no more loves Luke than you do. Luke will catch on."

I flinched at her words. "But I thought they were exclusive."

"Oh no—at least not on Amanda's side. She's barhopping two or three times a week. I've even seen her once or twice with Kale again."

Kale? Tire-store Kale? I took a deep breath and forced a smile. "I'm happy for you."

"Well, it's just a date." She eyed me curiously and fiddled with the edge of the table. "Why didn't you marry him?"

I gripped the rag in my hand and moved to the sink and rinsed it out before I answered. "I don't know. Brandon needed me, I guess." I set the rag in the sink and grabbed my bag, not wanting to look her in the eye. Afraid she'd notice the jealousy.

"I'm sorry, Mars. I forgot about all that." She pointed to the welt on my neck. "What happened?"

"I got stung by a bee," I explained casually, not ready for her to change the subject yet. "So, what are you guys going to do?" I asked, trying to make my voice sound casual.

"He has a friend with dune buggies. We're taking them to the sand dunes. Then we'll have ourselves a big old bonfire, just like we used to in high school." Her eyes grew excited. "You and Brandon should join us. It will be fun."

I went back to my stack of papers and started to actually sift through them. Newspapers, advertisements. Recycling. My list of people I need to help came up. I quickly slipped it underneath the stack before she noticed it.

"Brandon's gone hiking in Yellowstone. He won't be back until tomorrow," I stated shortly. "But it sounds like fun." I meant that. And now I did want to change the subject.

"Guess I better get going. That outfit might be a little wrong for the sand dunes, though. Are you sure you don't want a pair of jeans instead?"

"The ones with the really great denim wash?"

I blinked back at her. How did she know my clothes so well? "Sure."

I went to my bedroom and found the bag in the back of the closet. I called to her as I tore through the bag looking for the jeans. "The outfit is still in the washer, so if you don't mind, would you hang it out to dry when it's done?"

I pulled out a few additional sacks of folded clothes I hadn't seen before: "future payments" I could only assume. I stopped when my hand bumped against something cold and hard on the shelf in the back of the closet. I pulled it out. It was a shiny handgun. I'd never held a gun like that before in my life. A cold sweat hit my forehead. I stuffed it back where I found it. Something fell to the ground. A stuffed manila envelope lay shut with jute rope. I untied the rope and looked inside.

It was stuffed with hundred-dollar bills. Something twisted in my stomach. I thumbed through the bills. There was well over two thousand dollars. Was this my money? Was it Brandon's? What did we have that kind of cash in our house for? Was Brandon dealing drugs? Who else had large sums of cash—and guns—on them? I pulled out a hundred-dollar bill and shoved it in my pocket. I was sure this would come in handy. I replaced the sacks and the manila envelope and hurried out of the room, glad to be putting some space between me and that shiny black thing.

Darcy was still talking about Luke. When she took a look at my face she stopped.

"You feeling okay?"

"I'm fine," I lied. "You'll probably want these too." I held out the pair of designer jeans.

"Are you kidding?" she squealed in delight. "You are so forgiven!" She grabbed the jeans and tried them against her frame.

"Dylan will be waking up from his nap anytime now." My shoulders felt like metal weights were glued to them.

She looked up from admiring the jeans. "We'll be fine. Now get out of here, so I can start earning these clothes."

I pulled my bag over my shoulder, thanked her for watching Dylan, and then headed out the door feeling like I'd just given away my favorite $400 jeans.

Chapter Twenty-two

I was in a fog. Besides thinking of my clothes, all I could think about was the gun and huge pile of money stashed in the back of my closet. I entered the air-conditioned bank and made my way to the first teller. She was a stern-looking woman, midfifties, glasses, and short curly hair. She had worked at the bank ever since I was a little girl and used to hand me butterscotch or cherry-flavored suckers in clear wrappers. I realized I did not know her name. She smiled grimly when I walked up.

"Can I help you, Marlo?" She blinked through her glasses.

I hesitated, surprised that she remembered me. Then I remembered that I probably came in here a lot in this "glimpse."

"I need to check my balances on my accounts," I said quietly.

"All right, can I have your card, please?"

I pulled out my wallet and scanned the row of cards until I found a matching bank card. I handed it over. She swiped it through her machine.

"You do realize we are on the Internet. We could get you set up so you could do all of this from your home computer."

I scarcely could meet her eye. I wasn't even sure we had a computer. "My computer's down," I answered shortly.

"That's fine. Just want you to know all of your options. We also installed a new ATM in the drive-through. We used to have one in the lobby, but now we've added one out there, so it's nice and convenient for people."

"I was going to do that, but I've somehow forgotten my pin." This was true.

She looked at me funny. "I'm sorry, Marlo, but if you don't know your pin I'll have to ask for some ID. It's just company policy."

"Sure."

You never know when someone will have a face transplant and come into a bank looking just like me, I thought snarkly to myself. I handed her my ID. She scarcely took so much as a gander before returning it to me. She looked down at the computer screen and then, without looking at me, asked if I'd like a printout.

"Yes, that would be great," I answered. "I'd like a printout on all my accounts, please."

She hesitated, "And what other account would that be?"

"Don't we have like a savings account?"

She cleared her throat and shifted her feet a little. "Well, now, Brandon does have that one account from Kelly's insurance policy, but you are not on that account, and I'm afraid that without Brandon here I can't allow you access to it."

"Brandon has a separate account? How much money are we talking about?"

She shifted uncomfortably again and adjusted her glasses. "I'm afraid I can't give you any information, Marlo. You need to ask Brandon about that, okay?"

"Like hundreds of thousands of dollars?" I demanded, ignoring her privacy policy garbage. My neck felt hot; my head burned with frustration that once again I had allowed myself to get isolated in the financial department.

"Would you like a printout of your account?"

"Do I have my own account?" I asked, feeling more hopeful.

"No, dear. Just the checking account that you share with Brandon."

"Right. Yes, I'd like a history of our activity too."

She made a copy and handed it over without glancing at it.

"Anything else I can do for you today?" she asked with an embarrassed smile.

I shook my head. I glanced down at the paper and gasped. "What is this?"

Seventy-five dollars had been generous. Our checking account had only thirty-four bucks in it.

"Did we make a mistake?" she asked politely, glancing at the paper.

I scanned through the printout of our bank history going back three months and gasped again.

"Somebody made a mistake," I insisted. Our account never exceeded one thousand dollars, and generally hovered in the three- to five-hundred-dollar range, with small deposits of six to eight hundred dollars every week.

"This is a disgrace. I have thirty-four dollars to my name?" I cried. The man working in the next window, who had been pretending not to listen to our conversation, had stopped counting money and peered over his window with a look of surprise on his face.

I shook the paper. "How could Brandon do this to me?"

I waved the papers in Kathy's face. "I need to know how much money we are talking about in his little private account. Is it more than fifty thousand?"

She glanced over at her coworker. He looked back down at his stack of money and started counting again.

"Marlo," she shook her head, "I can't tell you. Besides I'd have to have his account number."

"Oh, come on, you know how much money he has. This is a small town. You'll at least know general numbers." I leaned in and ordered, "Just blink if it's more than fifty thousand." She sighed, and then did a long slow blink.

"More than one hundred thousand?" I mouthed.

She gave another big long blink.

"I think I'm going to be sick." I leaned against the counter and took three cleansing breaths. Kathy stepped back and turned her head, preparing for me to get sick across her booth. The lobby was nearly deserted. There was only one other employee sitting behind a desk working at a computer. I could only hope I hadn't yelled loud enough for him to hear me too.

"I'll sell the truck," I said under my breath.

Kathy cleared her throat and shuffled a bunch of papers in her hands. I waited expectantly, but she only cleared her throat and shifted from side to side.

"What, can I not do that? Do you know something else?"

"Well, I am the one that helped Brandon get his truck, and you were not a cosigner. Did you forget?"

I stomped my foot. How did I screw myself again? How could Brandon have shut me out like this?

"Are you saying I gave him my car?"

"Well, I don't know quite how it all worked out, but he came in with quite a bit of money from the proceeds of a previously owned vehicle. His loan was a very small one, and he paid that off soon after. I remember sending him the title." Her face turned like a trapeze artist from surprise to concern.

"Honey, you might want to go home tonight and have a long talk with your husband. I'm sorry you weren't made aware, but Brandon has to add you to his account in order for me to do anything for you. I'm so sorry."

"It's okay. It's not your fault that I'm so clueless." My face filled with color. I stuffed the papers in my bag, thanked her, and turned to leave.

I burst through the bank doors and nearly tripped over my own shoes in the process. "Stupid shoes!" I hissed as I tore off the high heels and chucked them at the next-door building. I'd had it with these shoes. I'd had it with designer clothes. No wonder Marlo in this glimpse was giving her things away. I wanted to rid myself of every superficial thing I'd ever owned. For once I wanted to wear something comfortable and flat, like a pair of Keds.

I glanced over at the building where my shoe landed. It was Grey's Opera House. The old Grey Opera house built in 1912 was built for traveling road shows that performed their vaudeville acts or small-time operas like the E. Forest Taylor company and Ralph Collinger company. In 1918 a fire damaged the Opera House and the Opera House was transformed into a movie house. At one time it was a candy store. In the thirties, the building went through another change—including a forty thousand-dollar remodeling package—to turn it into a seed packing plant, and later a sports complex with boxing matches. Today, it was a plumbing company and had been for as long as I'd been alive. But the exterior of the building remained the same, with the name "Grey's Opera House" etched into the stone of the old-fashioned three-story building. Above the plumbing store were several apartments. One of those apartments belonged to a certain old lady that I hoped to catch at home.

I stuffed my high heel back on my foot and clunked loudly up the steep wooden stairs toward the third floor.

I knocked on the first door, but no one answered. I moved to the next door. It was decorated with mossy-looking vines that crept around the grey door frame. The door opened without my even touching it. Sure enough, the old woman, whose name was still a mystery to me, stood in her familiar muumuu. Her mouth dropped in surprise. She went to shut the door. I jammed my leg in the opening to keep her from shutting it. The door banged painfully against my thigh. I bit my lip to keep from yelling.

"I just need to talk to you!" I explained through the small opening.

"You want me do it for you. I not doing nothing!" she warned through the opening.

"No, I don't. I just need to talk. Please."

The old woman seemed to sense a change in my voice. She eased her powerful grip on the door. I took the opportunity and opened the door wide and walked into the place the old woman called home.

Her walls were a perfect sky blue. The floors were covered in wheat and brick-colored Native American-styled woven rugs. I stood frozen in the entry as I took in an enormous black iron birdcage spanning the entire wall, floor to ceiling. Probably ten feet by ten feet and three feet deep. Sitting in a swing that hung from the ceiling sat a most magnificent raven. Its marvelous long-tailed feathers were a striking iridescent blackish purple. Its strong beak stood sharp against the blue silhouette. On the opposite end of the cage stood a large cypress tree. A carefully woven nest made of sticks and grass lay nestled and protected in the crotch of the tree. The raven let out a deep gurgling croak when I stepped closer.

"This is amazing," I sighed as I carefully made my way to the edge of the cage.

"My love, she's at my window like raven with broken wing," the old woman spoke with a thick accent.

I turned in surprise. "Is that Poe?" I didn't recognize it.

"Bob Dylan," the woman answered without missing a beat.

"Oh." I suppressed a smile. "I didn't know a raven could be domesticated."

She shook her head. "Not domesticated. Free to roam. But very clever bird. It know home. The raven is sacred. It create heaven and earth. It steal from the sun to bring fire to people. Raven drops good fortune when needed." She pulled a large cloth bag out of her pocket and dumped a clump of grain into a bowl and set it just inside the cage. "People call raven for help. We say to raven while hunt, '*Tseek'aal, sits'a nohaaltee'ogh*.'"

"What does it mean?" I asked.

"Grandpa, drop pack to me."

I laughed.

"It true. People talk to raven. You talk to raven. Ancestor raven will help."

"Well, tell ancestor raven that I'm screwed." I moved to the opposite side of the cage and sat in a small wooden chair. I pulled out the stack of papers that detailed my sorry financial state.

"I found out that Brandon sold my car and bought a big truck and never even put my name on it. Then I discovered that he has his own account with more than one hundred thousand dollars in it from Kelly's death, and I don't have any access to it. Nothing has changed. I'm no better with Brandon than I was with Cort. I'm an utter failure. Was this what you wanted to show me? That I'm a complete mess?"

The old woman sat in the chair opposite me, her hands tied together in thought. Then she stood and without a word disappeared into the next room. I sat and stared at the raven. I had been so upset only a few minutes before, but felt strangely calm now. Whether it was from the blue-painted walls or the black, silky winged bird watching me from its perch, I did not know. There was a bit of commotion in the other room as cupboards opened and closed and glass clanked against glass. Within a few minutes the old woman returned with a small wooden tray filled with two cups of something steaming.

"Hot cider," she explained as she set the tray on a small wooden table in front of me. "Take," she nudged.

"What will this do? Send me back to the present?"

"No." She seemed surprised by the idea. "Just plain cider. Drink, make you feel better."

"I've heard that before," I muttered before taking a sip. She was right. It tasted like hot cider. Steam rose from the cup and cleared my pores.

We drank in silence. Occasionally the big black bird would squawk something, and the woman would respond in a language I'd never heard.

"That's an unusual language. What is it?"

She shot a look at me, her eyebrows raised over her cup. "Haida. We are people who dwell along river."

"You know, I never have gotten your name," I realized.

"Hilma. I never thought you ask."

"Sorry," I blushed. "I've been very self-absorbed lately."

She grunted.

"Forget money," she said without looking up from her cup.

"Why?"

She shook her head. "Not important. What important is the part you play. You no respect yourself. You not know who you are. Cort define you; Brandon define you. You lose them because you lose you."

I closed my eyes and shook my head. "How do you know these things?"

"I not know. Raven knows. He tell me. He likes to meddle and help change. I just follow."

I set my cup down.

"You finish?"

"Yes, it was delicious." Sweat dripped down the back of my neck. She didn't have a bead of perspiration anywhere.

"Time to go. You have much to do and little time." She stood and ushered me to the door. "Forget money. It distract you from your purpose. I come tomorrow to take you home. There is little time."

My eyes widened; my mouth shot open. "Tomorrow? You promise?"

"There is little time. Now go." She opened the door and gave me a little push. I hesitated, not sure if I'd gotten the answers I needed. She gave a stronger nudge; the raven squawked again. I tripped over my feet and stumbled out into the hall.

"Okay, I'll see you tomorrow," I said just as she shut the door in my face. Well, that went better than I expected, I supposed. At least she didn't yell at me this time.

I pulled out my list and glanced over the names. Less than twenty-four hours? Did that mean I was off the hook? While that sounded good, I knew it wasn't true. I had lives to save. And there was still something nagging me. I couldn't get any more info from Luke or

Kelly. I needed to talk to Brandon. I walked back to the Escort and dialed his cell. He didn't answer. I left a message, asking him to call me as soon as possible. If he didn't get back in time I would miss him entirely. I needed answers about Kelly's death, and I needed Brandon. What could I do while I waited? I glanced at the phone to check the time. Less than twenty-four hours to do something important. But what? Who? Melissa. I would go there next.

Chapter Twenty-three

When I arrived home, Darcy had cleaned the house and ordered pizza for Dylan and me. She was wearing my favorite jeans and a grey blouse, and her dark hair looked ravenous against her milky skin. She looked great. I forced a smile and insisted she call me the next day and tell me all about her date. She grabbed the bag with what was now *her* miniskirt and gave me a tight squeeze. The old surge of jealousy crammed my chest with useless hot air. I wanted her to be happy, but just wished it weren't Luke she was so excited about.

"I'll see ya," she called from the doorway.

"Wait!" I called, unsnapping my sandals. I held them out to her. "I don't need these anymore, and they would go great with your outfit."

"Seriously? You know I love these shoes!" she squealed.

As I watched her drive away, I realized she had no idea the value of the clothes I was paying her with. I wondered what she would have thought if I'd told her how much I had really paid for those shoes. I was glad she didn't know.

I sat Dylan in front of the TV, put on a kid's video, and sneaked a quick shower. All the while I kept imagining Luke and Darcy in a dune buggy, laughing and having a great time together as they climbed the sand dunes, the hot sun resting in the western sky.

Why had the Marlo of this glimpse given up control again? I felt frustrated. Was it the loss of control I was upset about or the lack of a partnership? Equals working side by side. The old woman, Hilma, blamed my failed relationships on my inability to know who I was. So who was I? A sister, a daughter. I was once a wife. That didn't seem enough.

What did I even know about myself? What were my likes and dislikes? I for sure loved hot chocolate and hot cider, but I had to be honest. I had no appetite for coffee, even though I had pretended to like it while I was married to Cort. I wasn't sure if I liked fishing. I hadn't as a teenager, but some of my favorite memories where those fishing with my father. Maybe I would try it again. I liked seafood and a good steak, but I didn't think this was the kind of thing she was talking about. What could I do to know myself better? Go to a spa? Take a three-month hike through the park?

There was a bang at the bathroom door. I jumped. The sound brought me out of my daydream. I had forgotten the time and had been in the shower much longer than I had meant. I shut off the hot water and threw a towel around me, then I opened the bathroom door. Dylan was standing in the hall and pointing to the front door. His eyes were large and frightened. There was a knock at the front door. I poked my head around the corner. Through the window in the door I could see it was the pizza delivery guy. I rushed back to the bathroom and pulled the hundred-dollar bill out of the front pocket of my jeans. I wrapped the towel tightly around me and walked to the front door like this was a normal part of my day. The boy at the door was no more than sixteen. He stood with his eyes bulging at the blue towel wrapped around my wet, naked body. It didn't take long before he got his wits about him and averted his eyes.

"Hi, sorry about that. Here ya go. You can keep the change," I blurted as I shoved the money into his outstretched hand and nabbed the pizza out of his arm. He stuttered a thanks, and I slammed the door before he had time to say anything else.

"Come on, Dylan, time for pizza!" I called. He cheered for joy and followed me to the kitchen.

I cut up his pizza into bite-sized pieces and then grabbed a piece for myself and took a huge bite. Darcy had ordered us pineapple and ham. The crust was thick and crispy, and the mozzarella cheese was stringy. I extended my hand, pulling the pizza away, but the cheese continued to stretch. I finally had to cut it with my finger in order to separate it. Dylan was as engrossed in the pizza as I was, mostly picking off the pineapples and eating them one by one. I hadn't eaten much pizza when I was married to Cort. I'd been too afraid of the calories and fat content and had forgotten how delicious it was.

I changed into my second-favorite pair of jeans and a three-fourth sleeved black-and-white striped shirt and pulled on a pair of running shoes. I called Melissa and asked if it was okay if I stopped by. She hesitated and then quickly recovered, saying Brayden was having a late night with some little friends and she'd love for Dylan to join them. I buckled Dylan into his car seat and prayed that the car would start. It sputtered and choked, and then died. The gas gauge rested on E. I got out of the car and searched around for a gas can. I found a red one sitting next to a small lawn mower. I dumped what was left in the can into the tank and tried it again. It turned over on the third try.

"Thank you," I sighed.

I backed the car onto Bridge Street and made a quick left on Fourth North, and headed west toward Parker.

Parker was a small farming community just west of town and had about 300 people. My father's great-grandfather Parker had homesteaded the area a hundred years before as a stockman and rancher. He was the first to develop a way to support a canal irrigation system in this bone-dry area; an idea that had been tried, and then abandoned as impossible because of the sandy loam soil. As kids, we often heard of the difficulties our grandparents had trying to farm a land that many argued untamable due to the sand and volcanic rock. Every time a ditch or canal was created and water was diverted from the river, it would immediately sink into the soil. It wasn't until Wyman Parker thought to fill all the canals simultaneously that the water stayed in the canal. Something about the water table pressure kept the water from draining.

Today, Parker was a farming community whose sprawling fields kissed the very edges of the desert and survived in part because of the heavily irrigated practices. Various shades of green—sprouting alfalfa, potatoes, canola plants, and cornstalks—grew like green velvet along the rolling hills. It was where I imagined Brandon would build a home since his family had farmed there for nearly a century. It was also where Melissa and Troy had inherited a thousand acres of fertile soil from Troy's parents. And less than a mile from Melissa's picture-perfect farmhouse lay the beginnings of the world-famous sand dunes.

The secret of the farming success for the region lay hidden under the sand dunes. The hills, now covered in sand, were once active volcanic vents that poured red-hot lava over the land. Over the next two thousand years, the winds blew clear, shifting white quartz from the Snake River and deposited it over the hills creating dunes of sand; over ten thousand acres. Today, the dunes were a huge ATV enthusiast's paradise. The area even boasted a small lake and RV campground that was filled to capacity most summer nights. Hidden Lake provided a rare escape from the desert sagebrush and endless miles of sand. When the sun shone high in the cornflower blue sky and the white sand gleamed like millions of tiny crystals, I could have believed I was on St. Martins were it not for the interrupting noise of distant dune buggies. That's how it was in Idaho. We survived on active imaginations.

Melissa never complained about living near the dunes, except to say she had to dust her furniture all the time. And if there was a particularly bad windstorm, she'd find small piles of sand in the corners of her rooms that she either vacuumed or swept. Melissa labored assiduously to keep the wood furniture dusted and the floors cleaned. She was usually found with a broom or vacuum or dust cloth in her hand whenever anyone popped in for a visit.

Tonight, she traded the vacuum and broom for a late night with a group of little boys ranging from four to six. She seemed pleasantly surprised to see me.

"I've been thinking about what you said," I began when we were seated with cold lemonades on her back patio. The boys ran circles around a salivating black lab that bounded joyfully at the attention. Dylan sat on the trampoline, kicking his feet in the air and yelling unintelligible words at the others. He'd refused to get down as he was afraid of the dog, but was delighted to call out jumbled orders to the others.

"I shouldn't have said those things. I was having a bad day, and I'm sorry," Melissa said.

I set my lemonade down on the patio table. "I'm glad you did. I hadn't realized that I was unable to handle the stress. The whole thing with Dad was so upsetting, but I think I can fix it." I took a deep breath, hoping to get what I wanted to say out. "I know that sounds crazy, but I think I can make everything right again. But I can't if I don't make things right with you first."

She blinked back at me as if she wasn't sure she'd heard me right. It was the first time I'd really looked at her. Her brown eyes were outlined with deep lines and seemed swollen. Her beautiful oval face was long and narrow; her chin protruded more than it had been before. She had grown so thin.

"That is the first time you've ever said anything like that to me."

"I'm sorry if I've never acted concerned, but I have been."

"You were always so into your fashion. Into your money. All you ever talked about was what new item you'd just purchased for your home or what exotic vacation you and Cort had just returned from. At the time, Troy and I were saving up to build a home, and I had two little kids and was pregnant with Brayden. I was jealous of your life and angry that you couldn't see how self-absorbed you were being. Remember the time you visited and I'd just had Maura? You didn't even hold the baby; you just wanted to show me pictures of your trip to Bora Bora. I went in the bathroom and cried."

I was stunned. I hadn't realized I had personified the very behavior

I had long abhorred. I wanted to argue, yet I knew that everything she said was true. I looked around for Troy or the girls. "Where are the others tonight?"

"Troy's parents take them every other weekend. To give me a break."

"That's nice of them."

"Yeah, it's tough without Troy around."

"I can imagine. Where is he this time?" I asked.

Her eyes narrowed. Her stone face crystallized into a hard stare.

"Why would you say that?" she hissed. The kids stopped in their tracks and watched us.

I'd done it again. I'd obviously missed something big. "I'm sorry. It just slipped."

"Just slipped?" she snapped. She glanced over at the boys. They were still watching. She turned back to me and said in a much-lowered voice. "You forgot that my husband is dead and buried over at the Parker cemetery! I can't believe you!" She stood abruptly, entered the house, and slammed the patio door behind her.

I sat at the patio table absorbing the information that Melissa had thrown at me. An additional brick in my wall of shame. How could I have gotten Troy killed? What could I have possibly done?

The boys soon forgot the recent disturbance. Brayden turned on the sprinklers. The others ran through them, getting their shirts and shorts soaked.

"Hey, guys. Let's not get wet," I called weakly. Not one of them heard me. I was too drained to argue. And maybe this was part of the "late-night" routine. Besides, I had more apologizing to do. I carried our empty glasses to the kitchen. Melissa was taking out her frustrations on me by vigorously wiping down her spotless granite countertops.

"The boys are running through the sprinkler. Is that okay?" My voice cracked. She stopped and sighed, her shoulders slumped. "It's fine. I'm going to change them into their pajamas in a minute." She glanced out the window and caught sight of the boys running back and forth under the sprinkler. She sighed and threw the rag into the sink. Then she turned to me and folded her arms.

"Look, I'm sorry. It's just the two-year anniversary, and it's still so fresh. I really don't blame you." She leaned against the cabinets and watched the boys clamber onto the trampoline. They bounced into each other and into Dylan. He whimpered from the new commotion.

"I better go get him," I said.

I hurried outside and coaxed Dylan off the trampoline and carried him over to the sandbox. He immediately drove a dump truck down the middle, knocking over a large sand castle, the ruckus on the trampoline already a distant memory.

Melissa soon joined me. We stood side by side and watched the sun dip behind the distant western mountains. "Brayden will never remember his daddy. Maddy and Maura sometimes forget what he looked like, and me?" She pressed her finger against her lip and pounded her tightly balled fist against her chest. "I miss him so much that it feels like something is boring down in my chest, making it impossible to breathe, yet I keep breathing and that feels as bad sometimes. But I know I have to, for the kids."

Melissa held her fist to her chest a moment. I held my breath, not sure what to say. She took a deep breath and continued. "I know that you agreed to marry Brandon so that Dylan could have a mommy. I know that it's not really your fault that Dad had another heart attack, but sometimes I just wish that you hadn't talked to Brandon that night. You must have given him some inclination that you'd marry him." She grabbed a tissue out of her tan shorts and blew her nose.

"I was confused. I didn't know anything bad was going to happen. I just needed some time to figure out my feelings."

"Every time I see the river, I cringe. I hate going to Mom's place."

The river? I wanted to ask why. Then the answer came to me. My eyes widened. My jaw dropped, the pieces finally coming together. Troy was on the volunteer Search and Rescue team. If someone was in the river, Troy would have been the first to volunteer.

Troy had died trying to save Kelly. I felt sick.

Now I had three people to save. I glanced up at the orange-colored sky. A surge of panic hit me in the gut.

Melissa yelled for Brayden to turn off the water, which he did with little argument. We sat on the edge of the sandbox. Melissa tapped her hand nervously against the wood.

"I haven't been to church since the funeral," she finally said, so quietly I almost didn't hear her.

I was surprised. While my parents hadn't much use for religion themselves, Melissa had always gone to church, either by herself or with one of her friends' families. I had never given religion much thought, and Cort was agnostic. But to Melissa, it made life richer and more worthwhile. She used to try to explain it to me, saying it was like the salt in freshly baked bread, but the passion was absent for me. Sometimes I wondered if I was missing some religious chromosome, the same as the missing mommy chromosome, while Melissa had taken more than her share.

"Everything about church reminds me of Troy's death. I can't sing the hymns for fear of crying. And frankly, I'm just mad. Mad at my neighbors who still have intact families and mad at God for taking Troy from me." She paused, "And I'm mad at you."

"I'm so sorry, Melissa."

She wiped at her eyes. "I didn't do anything to deserve this life. My children didn't do anything to deserve losing their father."

"Is that what they teach at church? That if you are bad, bad things will happen?"

"No. Of course they don't, but it's one thing to talk about how to stay positive through our trials. It's another thing to actually experience them. It's all lip service until you go through it yourself."

"You're doing such a great job. The kids seem to be adjusting and happy. You're so strong. I don't know how I would ever deal with the things you've been dealt."

"I don't want to be strong. I just wish it had never happened."

I allowed her words to float through me. Something like a warm oven began to fill my heart. I knew what I had to do.

"You're right about me being self-absorbed. Things aren't going well for me and Brandon, either."

"Don't, Marlo!" She leaned across the sandbox and pointed a finger at me. "I'd do anything to get Troy back. You don't know what you have."

Now was my chance. I leaned in excitedly and began, "But what if I wasn't supposed to marry Brandon? What if I could go back and fix everything? You could tell me what happened that night and I could go back and stop it. If I could stop Brandon from whatever happened between him and Kelly, I could also save Troy, and in the end, I'd save Dad too!" My voice grew louder in my rush of excitement. I was so energized I didn't recognize the look of confusion on Melissa's face.

"Wouldn't that be nice," she said flatly. She wasn't buying it.

"I'm serious!"

"Why did you marry Brandon? It was generous of you, but it's been two years. You can't still be unsure whether you did the right thing. I don't understand it. Unless you're about to tell me it's Luke again."

My head shot up at his name. I couldn't help it. She rolled her eyes and groaned. "Marlo!"

"He's on a date with Darcy right now. They're at the dunes. She invited me and Brandon, but well, with Brandon gone hiking, I had to turn her down."

"Is that why you're here? You want to go spy on them?"

I shifted uncomfortably in my seat. It had crossed my mind, but it definitely was not why I was here.

"No. I really want to talk to you about the night of Kelly and Troy's deaths. I need to know exactly what happened. What time it was, where Kelly and Brandon were. Where Troy was. Everything."

"You know everything already. You were there yourself. Stop avoiding the real question. How did you plan on spying on Luke?"

"I . . . I don't know . . ."

She leaned forward and touched my hand. "Marlo, it was commendable that you married Brandon, but you're not being fair to him."

"Dylan needed a mother."

"But Brandon needs a wife. You've got to figure this out. Either stick it out with Brandon and make it work or end it. Sneaking behind his back is not okay."

Luke had said the same thing. "I know. If Luke and Darcy are right for each other, then great. I want to help make it happen. I guess I just need to know. It would make my decision easier."

The sun had nearly disappeared behind the distant purple mountains. I felt a chill run through the air. The boys were sure to be freezing in their wet clothes. Melissa must have had the same thought because at that moment she stood up and hollered at the boys to come inside.

The young boys, their faces smudged with pizza sauce, their hair wet and matted, their clothes soaked, scrambled off the trampoline and ran across the thick Kentucky blue grass toward the house.

We lined them up at the door and wiped them down with towels. Once they were suitably dried off we sent them off to find their pajamas while Melissa popped popcorn and started a movie. When the boys were snug and warm under blankets and the cartoon was playing, Melissa led me to her room. I followed obediently.

"These late nights are big deals," I admired, hoping to break the silence.

"We rotate, every weekend. Gives me a few nights a month to myself. And Brayden loves having his friends come to play. When you live in the country, play dates take a lot more effort, but nights like this one remind me why I stay out here."

Melissa's bedroom walls were painted a chocolate brown; her bed was covered in a silky peacock blue with tons of decorative pillows. She continued on into her equally roomy bathroom. I stopped and remembered the way it felt to own something this spacious and organized. Two separate sink cabinets, sunken tub, separate stone shower with two spigots, one in front and one in back. My hands lingered over the cold granite. Melissa was already through the bathroom and into a closet. She opened a large drawer and pulled out a handful of camos.

"These were Troy's. He wore them hunting. They'll be a little big, but you could roll them up. I'll watch Dylan. This will be the last time I help you, though. You've got to move on too, just like the rest of us."

I wondered what else I had asked her to do in the past, but decided it was better if I didn't know. "Mel, will you come with me? I don't know the sand dunes very well anymore. It's been so long I'll probably get lost."

Melissa sighed. Her face flushed as she dropped the clothes in my outstretched hands. "You better get changed." Without another word she shut the door behind her.

I glanced around the closet. Suits and button-down shirts lined the closet. This wasn't Melissa's closet, but Troy's. I could sense how difficult it must have been for her to let me in. I stared at Troy's camo pants. I'd never touched a dead person's clothes before. It felt strange. I pulled them over my jeans anyway. They were a little baggy. I rolled them up, and then tried on the matching jacket. It hung off my shoulders but worked. This wasn't a fashion show, I reminded myself.

I caught my image in the floor-length mirror. This was not something a grown woman should do, a supposedly married woman at that. I was surprised that Melissa was even supporting this crazy idea.

Melissa poked her head through the door. She paused when she saw me dressed in her dead husband's clothes. She cocked her chin up, perhaps for courage. A tiny crack of a smile spread across her lips. "Okay, we're set. I called Amber from across the road. Do you remember Justin Ricks?" I nodded. "His daughter. She babysits for me. She'll watch the boys while we're gone."

She retrieved another pair of camo pants out of the open drawer and slipped them on. Melissa was taller than me. She hardly had to roll the pants up at all. I pulled my running shoes back on while Melissa searched for shoes of her own.

She opened the top drawer and pulled out two headlamps.

"Here." She shoved one into my hands. "These might come in handy." She still couldn't look me in the eye. I wondered if it bothered her to see me in Troy's clothes, or maybe she was disgusted that we were doing something so silly in the first place. I didn't blame her. Even I was having second thoughts about spying on Luke and Darcy. But I was in too deep now.

I waited in the garage as Melissa gave Amber instructions. Seeing two women dressed in camouflage would have raised too many questions. Though knowing how young people think, she might have just written it off as typical strange adult behavior.

"What did you tell her?" I asked when Melissa finally opened the door, four-wheeler key jangling in her hands.

"I just said I had to check the head gates at the canal. Her family farms; she won't think a thing about it. The boys' families will be here to pick them up in an hour, so let's hurry." She was already loading herself on a four-wheeler and turning the key over. "Get on back."

A rush of exhilaration rippled through me as I climbed behind Melissa and grabbed the side bars, *Thelma & Louise* style. Without another word, she turned the throttle, and the machine blared down the now-darkened road.

Chapter Twenty-four

I realized as we traveled down the very dark road that bringing Melissa had been more than a good idea. I had no idea where Luke was and would have only gotten myself lost. Melissa seemed totally at ease as we flew down the empty road. The wind snapped against my face, but I was surprisingly warm in the fatigues. As we came over the first big hill we caught sight of a large bonfire in the distance.

"What do you think?" I asked.

"They're probably past the resort. That's where everybody goes. We'll pull off the road once we've passed the resort."

"Sounds good," I agreed.

Melissa hit the throttle and never slowed down until we passed the resort.

"Could we get in trouble?" I yelled over the howl of the wind.

"Not if we don't get caught," she yelled over her shoulder. I couldn't help but smile at Melissa's newfound attitude. The girl who never did anything wrong. Who preached to me about the dangers of sneaking out at night or sloughing school. Melissa had lived her life so rigidly I wondered sometimes if her head might pop off, it was on so tight. I wondered if this was the first bad thing she'd ever done. Somehow I doubted that now.

We came upon a row of cars lining the sides of the road. One had a trailer with dune buggies strapped down on it. I recognized Luke's Explorer. I swore. Melissa squeezed on the brake.

"Is that them?"

"That's Luke's Explorer! They're going to catch us, and we're going to look like idiots!"

"Speak for yourself. I have no intention of getting caught," Melissa promised as she eased the four-wheeler behind one of the craggy old junipers that grew out of a small sand hill. I peeled myself off the four-wheeler. My legs felt shaky. I shivered nervously.

"Our best bet is to climb this hill," she said, as she pulled out a pair of binoculars from the pocket of her jacket.

"Are you kidding me? Binoculars? You are brilliant."

"I know a thing or two about sneaking around," she said matter-of-factly while climbing, hand and foot, up the hill. I wondered if it was possibly true. And how I couldn't have known about it. I shrugged in amazement and scrambled up the hill to catch up.

The bonfire was in perfect position from where we lay hidden. With Troy's binoculars we could make out faces as the four couples sat in camping chairs around a large fire that seemed to stretch its flames in our direction, like a body detector trying to pull us out of our hiding spots. I wormed my way to the edge. Sand spilled over the top. The shifting sand sent a random stick end over end down the front side of the hill. I kissed the sand with my face as it fell to the foot of someone's camping chair. When I dared look up no one below seemed to have noticed the disturbance in the sand. The stick lay undisturbed.

"Nice one," Melissa spat in disgust. She passed me the binoculars. "Get your look so we can get out of here."

I bit my lip to keep from saying anything smart. Melissa had been more prepared than me from the get-go, and I knew I really didn't have much to say that wouldn't sound ungrateful. I took the binoculars and searched the faces until I caught Darcy's. She was smiling broadly, her hair back in a ponytail. She was naturally beautiful, and she looked like she'd had a great time. I followed the direction of her eyes. Luke's face filled the round windows, his mouth turned up pleasantly as he spoke. My stomach did a little whoopty-doo. The crowd laughed out loud. I ached to be there, to hear him talk. I felt so jealous I was angry. I wanted a part of that life. If not with Luke, someone like him. More important, I wanted to be self-assured like Darcy was.

Hot tears seared in my eyes. I dropped the binoculars. I had no right to be intruding on their party. It was immature and invasive, and I would die if Luke found out.

"Let's get out of here," I pleaded when I wiggled back to where she was hiding.

"Did you find what you were looking for?" she wondered, a softness in her voice I hadn't heard in a long time.

"I don't know. This was stupid. I'm sorry I made you do this." I handed the binoculars back to her. She replaced them in the case. As quiet as we could, we slid back down the hill and pushed the four-wheeler away from the party. My shoes were filled with sand. I was tempted to stop and dump them out, but I could sense we were on borrowed time, plus the four-wheeler was heavier than we'd anticipated. It took all our efforts to move it toward the road.

When we came around the bend I froze. Luke's Explorer's hatch was up, the light on. Luke came around the back. Cooler in both hands. His eyes caught mine. I stood with both feet buried in the sand. Melissa sighed loudly knowing our cover was blown. My heart was in my throat. I couldn't look away or speak.

Luke regained his senses quicker than I did. He slid the cooler into his car and with a soft click, shut the hatch. His eyes went from the four-wheeler, to our camouflage garb. He walked toward us. My legs were sinking deeper into the sand. I didn't dare move.

"Hello, ladies. Out for a midnight ride?" He sounded like the officer that pulled me over that first day I arrived home. The guy I happened to like, and also happened to be spying on, was also a police officer, and neither Melissa nor I had worn helmets.

Sure enough that was next. "Are we wearing helmets tonight?" he asked syrupy sweet, his hands rubbing together, like a toad about to get the fly.

"Is there a law about that?" I asked, my voice still low enough to keep from attracting more attention.

"I am going to kill you," Melissa threatened into my ear with spine-tingling venom while simultaneously digging her fingernails into my jacket. I ignored her, thankful to have the camouflage jacket to protect me, and kept on smiling.

"It's dangerous out there. This ATV is licensed to ride on major roads, I presume."

"Yes, Luke, it is. You know that," Melissa said.

"I didn't realize you had a farm out this direction. Is that what you two are doing out here? Farming?"

"Yes. We were absolutely farming," Melissa conceded, giggling. I tried to shush her, but she couldn't be stopped. She snorted out her nose and burst out laughing. Tears poured out of her eyes. I started to giggle. I met Luke's look and saw a smile crack his face.

"I'm going to look the other way about this, but let's stay on the right side of your farm from now on, okay?" Melissa giggled again. I jabbed her ribs with my elbow, and she let out a loud "Ouch!"

"Okay," I agreed with a muffled laugh.

"Nice camo, Marlo," he teased as he passed by and disappeared behind the hill again. The hairs on my arms rose.

"I really am going to kill you," Melissa threatened with a suppressed grin, "Now get on." I jumped on the back and without caring who heard, Melissa turned the key, punched the gas, and tore out of there, like two ladies out of hell, kicking dirt, sand, and rocks off the tires as we went flying down the road, our hair flapping in the wind, threatening to tangle together. I started to giggle, then Melissa joined in. We laughed so hard that we had to slow down to keep control of the vehicle.

"That was the most fun I've had in a long time," Melissa sighed once we'd said good-bye to Amber and all the little boys. She sat slouched on her black leather sectional, some fruit drink she'd concocted in her hands. I sat with one foot up on the table, feeling strangely exhausted while Dylan slept soundly under a blanket across my lap.

I giggled at the memory of the two of us spying with binoculars and rubbed my hands in my face. "I'm glad you feel that way, because that is about the most embarrassing thing I've done in a long time."

"I can't believe we got caught."

"I know. How will I ever face him again?"

The room turned silent. Each of us thinking the same thing.

"What are you going to do, Marlo?"

"I don't know yet." I sat up. I shifted in my seat so I could face Melissa.

"I need to ask you something. Will you tell me what happened the night Kelly died? Did she and Brandon get in a fight? How did Kelly end up in the river?"

"Whoa. Where did that come from? Did you hit your head or something?"

"Yes!" I latched onto that excuse. "That's exactly what I did. And let's just say it is important that I know what happened."

"You're not going to try to tell me that you can go back and change everything again, are you?"

I paused, my mouth half-opened. "No."

She shook her head. "I'll humor you. Then will you stop?" I nodded eagerly. "Brandon and Kelly got in a fight. I think he told her he was leaving her for you. She was distraught. She left; he went after her. They ended up at the park. That's where everything gets hazy. Brandon says she fell into the river. Some people think he pushed her. Including that Amanda chick that was Kelly's best friend. She's been trying to ruin the two of you ever since. Is that good enough?"

"And Troy?"

Her voice went soft. "Troy got called to the river. He is—was—one of two other scuba divers on the rescue team. His kayak got stuck on a log, and when he went under to push it out, his equipment got stuck on something and he found himself jammed under the water. He'd been in the water too long and it's so cold, even in July. His fingers got too numb or the current was too fast. He couldn't get his BC off." At my confused look, Melissa said, "BC—it's like a jacket or vest that helps him stay afloat. It got stuck, trapping him. And he couldn't get free." Melissa gasped back a sob. "Now is that enough?"

"Oh, Melissa," I sobbed and threw my arms around her neck. Even though a part of me knew this was just a temporary thing, I mourned with my sister. I loved Troy too. He had always treated me with kindness and respect. The idea of him struggling, suffering, was painful to imagine. We cried in each other's arms. I wondered if I had ever properly grieved in this glimpse. Had I ever let Melissa know how sad I was about losing a brother-in-law? Maybe that was why she had always seemed upset. She didn't think I cared.

"If I could take it back—stop it from happening—you know I would. I would do anything."

"Don't make yourself crazy thinking what you could have done differently. You have to move forward. I've got to move forward. If I've learned anything tonight I've learned that," Melissa avowed as she wiped a tear from my cheek. Her eyes glistened. She attempted a smile. She was so strong, this beautiful sister of mine.

"I better get going." My mind was reeling with this newest information. I said good night and gathered our things. Now I had to add Troy to the list of people I had to save, but it still all went back to saving Kelly. If I could just keep her out of the water everyone else would be saved also. I knew now what I had to do. I'd finally found the old woman's bone.

I stood at the door with Dylan slumped heavily over my shoulder. Melissa stood beside me. "Thanks for everything tonight. It just reminded me how much I love my sister." I hugged Melissa again. Her bony frame felt so foreign from the Melissa I had always known and loved.

"I needed it too. I've been so caught up in my own sadness I've forgotten how to live. Maybe we could do it again sometime."

"Ah . . . let's do something else, like go on a trip or spend the weekend at a spa. No more spying on old boyfriends."

Melissa laughed. "Amen."

I carried Dylan, slumped and out cold, to his car seat. He squirmed and cried out as I buckled him in, but once I tucked his blanket in around him, he fell back asleep. I turned the key. The car sputtered and choked but finally started.

The road was dark, and the beams on my car were weak. A few houses provided a small source of light along the country road. I checked the gas gauge. It was hovering near empty. I offered a silent prayer that we'd make it home.

I glanced in the rearview mirror. Orange parking lights from a truck glowed ten feet behind me. Was it Brandon? A lone street lamp lit up a driveway. It sent light across the road. It was an older Chevy with fog lights on top and a big square front from nineteen eighty-five. The truck's lights turned on. Then they flickered from high beam to low beam. I twisted my palms nervously on my cracked steering wheel. The lights flickered again. A signal for me to stop. I pulled the car over and turned the key off. I must have known them, but if someone wanted to talk to me they could show themselves first. Sure enough, a dark shadow emerged and slowly walked toward my car. A pair of long legs held up by nine-inch heels came into view.

Are you kidding me? What did she want? I looked around for the lock button, but there was no lock button. Manual locks? What century was this car from anyway? Thankfully, Dylan was sleeping peacefully. The last thing I wanted was for Amanda to wake him up. I got out of my car.

"I just drove by your house. It was all dark. I was afraid you and Brandon finally got smart and shook this town."

"Shook this town?" I laughed. She was like a comic-strip character.

Amanda didn't find it funny, however. She leaned in. Her eyes were glossy. Her breath reeked of alcohol and cigerettes. She peered through the car window. "Where's Brandon? I told him I'd be coming today. Where's he hiding?"

"I told you, he went to Yellowstone. He'll be back tomorrow."

"By the way, that was a real cute stunt you pulled today with Luke. Real cute. Now you can nicey-nice and hand the journal back to me, or I will make your life very miserable."

"What are you going to do, Amanda?" I put on a hard, brave face, but there was something off-kilter enough about Amanda that an ounce of fear began to rise in my spine.

Amanda cursed and pulled out a cigarette from between her breasts and lit up. "Are you serious?"

She took a deep drag, and then zeroed in on me. "Brandon has pushed us past our limit. And I, for one, have had enough. Let's see how he feels tomorrow when he discovers his wife and child are missing."

My stomach flip-flopped. Certainly she was bluffing, but there was something unnatural in her stare. I couldn't see past the gloss of her eye.

"Good night, Amanda. I'm talking my little boy home to rest, and by the looks of things, you need to, too."

Her eyes flashed with fire. "*Your* little boy!? That is Kelly's child. If anyone should be raising him, it's me!" She paused and puffed lightly on her cigarette, as if consciously aware of her Greta-Garbo stance. "Did you know Brandon and I dated first? Before he even met Kelly?" She took another puff. "Kelly was my best friend, but Brandon fell for her pretty hard. I forgave them. You can't fight love, right?" she laughed.

Amanda looked over her shoulder and out into the star-filled sky. "He threatened to leave her the night you came home. The night Kelly mysteriously ended up dead in the river. Strange, isn't it?"

I'd had enough. Amanda was up to no good, and I was defenseless. The game was up.

"I don't know if you are implying that I had something to do with her death or if Brandon did, but you are wrong on both counts. Now, excuse me." I spun around and opened my door. Amanda stepped ahead of me and slammed the door shut with her high-heeled shoe, barely missing my hand in the process.

"I'm not playing games here, sis," she threatened.

"Neither am I," I warned, the blood hot in my veins. I glanced over my shoulder into the backseat, relieved to see Dylan was still sleeping.

She dropped her cigarette inches from my shoe. Slowly, she removed her foot from the door and twisted it on top of the smoldering cigarette. She blew the remaining smoke in my face.

"I saw him at the Lucky Star Bar that night. He told me about seeing you. He looked completely broken up about it. I saw you together at the Sand Bar. I tried to catch up to him after he left you, but he didn't even see me. Walked right past me."

She paused and looked up at a distant star. A light breeze blew through her wispy hair. She tucked the loose piece behind her ear. "He went home and told Kelly he didn't love her anymore and that he was going to leave her. Kelly was devastated. She loved him and would have done anything to keep him. She threatened to kill herself if Brandon left her. Brandon was such a heartless bastard. She called me and told me to get the baby. Brandon followed her to the park. We both know what happened next." Our faces were inches from each other. I held my breath to keep from smelling her stench.

"How does that make you feel to know you broke up a family and killed the mother of that sweet, sleeping child?"

I took a step backward. I stuck out my chin and glared back at her. "It was an accident. End of story. Now move away from my car or I'll call the police."

"I'm not done with you."

"Yes, you are," I said as I reached past her to open the door. She grabbed my arms and twisted them hard behind my back and slammed me against the car door. Pain slashed through my shoulders. I yelled out. A door opened and closed. The sound of hurried footsteps in the gravel filled the air. I turned toward the sound.

"Amanda, what are you doing?" a man's voice called out. I squinted my eyes. The truck lights were too bright for me to see who it was. Finally he blocked the headlight with his frame. It was Kale. His worried face failed to meet my pleading eyes.

"I think it's time we taught Brandon a little lesson," she explained. "He promised he'd take care of us by yesterday. She says he's still gone. He needs to know we're serious. I'll take Dylan, and you take her."

He ran a hand nervously through his hair. "We can't kidnap them."

"We're not going to hurt them. At least this time. And he won't go to the cops. He knows we'll tell them what you saw the night Kelly died."

He looked from me back to the car. Amanda's bony arms were much stronger than I would have believed. I grimaced and wondered if my arms might rip off.

"Amanda, let her go."

"Shut up, Kale! Without me, you wouldn't have gotten a dime from Brandon."

"This is crazy!" he said.

"Just go get me something to hold her still."

Kale shifted his weight. He swore and shook his head, mumbling something about "Never . . ." to himself. He ran a hand through his hair again and squeezed his fingers into a fist.

"Kale!" she yelled. He snapped to attention and disappeared toward the truck. In the meantime, Amanda's protruding elbow had wedged itself between my shoulder blades, sending shooting pain down my spine.

In less than thirty seconds he was back with a roll of duct tape.

"Kale, don't!" I screamed. I dropped to the ground and attempted to wiggle out of Amanda's grasp. Dirt and gravel dug into my skin. Something sharp against my back sent me flailing. I fell prostrate to the ground. It was Kale's knee, jamming hard into the middle of my spine. I hollered and kicked, but he was stronger. I thrashed around, but once his strong arms were around me I knew I had no chance. He covered my mouth with a strip of duct tape. Then he moved to my wrists and wrapped them behind my back with duct tape.

The Escort started up without even a hiccup. I wondered if Kelly's car had it out for me too. Amanda yelled something back to Kale, and then spun out, flipping gravel that pelted my face and left tiny welts. I closed my eyes and held my breath. My lungs burned. I needed air. I opened my eyes. The Escort was down the road, leaving a cloud of dust in its wake. Something like a falling tower crashed inside me. That Escort held the most beloved thing, person, existence, I'd ever known. I couldn't believe this had happened. I had lost Dylan. Tears trickled past my eyes. I attempted to roll over. Something sharp stung my arm. I moaned in pain and stopped moving. Kale cursed under his breath as he picked me up and carried me to the truck bench.

"Stay down, okay?" he demanded, laying me down. I lay on the bench, my feet off to the side. Kale still refused to meet my stare. He ran a hand through his hair as he drove through the dark night.

It wasn't until the streetlights became consistent beacons—lighting the shadowy spaces around me—that I realized my hands were shaking. The worst had happened. I had been kidnapped. And worst of all, Amanda had taken Dylan.

Chapter Twenty-five

There was no use in crying. Besides, it was impossible to breathe and cry at the same time. I had to remain calm. While Kale drove, I put the pieces together in my head. Brandon had been unhappy in his marriage. He said Kelly was unhappy. I'd read in her journal that things weren't great, but were they bad enough for her to kill herself? Amanda blamed Brandon for Kelly's untimely death. She had implied that he had caused it. Had he pushed her into the river? I couldn't believe it. Why would he kill her? To be with me? I hadn't promised Brandon anything that night. Besides, couldn't they have just gotten a divorce? And what about Kelly? Amanda had made her the victim in all of this, but I hadn't gotten that impression from her journal. She was keeping secrets of her own. And what had Kale seen that had him willing to kidnap people? What had really happened? What was Brandon supposed to do and had not done yet?

What about the money in the back of the closet? And the gun? Was it possible that Kale saw Brandon kill Kelly? Was Kale blackmailing Brandon to keep him quiet?

And what did Amanda think she was going to do with Dylan? She was crazy. She wouldn't last one day taking care of him.

I glanced down at my bound hands and squeezed my eyes shut, willing this moment away. Where was the old woman now?

I turned my head a little to look at Kale. He must have felt my stare; he glanced down at me. His eyes were red, his forehead a row of worry lines. Maybe it wasn't too late for Kale. If I could reason with him, maybe he'd help me find Amanda and get Dylan back before she could do any real damage.

I mumbled unintelligible words to get his attention.

"Hold still," he said quietly. His hand came down and swiped the tape off my mouth. It stung like fire. Much worse than the bee sting. I was so grateful to breathe through my mouth again that I ignored the sting. I just had to get Kale to work with me and not against me.

"I'm sorry, Marlo. Damn if this hasn't gotten out of hand." Nervously, he threw his hand over his hair again. "I don't know what the hell Brandon is doing! We had a deal. And now Amanda has lost her freakin' mind." He blew air threw his mouth and punched the steering wheel with his palm. "I'll take you to my place until Brandon pays me the money he owes me. I'm not going to hurt you. We're friends, remember?"

"We *were* friends until you decided to kidnap me and let that bimbo take little Dylan. What were YOU thinking?"

He was silent. He sped up. By the consistent street lamps I knew we were driving through town. Speeding, to be exact. Would serve him right to get pulled over, I thought smugly to myself.

"Kale, I don't mean to sound ridiculous, but should I know what this is all about? What is the money for anyway?"

"I don't know what you know. Brandon says you have no idea. And you've never acted different around me. Amanda pretty much told it how it is. I saw Brandon push Kelly into the water. But there are things Amanda doesn't know. She thinks Brandon threatened to leave Kelly, but that wasn't what happened. Kelly was leaving him."

"How do you know that?"

"Because we were leaving together. She was supposed to meet me in the park. I was there waiting for her. I saw Brandon running after Kelly. He was trying to stop her from leaving."

"If Brandon was trying to stop her from leaving, why would he push her in?"

He shrugged, "I don't know. I guess he felt if he couldn't have her no one could."

"Why didn't you tell Amanda about you and Kelly?"

"Because Kelly died. There was no use telling her about the two of us. The less anyone knows about me being in the picture, the better for Brandon and me. We worked out a deal. He pays me, and I keep quiet."

"How did Amanda get involved in the first place?"

"How?" he laughed self-deprecatingly. "How does she weasel her way into anything? She caught Brandon and I arguing. She worked out a deal and insisted on being a part of it or she'd go to the police and tell them that I was blackmailing Brandon."

I started to push myself up with my elbow, but Kale laid his hand against my shoulders. "You gotta stay down, Marlo. This sucks for both of us, but I can't let you go yet. You talk to Brandon. It won't do him any good to have you go to the police."

He was right. Going to the police would only make things worse.

"What about Dylan? Amanda has no idea how to take care of children. If you were Dylan's father, would you trust that creature with your child? She is totally clueless."

Kale remained silent, lips sealed, staring straight-ahead.

"Come on, Kale, you know I'm right. Please don't let her take Dylan!" I begged. He refused to look at me. I sank back down and thought about what he'd told me. Something heavy seemed to plant itself in my gut. Brandon murdered his wife the night we were together. How could he have been so stupid?

But something didn't sit well with me. If he was going to leave her, and she was going to leave him, why would there be a need for anyone to die at all? Couldn't they have just shaken hands and been done with it?

Kale's truck pulled into what I assumed was a driveway. He inched his way into a garage and shut the truck off as the garage door rumbled down behind us. Except for the yellow light of the garage door opener we were in darkness.

"Here, let me help you," he said, placing his hands under my armpits and lifting me into a sitting position. I'd been taken to the second location. The worst mistake a victim can make. I surveyed the garage. Raw fear crept over me. What if he hooked the gas up and locked me in here? My hands trembled at the thought of all the horrible things he might be capable of. No amount of self-defense was going to save me now. He was much bigger than me. I took small breaths. My head felt woozy. I would hyperventilate if I didn't calm down.

Kale wasn't a killer. But I didn't think Brandon was, either. But if he was paying off Kale he must have been guilty. My heart nearly broke to think of him being capable of murder. My heart broke for poor Kelly, poor Dylan.

"What's Amanda going to do with Dylan? He is a sweet little boy who doesn't deserve any of this," I lamented as Kale led me into the house.

"Hell if I know. None of this was planned. Yeah, she was pissed that Brandon had gone AWOL, but I didn't expect this."

He turned on a lamp and sat me on an old plaid sofa. One wall was covered with baseball hats. A long shotgun sat on a rack on the opposite wall. A deer head beside it. A TV sat on a simple stand opposite the sofa. There was a faint smell of spilled milk and cologne.

"I'm really sorry, but I gotta leave your hands tied. Just until I talk to Brandon and we get this straightened out." He paced the floor in front of the sofa.

"Kale, this is kidnapping. This is a felony. Real jail time. You don't want to do this."

"Well, I don't have much of a choice now, do I?" he yelled in frustration. He cursed and kept pacing. His phone in his pocket rang.

"What?" he answered. He disappeared into the other room. I couldn't hear his words, but I assumed he was talking to Amanda. I tried wiggling my hands out of the tape, but he had done a dandy job wrapping it so tight the only thing I could do was clasp my hands together. Maybe I could swing them across his head and knock him out.

He came out of the room, stuffing his phone in his pocket and rubbing his neck. He finally met my eye.

"She wants me to leave Brandon a note telling him what's going on. I can't have you running off, so I'm afraid I'm going to have to tape up your legs. I'm really sorry."

"Don't do it, Kale. The deeper you go, the worse it's going to get for you."

"No, it's not, because Brandon will tell you not to go to the cops. You don't want him to go to prison, do you? Being Dylan's daddy and all?" His face turned red. He looked off to the side and coughed uncomfortably, then he disappeared through the garage door and in a few minutes returned with the roll of tape. He avoided my eyes as he strapped my legs together. Then he reached behind the sofa and grabbed a quilt and laid it over me.

"Did your grandma tie this quilt for you?" I mocked.

"Nope, old girlfriend," he explained without meeting my eyes. "Try to get some rest. And pray that Brandon cuts his trip short."

"Kale!"

He spun around to face me.

"Please get Dylan away from Amanda. Please!" I begged. His face was red. His eyes seemed tired. He didn't say a word. He just turned back around and exited through the open garage door. The garage door went up, an engine roared to life, and then the garage motor chugged again. Soon all became silent. I stared at the popcorn ceiling making my plan.

Did he really think I would just sit here and wait for him to return? I brought my hands up and bent my arms so I could dig through my pocket, hoping my phone was there. It wasn't, nor was it in the other pocket. It was most likely in my purse, which was still in the Escort. I rolled myself and the blanket off the couch. Then I wormed my way out of the quilt. I needed to get to a phone. I glanced around the room. A phone cord fell over the side of the kitchen counter.

I slithered myself across the dirty brown carpet toward the kitchen. Once there, I rocked on my butt and rolled to the side. I raised my hands above my head trying to knock the cord down. My fists got tangled in the cord, and I yanked at it. My sore shoulder screamed. I moaned. I yanked harder. The phone came crashing down and caught the back of my head before falling to the ground. The phone lay to one side as the tone rang through the empty room. I lifted my fist to dial 911, but stopped. What about Brandon? Murder was worse than kidnapping. But the thought of Dylan with Amanda was more than I could take.

I dialed 911 and reported the Escort stolen with a little boy inside. When they asked where I was I hung up. I could fend for myself. Dylan could not. I made another phone call.

"City and state, please," the female operator requested. I leaned my head into the phone and answered.

"Name please."

I was silent.

"Name please," the operator called out again.

I gave her Lukes name and hoped I hadn't just made the biggest mistake of my life.

"Have a good evening," the operator called pleasantly as she connected me.

Five minutes passed. I kept my eyes glued to the front door. I was nervous. It wouldn't be long before Kale would be back.

I heard the sound of a garage door. My heart flipped into overdrive. It was too late. Kale was back. Where was Luke?

I stared at the front door, willing myself to hear a knock or Luke's voice on the other side, but there was only silence. Just as the door to the garage opened and a tense-looking Kale walked in, the telephone rang. My eyes darted from Kale to the phone.

"What did you do?" he asked gravely, his turquoise eyes turning black.

I refused to speak.

"You called the police, didn't you?" he accused, shaking his head. He cursed and covered his mouth as he looked at the phone.

"I just want to make sure Dylan is safe," I explained. "I didn't tell them about me." The call went to the machine. We both watched it. I prayed that if it was Luke he would just hang up, not say anything. A woman's voice began speaking. They'd received a 911 call from this phone number reporting a kidnapping. They'd sent officers to this location to verify.

Kale cursed again. "You've really done it now, Marlo!" he yelled. He continued to curse as he paced in front of me. I flinched when he stomped over to where I sat on the floor. He grabbed my arm and legs and flipped me over his shoulder like a dead animal and went into the garage. Fumbling in the dark he finally found the car handle, opened it, and dropped me on the seat, pushing me aside. He slid in beside me and started the car in one swoop. The garage door slowly rose. I could smell the gas fumes filling the car. My heart thudded in my chest.

"Where are we going?" I asked, raising my head.

He refused to speak as he slowly drove down the road.

"Kale, I had no choice. Amanda took Dylan. It's called kidnapping. This is serious."

"Shut up!" he yelled, holding a hand to his temple.

I pressed my lips together. Kale clenched his jaw. Signs and street lamps reflected off the windshield as he drove through town. I had no idea what he was going to do to me, but I only felt sorry for him. Whatever his faults were, his worst was listening to anything Amanda said.

"You don't think Amanda would hurt Dylan, do you?"

He rubbed his hand against his head and laughed in his throat. "You need to understand Amanda. She loved Kelly. She worshipped Kelly.

Kelly could do no wrong, even when she stole Amanda's boyfriends away. Amanda always forgave her. She'd never hurt Kelly's child."

I nodded my head. "I just can't believe it about Brandon. Something about it just doesn't add up." I closed my eyes and stared at the dashboard.

I turned to Kale. I remembered the money in the back of the closet. I leaned my head against the door to get a better look at him. "Listen, I know where Brandon put the money."

"How much?"

"I didn't count, but it looks like it could be a couple thousand dollars."

"Not enough. Now, with everything that's happened, I want a big lump sum, no small monthly payments anymore."

I shoved my shoulders against the door and pushed myself up as far as I could. "Come on, Kale. Brandon will be home soon, the police are searching for Dylan. Help me and I'll help you. They're after Amanda, not you. Help me get Dylan back and I'm sure Luke will work out a deal for you."

"Did you call anybody besides the police?"

"No," I lied. We headed out of town. Where on earth was he taking me?

"So that Explorer following me isn't Luke's?"

I cranked around to look out the back window. Kale pushed me back down. My feet, still bound with tape, had fallen dangerously close to the gas pedal. I slunk down further to see how fast we were going. The needle hovered around forty-five miles per hour. I tried to calculate the chance of me dying if we wrecked. Or how badly I'd be hurt if I forced myself out of a moving vehicle. My hands and feet were tied together. I was no stunt double. Neither sounded like good options.

"I'm sure it's a coincidence," I said casually, hoping he'd forget about it. "Kale, where is Dylan?"

"He's with Amanda. I already told you, she would never hurt him."

"She doesn't know how to care for him. She won't even know what a bankee is. Or a dink, or a kook. He's probably crying for me right now."

Kale glanced over at me. A lone street lamp reflected across his face. His aqua-colored eyes reminded me of something. They seemed to soften. I opened my mouth. He quickly turned his head away.

The truck pulled to a sudden stop. I pushed myself up and looked out the window. The moon, high in the black sky, spread a large blanket of light in front of us, illuminating mountainous hills of sand.

"What are we doing here?" I asked, suddenly worried for my life.

"I figure you won't be in the way out here."

"Kale, please, I'm begging you not to do this. You leave me out here and you are as guilty as Amanda."

"I don't have a choice!" he yelled, his neck pulsing. "You've called the cops, and you probably called Luke. I think I lost him back there, though." He peered out his rearview mirror.

"And don't worry, I'll be with Dylan. I promise he'll be okay. When Brandon gets home he'll see the note. He'll know what to do." He turned and looked at me with brooding eyes. "I'll probably never see you again. I just want to say I'm sorry for this." He exited the car. Soon he was around the other side. He opened my door. Then he threw me back over his shoulder and started walking. My butt was high in the air. Rage flashed through me.

"Help!" I screamed. I shook my body. He held me tighter. I wriggled, but it was no use. He lay me down in the sand. A cool wind blew, dusting me with sand pellets. I turned my head and spit.

Kale pulled off the green and black flannel jacket he'd been wearing and placed it around my shoulders. He knelt down in front of me and said, "I never loved any woman like I loved Kelly. We were going to be together. Me and her and Dylan. I'm only getting what is rightfully mine." He stood and walked back to the truck.

"Kale!" I yelled. He stopped and glanced over his shoulder at me. "None of this will bring her back."

He stared at me for a minute. His liquid eyes swirled. That familiar feeling tugged at my heart again. He turned back to the truck and climbed in. The engine roared to life. The truck chugged back down the dirt road. Its taillights the only sign of civilization for miles.

Chapter Twenty-six

Once the truck disappeared there was only terrifying silence. Occasionally the wind rustled the sagebrush or a strange noise echoed across the star-filled night. Out here in the desert the sky was lit up with stars, like there had been a recent explosion. I couldn't remember ever seeing the millions of shimmering white lights like this very moment. A gust of wind blew through me. I shivered. Something moved in the grass. There were snakes in this part of the desert. I closed my eyes and said a silent prayer that the Explorer Kale had seen had indeed been Luke's. I sat with my knees tucked to my chest and worked the duct tape wrapped around my wrist with my teeth. I should have done this when I was waiting for Luke to come, but I hadn't thought ahead. I wasn't used to being kidnapped. Lucky for me I had pointy teeth.

I spotted headlights coming down the road. I rolled to my knees. I continued to gnaw on the duct tape. My teeth sliced through the first layer. The vehicle passed the dirt road without turning. My stomach sank as I watched it continue down a main road. Even if someone was trying to find me, it would be easy to miss the small rut-filled road that veered east. I kneeled down next to a large volcanic boulder and continued to gnaw the duct tape. The taste of glue and tape was strong in my mouth, but I could feel the tape weakening between my teeth.

I worked on it for twenty more minutes. Finally the tear went all the way through. I snagged it in my teeth and pulled in the opposite direction with my fists. It made a small ripping noise as it split down the middle. I grimaced as I separated the tape from my skin. There was no time to dwell on the stinging skin. I bent over and found the edge of the tape around my ankles and quickly unraveled my legs. I grabbed the jacket and started running down the dirt road. Fear burst through my body. I ran hard on the dry dirt. My hair whipped across my face. My feet slipped in a rut, my ankle burned. I kept going, my arms flailing. My shoulder pounded with the jarring movement. Headlights appeared in the opposite direction. The vehicle had turned around. Adrenaline surged through me. I was in a race against the headlights. My legs turned quickly as I rushed down the road, waving my sore arms. I waved the jacket over my head and screamed, hoping the window was down. Closer now, I was almost sure it was Luke's car. It wasn't slowing down. I scooped up a small rock and wadded the jacket around it. Just as the car passed, I threw the jacket as hard as I could toward it. It flew high into the black sky and came down against the side back window of the car with a small clink. I cringed. I hoped I hadn't broken anything. Brake lights flashed.

"Stop!" I yelled. The car screeched to a halt. Luke jumped out of the car and ran toward me. I stumbled toward him, all my energy suddenly drained. He caught me in his arms. I collapsed into his, breathing too heavy to speak. He ran his hands over my hair, soothing me with soft words that everything would be all right.

He pulled my face up to meet his and examined me. "Are you okay? I'm sorry I couldn't get there in time."

"It's okay," I said, still reeling from the run. "Have they found Dylan?"

He shook his head. "I pulled onto Kale's street just as he turned on Main Street. I kept a low profile, but he lost me."

"Luke, it's okay. I'm fine. I just want them to find Dylan."

He helped me into his car. He handed the jacket to me. "It was a good thing you did that. I don't think I would have noticed you if you hadn't."

"It's Kale's. He let me borrow it. I'm just glad that I didn't break your window."

I told him what I knew about Kelly and Brandon, and in turn, Luke told me all he knew about the search for Dylan. The police were staked out in front of Amanda's apartment, but she wasn't there.

"They have an Amber alert out for Dylan."

I felt a tiny flutter of relief.

"I can drop you off at your house or leave you at my place. What do you think will be safer?"

"Take me to my house. That way I'll be there when Brandon gets home."

"Are you sure?" He hesitated.

"Yes. I'm sure," I promised. I stared out at the passing sand dunes and wondered what would happen when I confronted Brandon.

"What do you think will happen to him?" I asked.

"If he murdered Kelly he has to be held accountable, no matter how much you care for him."

"I know," I said quietly. I rubbed my eyes and suppressed a yawn. My eyes itched. It was after two o'clock and the adrenaline wasn't pumping through me any longer. I yawned and lay back on his headrest. I wasn't sure what I would say to Brandon, but the time for lies was over. Dylan deserved the truth.

When we arrived at the house, Luke insisted on giving it a sweep, just to make sure it was safe. All was still. Too still, really. It meant Dylan was still missing.

I turned to Luke. "Will you call when you hear anything about Dylan?"

"Of course I will."

We said good night, and then he left.

I locked all the doors. My hands shook as I pulled off my running shoes still full of sand. Then I immediately collapsed onto the couch. Tired, sad, and completely out of energy. I was exhausted. Despite my desire to do otherwise, I fell asleep immediately.

When I awoke the sun was streaming through the window. I shot up, but my body screamed foul when I did. Every muscle ached. My shoulder especially. I moved more carefully to the kitchen. It was just after eight in the morning and not a single call about Dylan. I got a drink from the sink and peeked out the window. My hands flew up to my mouth. The old woman, Hilma, in yet another colorful muumuu, was carrying a large red bag and making her way slowly up the driveway.

I flung the door open. "What are you doing here?"

"Time to go. Happy?" she called.

"Time to go? I don't think so. Kind of in a panic right now."

She didn't seem to hear me, "Good time to get out Dodge, right?" she winked. She pulled the familiar bottle out of her bag and held it out to me.

I stepped outside and stopped her in the driveway. "Kale and Amanda have kidnapped Dylan, and Brandon murdered Kelly! I can't leave yet."

The woman's eyebrows raised. She held the bottle out to me. "So what? All a glimpse. One drink and poof, never happen."

I shook my head at her and snatched the bottle out of her hands. "You can't tell me that Dylan isn't real!" I yelled, the emotion sharp in my voice. "Or that Brandon is only a glimpse or that none of this matters, cause it matters to me! This is too important to me to just leave it unfinished like this. I'm not leaving until Dylan is safe and sound, and that's final!" I threw the bottle onto the driveway. It broke into several large pieces. The brown liquid seeped between the cracks and disappeared.

The old woman cursed in her unfamiliar language. I was glad I had no idea what the words meant, though I was certain by her angry tone they weren't nice.

"What you do that for? Now I have to go home and do over. Raven not like this."

"You tell Raven I'm not drinking anything until I'm finished here."

The old woman's eyes became slits. She pointed her long wrinkled finger in my face. "You have no choice in matter. You learn what you need to know. One hour. Or you never go home." She spun around and hobbled back down the sidewalk, mumbling in her native language.

Like a miracle, Brandon's truck pulled into the driveway as soon as the woman disappeared. I had his door opened before he could.

"I need to talk to you," I said as calmly as I could.

He was covered in soft dirt. "Hi," he smiled shyly. "Is everything okay?"

"No. Nothing is okay." I glanced over my shoulder. Cars passed by. Outside was the best place for us to be. That way, Brandon couldn't do anything too drastic when I told him what I knew.

I took a deep breath. "I don't know where to begin." I sighed, tears filled my eyes. My hands pressed against each other in prayer. "I need to know what happened the night Kelly died. I need to know if you pushed her in. I know about Kale and Amanda blackmailing you. They've got Dylan, and they want all the money."

He raised his hands to slow me down. "Whoa, whoa, whoa! Start over. They did *what?*"

My hands dropped to my sides. I told him the rest.

"They kidnapped me and Dylan. It was Amanda's idea. She just went nuts and took Dylan. I got away, but they still have Dylan. They want all the money now. No more payments. They know they are in a lot of trouble." I shifted nervously.

Brandon's face grew dark. He slammed the truck door and stomped toward the house.

"No. Not inside. I want to talk to you out here," I demanded. He turned and gave me a quizzical look.

I took a deep breath. My hands shook. "Brandon," I shook my head, my face pleading, "you've got to tell me everything. I have to know the truth. You have to tell me exactly what happened that night at the park.

I've heard Kale's side and Amanda's side and still something is missing. I want to hear your side."

Brandon looked over both his shoulders. "What did Kale tell you?"

I repeated what Kale and Amanda had said, then I added that I'd read Kelly's journal. This stopped him midstep.

"You read her journal?"

"Yes, I know I shouldn't have," I said, a sudden fear rippling through me.

"So you know everything."

"I don't know anything. Kelly didn't write down what happened that night in her journal!" I said with exasperation. "I need to hear the truth from you so I can help you."

He covered his face in his hands and rubbed hard. He groaned and made his way to the steps. I followed him. He let out a large breath of air, then he bit his lip. I waited in silence.

"Kelly had been acting strange. She was depressed one minute, excited the next. I never knew what set her off. I found her journal one day. I read it. I'd always known there was someone else, but I didn't know who it was. She, of course, denied it. Said I was being childish and jealous. But eventually she admitted it. Then I saw you at the party. You were beautiful and radiant, and you reminded me of what I never got. What I didn't have. I went home and found Kelly sitting in the dark. She asked me if I was happy, if I loved her. I did love her, but I wasn't happy. She told me she wasn't happy either. 'What a sorry pair we are,' she said with a simple cock of her head. Then she told me something that made me so angry, that hurt so badly." He stopped speaking. He leaned forward and covered his hands in his face.

"She told me that Dylan wasn't mine, that she'd known it since he was practically conceived. But at the time she was engaged to me. And she knew I'd make a good daddy. So she didn't tell the father, and she let me think the baby was mine. After Dylan was born, the phone calls started. I pretended not to notice because I didn't want to lose her, but that night she told me that the father knew about Dylan and that she was leaving with him. I asked who the father was, how she was so sure that Dylan wasn't mine. She just laughed. Laughed, of all things. Like it wasn't that big of a deal. She told me that Dylan looked just like his daddy; had his same aqua eyes."

Brandon stood abruptly and paced the driveway. "She called Amanda and told her to come watch Dylan. Amanda came like the lapdog she is and took Dylan. I panicked. I was sure she was going to take Dylan away from me. Kelly promised that everything would work out, but she had to go. I followed her to the park. I said some things I shouldn't have said. Hurtful things. And then she became very sad. All the light went out of her eyes. She walked to the edge of the river."

"At Keifer Park?"

He nodded. It was the same place the old banker had jumped to his own death at the start of the Depression, so many years ago.

"She just stood there, one foot on a rock, the other dangling over the edge. Then she turned around and said she was sorry. I could tell she was going to jump, so I reached out to stop her, but I was too late." He grew silent. He bit his bottom lip and stared down at the ground.

"It was Kale, wasn't it?" I said. Brandon looked up at me, his brown eyes swimming in tears. His lips quivered. He pressed them together and nodded. A single tear trickled down his face.

"Why didn't you just explain what happened?"

"I did, but he didn't believe me. He threatened to take Dylan away from me. I begged him not to, told him that it had been an accident." Brandon stopped speaking and took a deep breath. He clasped his hands together and stared at the house next door. His eyes seemed far away. "Eventually Kale stopped harassing me. But only because he had a new idea. He'd let me keep Dylan and not say anything about what he thought he saw if I paid him some of the insurance money."

"But paying him off makes you look guilty. Besides, maybe Kelly was wrong. Maybe Dylan is really yours."

He shook his head and walked to the window. "I did the math. I was gone for a month fighting fires with the Forest Service trying to make a little extra money for the wedding. There's no way he's mine. Besides, I am guilty in a way. I didn't stop her. I didn't save her."

"I'm so sorry, Brandon, for everything." I reached out and touched his hands. I knew he was telling the truth.

He turned his moist eyes toward me. "The worst part is I didn't go in after her. You saw it happen. You'd been across the river at the sandbar and heard us fighting. You saw her fall in, and you yelled for me to stop. I didn't go after her because you asked me not to. I could have saved her. I swam in those waters all my life, but I was a coward and I let her drown."

I'd heard them? How was that possible? "Why was I still there?"

He shook his head. "You told me you had forgotten your slippers, and you went back to get them. Don't you remember?"

"Right. But you don't know if you could have saved her."

"I'd have rather died trying than living like I am now. And then look what happened to Troy. I should have gone in after her." His eyes seemed to look right through me, as if I weren't really there. I hugged him hard around his neck. I wanted to tell him that I was going to right everything and bring Kelly back. Instead, I answered, "We'll get him back," thinking of all the people I had to save.

"I know. I just want the truth out. I want this all to be over."

Just then a patrol car pulled up. We jumped up. Luke stepped out. He was dressed in his uniform. A second patrol car pulled up behind him. I grabbed Brandon's hand. Together we walked toward them. Luke swung the back door open and pulled out a very tired Dylan from the backseat. He walked toward us, a smile on his face.

I ran to them and wrapped Dylan in my arms. Dylan rubbed his eyes with his chubby hands. When he recognized Brandon he called to him and started to whimper. Brandon ran toward Dylan. Dylan leaned forward, both arms reaching for Brandon. Brandon took Dylan from me and pulled him into a tight bear hug, kissing his tired little face and curly matted hair. A tear streamed down Brandon's face. Tears filled my eyes. Luke stood aside and watched the reunion in silence.

"How did you get him back?" I finally managed through the lump in my throat.

Luke smiled and rubbed his temples. "Amanda and Kale are probably the worst kidnappers in history. I went to Amanda's parents' house. The Escort was hiding in the garage. Kale's truck was in the back field. When I knocked on the door I could hear Dylan crying. Amanda must have known it was me, because she opened the door." He let out a small laugh. "She looked exhausted. Dylan had cried all night. I don't think either one slept more than an hour. Her parents washed their hands of the whole affair, but we took them to the station too. I don't think she knows the slightest thing about taking care of children—you should get a whiff of that diaper—and was sorry for her bargain. Anyway, they're all at the station. Officer Koons wants to talk to you both about the whole thing."

Dylan leaned his way into my arms. His hand wriggled down the front of my shirt. His skin was warm and soft. He nestled his head into the crook of my neck. Tears trickled down my face. I could hardly breathe. I excused myself and walked away from the others. I squeezed Dylan tight, kissed his soft hair and forehead and rosy cherub cheeks. I wanted to remember everything about him; the way he breathed with a slight open mouth when he was asleep, the way he wrapped a fistful of my hair tightly in his little hands, or how his remarkably soft skin, unscathed by life's harsh experiences, felt like crushed velvet against my own callous-hardened skin. I leaned my nose against his neck and breathed him in, like I might take a piece of him with me if I breathed long enough.

There was a deep throaty squawk overhead. I glanced up into the blue early-morning sky and recognized the iridescent long-tailed bird with its graceful upbeat wings soaring above my head. Brandon and Luke and Officer Koons were talking. They didn't notice the bird, or me, as I wiped the tears from my face and cradled Dylan in my arms for one last time. I didn't need to see the old woman. I could feel the weight of her stare, like ropes of steel wrapping me into a net and pulling me to her. I kissed Dylan one last time on the head, then I walked over to Brandon and handed Dylan to him.

"I've got to go for a minute," I explained in a hushed voice. I couldn't speak anymore, too afraid I would sob in front of them all.

Brandon hesitantly took Dylan. "Where are you going?"

"I've got to do something. I'll be right back," I choked out.

I leaned up and kissed him gently on the cheek. I glanced at Luke, and then walked around his truck, leaving everything that mattered to me behind. The old woman was standing in the middle of the sidewalk. Her arms were folded, her face softened, a look of genuine understanding in her eye. I walked toward her. I wanted to glance over my shoulder, to get one last look at Dylan and Brandon and Luke, but knew I had to move forward in order to change the past.

I took the bottle from her outstretched hand and took a deep breath. My hands shook. *Focus,* I told myself. *And have a thankful heart.* Then I emptied the bottle of its contents.

Chapter Twenty-seven

The first thing I recognized was the scent of wet earth. I lay in a fetal position, my shirt soaked from the rain that pitter-pattered against my skin. I glanced up. Hilma was gone. I felt for the welt on my neck. It was gone. My stomach flip-flopped. It had worked! I was back. My father was sleeping soundly in his bed, as was my brother-in-law. Safe and alive. And Kelly—Kelly was still alive! I stood and wiped my muddy hands against my damp jeans. I searched across the river toward the park. Brandon told me I had been on this side of the river and heard them arguing, but I hadn't been able to stop it from this side. I had to get to the park. I had to intervene before their fighting escalated. I glanced down at my bare and muddy feet. I racked my brain trying to remember if I'd had shoes. I remembered digging my feet into the sand, just before Brandon had arrived. The rain was nothing more than a trickle then.

I ran across the grass toward the stairs that led down to the river. I turned in a full circle and finally spotted a small black clump near the stairs. I hurried over and grabbed the slippers. They were soaked through. I'd never be able to run in slippers. I ran up the hill in my bare feet toward the road. The lamppost shone down on the wet pavement and gave off enough light that I could find my way to the backyard. My fingers shook as I opened the sliding door and slipped silently into my parents' house. All was quiet. I stopped at the top of the stairs and stared at my parents' bedroom door. I wanted to open it. Just to check and see. A distant clock tick-ticked, reminding me that I had only a little time. I returned to my room and grabbed my over-the-knee boots and pulled them on. These boots were ridiculous, but there was no time to look for anything else. At least they were better than slippers. Or bare feet.

I shivered. I wished I had a jacket to put on, but the room was encased in darkness. A clock counted down the seconds from somewhere in the distance. I needed to get to the park. I crept outside and walked through the very dark yard. When I finally saw the street lamp's halo ahead of me I broke into a run.

The boots made my running awkward. The bang of my steps echoed against the sleeping houses that were shrouded in blackness. I ran through the darkness straight toward the street lamp. Its yellow glow gave me hope. If I could keep Kelly out of the water everything else would fall in place. I quickened my pace, the fear of being too late overriding my own weak running. I struggled for breath as I pushed my arms harder, willing myself on. My legs felt like rubber bands, barely able to keep up with my will. *Save Kelly, save Kelly,* I said in my head with each step. I splashed through the puddles and streaked mud and water up my back and across my soaking jeans. My knees threatened to buckle. I swallowed back bile.

I rounded the corner of Bridge and Main and scanned the road. The streets were empty. Businesses dark. I leaned over panting. My stomach was a fit of nerves. I glanced around and saw no one. I started running again, aware I was under a constant flood of light from the many street lamps. I didn't care anymore. I needed to be seen if I was going to stop it.

The park came into view. I was almost there. My heart thudded in my chest. I crossed the wooden bridge. Crows cawed as the thud of my boots woke them. I hoped it was loud enough to catch Brandon and Kelly's attention. I peered ahead to the park. It seemed empty. I took a couple deep breaths, hoping to bring my heart rate back to normal. Nervously I ran my hands through my wet hair, hoping to calm myself down.

Movement caught my eye. It was a truck. It had been parked in the corner of the parking lot, and I hadn't seen it until a brake light went on. It looked like Kale's truck. My stomach churned. I shoved off my feelings of doubt and fear. There was no time to second-guess myself. I crossed the parking lot. My hand shook as I knocked on the window. Cigarette smoke billowed out when the window rolled down. Kale sat in the driver's seat. His face turned red when he recognized me.

"Marlo, what's up?" he asked with trepidation.

"I know why you're here. This sounds crazy, but something bad is going to happen to Kelly. Have you seen her yet?"

His eyes flashed wide. He stuttered, unable to speak.

"Don't ask how I know—just tell me if you've seen her yet."

"She was coming to meet me, but I haven't seen her yet," he answered.

"Good. Maybe I'm not too late. Come on."

"Marlo, wait!" he called.

I didn't turn around, and I didn't wait to see if he'd follow. I didn't really care. All I needed was to interrupt their fight. That would be enough to throw them off, and then the future would be altered forever and I could save them all.

A sound ricocheted off the trees, and my blood turned cold. A shout or a sob. A sound of distress. It was followed by a deeper voice. I froze at the sound; my flesh became tiny crystals of ice. I shuddered. Something rolled sicklike in my stomach. I took off in the direction of the river. Kale called to me again. A car door opened and slammed shut. I made my way down the road toward the shadowy park. I followed what I believed was the outline of the river, struggling to see past the dark blotches that were the playground.

The park was an island surrounded by water. On the left side a retaining wall controlled a quick-flowing canal. Straight-ahead, on the east side of the river, lay the sandbar. The right side remained open to the river, which dropped ten feet over man-made falls, and then cascaded further down a hill over large volcanic rocks and boulders, leaving a cliff about twenty feet high on the right corner of the park. I listened for sounds. Voices rose louder. My heart nearly burst through my wet shirt. I shivered and groped along the large jungle gym and headed toward the voices.

It was then I caught sight of two dark shadows nearly hidden behind several thick pine trees along the back right corner close to the water. Brandon had Kelly by the arms. He was yelling something and shaking her—her short hair whipped in the air. Kale appeared from the bridge. He ran toward them. Bile rose in my throat. I screamed a weak dreamlike scream. Brandon must have heard me because he turned and let go of Kelly.

Kale was immediately upon him. He pulled Brandon away from Kelly and shoved him across the grass. Brandon skidded on his knees. He pulled himself off the ground and dove for Kale. Kale stumbled and fell hard on his head. Arms flew, fists connected; a tangled knot of flesh and bones. Their large forms and sheer force filled me with a sickening dread. Flashes of grunts and heated, ugly words shattered the darkness. Two grown men fighting like enraged wolves for their rightful spot in the pack.

I glanced up at Kelly who was still standing on the edge. She turned her face away from the fighting. Her thin sundress fluttered across her body like a loose scarf that could easily be whisked away in the wind. She looked calmly over the water. I watched her foot reach out and hover over the water. I screamed. Brandon and Kale froze. They looked at me, and then followed my horrified gaze just as Kelly disappeared into the swarming black mass of the river.

Brandon yelled Kelly's name. My hands pressed against my face in disbelief. Stunned. Mortified. I was supposed to keep this from happening.

Brandon ran to the edge. I screamed Brandon's name. He hesitated. He looked back at me. I remembered what he had said in the glimpse. I bit my lip and closed my eyes. I heard the splash of the water. My eyes flew open. Brandon had disappeared over the edge. My stomach churned. The sound of a running faucet filled my ears. Everything began to spin. Something ripped my chest wide open. It felt like my soul had been torn from my body.

Kale rushed toward the bridge. I leaned over and vomited. I was in shock. I couldn't make my legs move. I needed to get a hold of myself, but I hadn't strength enough to pull myself off the wet grass. I shook all over. Something like a sob escaped my lips; all hope drained from my body. I had been completely worthless. I had failed to keep Kelly out of the water, and by so doing, had sent Brandon in after her.

It seemed like I sat there for a very long time, too long in the world of life and death. I considered calling 911, but knew that would only bring Troy out of the bed he shared with my sister. I knew what would happen then. I couldn't yell or speak. I moaned, "No, no, no," over and over, as if my denial might bring Brandon and Kelly back. I wanted to find that old woman and strangle her for making me believe I could have any effect on the future.

Kale ran from the footbridge toward Bridge Street. Troy would get out of bed, and I had to try to save him. Maybe it wasn't too late. I just had to focus. I stood up, hoping to get my bearings. I ran across the bridge and up to the road. It was empty, everything around me quiet. I had always imagined a scene so horrible filled with screaming and yelling, sirens blaring. Instead, everything was eerily silent. Kale ran toward the fire station that sat across the street—the back of its red brick building butted up to the river—its flag waving like a beacon of hope. I ran after Kale—my fumbling legs churning slowly as everything seemed to move in slow motion.

The door was wide open. Kale was already inside. As I rushed in, every sight and sound became vibrant and focused. The florescent lights screamed, a distant TV blared.

Kale shouted to a young man sitting behind a counter looking sleepy-eyed and confused. "Two people. They both jumped. Yes."

The man muttered to himself as he shuffled some papers. A rookie. It seemed as if he was trying to remember step number one.

"We need Search and Rescue!" Kale shouted. "Call Mack. He'll know what to do!"

"I know, I know," the other man yelled as he came alive to the gravity of the situation. Kale swore and spun around in disgust. He caught sight of me and turned silent. His lips became pursed. He ran a hand through his hair.

"Bo, here, doesn't know what the hell he's doin'," he grumbled as he placed his hands on his hips and walked away.

"This is Bo. We've got a 680 at Kiefer Park," he called into a two-way radio.

"This is dispatch," a woman's voice responded from the police station down the road. It was static to me, but the guy named Bo seemed to understand as she called out the Fremont County Search and Rescue members and the sheriff's department. Bo paced as he barked orders for a boat, scuba gear, and for someone to call the power plant located just up the canal from the fire station to lift the grate and lower the canal. The man disappeared. An alarm sounded.

I stood glued to my spot, nervously rubbing my fingers in my hands and wiping off the dried mud stuck between them. I kept thinking about the call to Search and Rescue. The call that would send Troy into the river. My mind raced thinking of a way to keep this domino effect from taking place. Kale finally turned to me. We stood staring at each other. His face was hard and angry. Without a word to me, he turned and stormed out of the building.

Men appeared out of nowhere. A truck started up. A police siren rose in the distance. I watched as stoic faces rushed past me one by one without a word, life vests secured, scuba tanks pulled on as they disappeared out the door. I followed them. I was completely helpless. A truck passed by. It had a specialized red and grey pontoon raft on the back. I heard one man talking to another about pulling the boats into the river from the sandbar. Two other men, both in their late fifties, both in scuba gear, lifted an inflatable kayak. One yelled for me. I hurried over to where they were cinching large coiled rope around their waists.

"How long have they been in the water?" a burly man with a mustache and beard asked me.

"Probably five or six minutes," I answered.

Five minutes was a lifetime. And they still had to get boats in the water. I heard my name called out. I spun around and recognized Troy running toward me.

"Marlo!"

My stomach dropped. My mouth went dry, my tongue felt numb. "Troy," I cried.

"We're getting conflicting reports. Some say it was a man that went into the water; others say it was a woman. Did you see who fell in?"

I explained what happened. Troy nodded in understanding and turned to leave, carrying a large coil of rope on his shoulder.

"Troy!" I yelled, my mind spinning on how to keep him out of harm's way. "You're not going in the water are you?"

"There's only three of us scuba-certified right now. But don't worry, I'll be tied to the boat, and I'll have these guys helping me," he reassured me. He turned to leave.

"Troy!" I yelled again. He spun around, but continued to walk backward. "Don't go in the water. Please. I'm begging you. Don't do it. It's too risky. The water's high and fast, and I'm afraid something terrible will happen to you."

He flashed a sympathetic smile. "You sound just like your sister. I'll be careful. We've got to worry about those two people already in the water." And with a small nod, he turned and disappeared behind the firehouse.

Chapter Twenty-eight

I ran back to the bridge. At that moment the pontoon zipped around the corner of the park, a large spotlight shining in my direction. I threw my hands over my face to shield my eyes. The clearing under the bridge was low. The boat slowed, and the men ducked their heads as they passed underneath. They scanned the riverbanks. Sirens blared into the night. Tears spilled down my face. First Kelly, then Brandon, and now Troy. This was a nightmare. I didn't stop anything. I'd only made things worse.

"Marlo!"

I turned. Luke rushed toward me. He was wearing the same dark jeans and blue polo from earlier, but his disheveled hair gave away the fact that he'd probably been awakened by the distress call.

"Are you all right? Did you see it happen? Was it really Brandon and Kelly?" His brown eyes scanned me over once. He put his arm around my shoulder and led me over to his patrol car parked along the side of the road.

"Kelly jumped into the water, and then Brandon went in after her." I squeezed my eyes shut, the vision of Brandon glancing back at me once, and then jumping in flashed in my mind again. "Do you think they'll find them?"

"They are doing everything they can. They just sent a boat in from the Sand Bar, and the power plant is lowering the water in the canal and lifting the grate so the guys can get through."

"How can they see anything?" I gibbered, peering through the dark and wet night. I could barely see Luke's car.

"They've got big spots on their boats and lights on their helmets."

He led me to his car. I pulled back on his arm. "I can't just sit here," I explained, shaking my head. "I need to do something." My head pounded, I rubbed my temples and turned to face Luke. "Honestly, what chance do they have of surviving?"

I caught a small movement in his eyes, the way eyes do when deciding whether to be honest or not. I grabbed his arm. "Tell me the truth!"

"Search and Rescue called John Baxley. He's got a helicopter. He'll fly over the river. I just wish we could see better. The night couldn't be any darker." We both lifted our faces to the black sky, wishing the moon would lend a hand and finally show itself.

A voice came over his radio. I jumped at the sound. It was difficult to understand, but when the woman finished speaking Luke took my hands and walked me over to the sidewalk.

"What did she just say?"

"They've sent in a jet boat. We'll see it on this side, and then they'll take it down past the island. I'm going down to search. You stay here so I can find you when I know anything."

"No! Please take me with you! I can't just sit here knowing you are all out there. Isn't there anything I can do to help?"

He pursed his lips together. His eyes peered into mine. Finally he opened the passenger-side door and nudged for me to hop in. Once in the car, he spoke into his radio, announcing his response to the northern side of the Egin diversion canal. He flipped his lights on and pulled a U-turn back the way he'd come. He turned left at the red light and flew down deserted Main Street, his lights silently flashing. After a mile he pulled left down a small gravel street and drove to where it dead-ended against a tall chain-link fence that blocked the canal on the other side. He leaned over, opened up his glove box, and pulled out a large flashlight. He grabbed a smaller light from his pocket and threw it to me. "Keep close," he ordered as we made our way to the twelve-foot fence. "We're going to have to climb. Will you be all right?" he asked. I nodded, wishing I had brought pointier shoes as I struggled to fit my round toes in the small crisscross openings.

Luke made it across first. I followed close behind. He reached forward and held my waist as I jumped to the ground. "You okay?" he asked.

I nodded.

"Let's go this way," he said, shining his light down the side of the bank.

The grass along the bank was thick and wet from the recent storm. I was glad I had worn these long boots until they gave way against the slick mud. I let out a small scream and grabbed for the nearby chain-link fence. Luke spun around to find me clinging to the metal, the flashlight in the grass.

"I better get you back to the car. We don't need another body in the canal," he said sharply, reaching down and weeding through the grass for my flashlight.

"I won't let it happen again," I promised, reaching for the flashlight. Luke got it first, and he didn't let go. His face was hard with unmovable determination.

"No. This was a bad idea to bring you along. I can't risk anything happening to you. Come on." He grabbed my wrist and pulled me the way we had come. I grabbed onto the fence and held tight. "There isn't time to argue, Luke. We've just got to keep going. Please!"

"Let go of the fence, Marlo, or I will pick you up and carry you." The face glaring back at me was unfamiliar and scary. I let go of the fence and turned to leave.

"I'll find my way back by myself," I sulked, angry tears stinging my eyes.

"Marlo, I only want to protect you. Go back to the car and if you hear anything on the radio, honk, okay?"

My boots slid again. There really wasn't anything I could do. Holding tight to the chain-link fence, I carefully retraced my steps.

I sat down in the passenger seat and let the tears pour down my face. I couldn't even help with the rescue efforts without it becoming about me and my inadequacies. I wanted to save Kelly. A woman I had never met, but who was the mother of a little boy that I had fallen in love with. I wanted to give her the opportunity to love him. I wanted her to hear her son ask for his bankee and a dink. To watch him tear up the road on his Big Wheel and read him stories and rock him to sleep at night. I wanted her to be able to cradle her little boy and have him burrow his head into that small part of the neck that he loved while playing with her hair like he did with mine.

And I wanted to save Brandon. Poor misunderstood Brandon, who only needed more time to believe in himself and raise his little boy and learn that he did love his wife, just like he told me he did. And I couldn't even think about Troy. My poor sister was probably in her home wringing her hands with worry.

There was a sudden loud chopping sound above me. I glanced out the window and saw a large helicopter with a bright spotlight attached following the path of the canal. It flew by me and continued on down the river. It made me sick to see it, yet gave me some comfort to know there were many others that wanted to save Brandon and Kelly too. Many that had the resources and skills for such a search. Luke had been right. It wouldn't have helped any to have me fall into the canal.

I watched the helicopter become a small speck of light and veer south, probably going to the other leg of the river. With so many legs it was difficult to say which they might have gone down. I tried to remain hopeful, imagining Brandon catching Kelly and carrying her safely to the bank. There was still a chance, but as the clock ticked, their chance of still being alive diminished.

I wiped the tears from my eyes, and then clasped my hands together. There was only one thing I had left to do. Thinking of Melissa, I closed my eyes and bowed my head, feeling slightly self-conscious. I prayed out loud. "Please, please, please, save these two people. Heavenly

Father, they need each other. Their baby needs them. They are so young. Please help us find them." Even after the prayer was finished I continued to murmur "*please, please, please*" until I ran out of tears and energy. After fifteen minutes, a spot of light came dancing along the fence line. Soon Luke appeared over the fence, his face grave. I was afraid of what he might have found.

"Hear anything?" he asked grimly as he turned and backed the car around.

I shook my head, recognizing the worry on his face as a very bad sign.

"Let's head over to the island. I'm going to try to hop on a boat. You'll be able to walk the bank easier over there. It's a lot safer," he added, giving me a quick look of concern. He opened his mouth to speak, and then pressed it closed again.

The familiar voice crackled over the radio. The sound was muffled, but Luke seemed to understand what was said. He whistled and inhaled sharply.

"What? What did she say?" I demanded, my heart in my throat.

"They're postponing the search until morning. It's just too dark and dangerous for them to dive or go over the more treacherous parts of the river. I'm sorry, Marlo."

I threw my hands into my face and cried out. "No!"

"Troy's a diver. You don't want him in these waters at night, right?"

I stopped at his words. Troy. Troy was still okay! At least we had a second chance with him. I'd just have to make sure he didn't dive tomorrow. That was what I'd do. Beg Melissa to keep him away from the rescue efforts, though I knew that nobody would be able to keep Troy away from what he considered his duty. But I would try. I pulled my hands away and met Luke's concerned stare. "You're right. At least Troy is safe. And if Brandon and Kelly are all right, they'll hold on to something, or they'll help get each other out of the water, right?" I asked holding on to hope as best I could. Luke looked out his window, his hand gripping the wheel, his left arm perched on the window ledge.

"Here, I'll take you home," he said, putting the car in drive and flipping it around.

"No, don't. I don't want to go home yet. I won't be able to sleep, knowing that they are out there somewhere." My voice trailed off, a thickness oozing in my stomach.

"Where do you want to go?"

Where did I want to go? Find Brandon and Kelly. Discover them safely protected under a tree, bridge, or some ledge. I sat in silence as Luke pulled onto Main Street. I thought of little Dylan and Amanda watching him, or not watching him. The image put a sour taste in my mouth. I told Luke where I wanted to go. He shrugged and turned left on Bridge Street. He parked on the side of the street. The Escort sat in the driveway.

I made my way toward the side door. Luke hesitated behind me. I motioned for him to hurry.

A light in the kitchen shone. I could hear voices on the other side. Loud and distraught. A woman's voice.

"How could you let this happen? Why didn't you stop him?"

"Oh, so now it's *my* fault!" I recognized Kale's voice. Luke was at my side. I knocked loudly on the door. The voices went silent. I waited, and then knocked again. The door opened a crack. Amanda's tear-stained face peeked through. Recognizing me, she stiffened, shoulders straight. Kale was at the table, his face buried in his hands.

"Did they find them?" she demanded.

"No. They've called off the search until morning. I was worried about Dylan." My eyes flew up to meet Kale's distraught eyes. He must have been crying too; they were so bloodshot their aqua color seemed to stand out more. Dylan really did have his eyes.

"Dylan's fine," Amanda said curtly. The familiar kitchen hadn't changed much, except for the dishes that were piled high in the sink, and the magazines, mail advertisements, and a half-emptied box of powdered donuts that littered the table.

"Have you called Brandon's parents?" Luke asked.

"They're on their way," Kale explained.

There was an empty beer bottle next to Kale's elbow. He continued to stare at the table.

"Did you see what happened?" Luke asked Kale.

"They were fighting. It looked like he might have pushed her. Then he jumped in after her."

"Brandon told Kelly he was leaving her. For you! He broke her heart. I knew he wasn't good for her," Amanda blubbered through her tears.

"She jumped in. Brandon didn't push her. And Brandon didn't tell her he was leaving her. Tell her why you were there, Kale. Tell her."

"What?" Amanda asked.

Kale shuffled his feet under the table. He pulled back a long drink, and then looked Amanda in the eye.

"She might have jumped. But I don't understand why, because she promised to run away with me. She told me that Dylan was my son."

Amanda gasped. "Shut up!" she yelled, pointing a finger in Kale's face. "She would have told me if that were true. Besides, I thought you were over her!"

"It doesn't matter," Kale moaned into his hands.

The door opened. It was Brandon's parents, older, their weathered faces grey.

"Marlo? I thought you were in California somewhere," Brandon's dad said, recognizing me first.

"I came back today. I'm so sorry this happened, Mr. Jensen."

Mr. Jensen nodded. He turned and thanked Amanda for watching Dylan and promised to let her know the minute he heard anything. He glanced over at Kale.

"Thanks for stopping by."

Kale nodded but couldn't face Mr. Jensen. Amanda and Kale silently walked out without another word.

Luke turned to Brandon's parents and explained what he knew about the rescue efforts. I heard a faint cry from the back room. Brandon's parents were engrossed in the conversation. I hurried through the darkened living room toward Dylan's room. My heart pounded. I turned the doorknob and quietly peeked into the room. The nightlight next to the crib cast a small yellow glow against the familiar yellow stripes and tumbling giraffes and elephants. I tiptoed to the crib and leaned over. A little baby lying in a simple onesie and holding his feet in a happy baby pose stopped fussing when he saw me. He was not the two year old I had grown to love, but the newborn Kelly had struggled to care for. His room was stuffy, and his head was damp from sweat. I picked him up, his thin wisps of hair lay plastered to his skin. I cradled him in my arms. He snuggled against my chest and stretched his tiny hand toward my hair and held on tight. I stared into his searching blue eyes and wondered if he recognized me. At that moment, Brandon's mom appeared in the doorway.

"Is he awake?" she asked gently.

"I think he's hungry," I said. She disappeared for a moment and returned a minute later with a warm bottle in her hand.

"It's nice of you to help, Marlo. I don't know what got into Kelly's head, or Bandon's, for that matter, but I appreciate your help," she said gravely while reaching for Dylan. I squeezed him tightly between my fingers and gazed into his searching eyes. I only wanted one more minute with him. Mrs. Jensen's outstretched arms beckoned like a lighthouse in a storm. I could no longer feign ignorance. I smelled in the newborn scent of hope and perfect love. I kissed his velvet cheek and slowly laid him in her arms.

"Brandon loved Kelly, Mrs. Jensen. Whatever else was going on, he was willing to risk his life for her. I only hope they can find them both alive."

She nodded but could not speak. I turned and left. A huge knot tied itself around my chest as I silently said good-bye to Dylan.

"Where do you want to go now?" Luke asked when we were back in his patrol car.

"Home, I guess," I said, feeling completely empty now that I had left Dylan behind.

"So, do you want to tell me what happened? How you ended up at the park with Brandon and Kelly?"

What had happened? How was it possible that I had only returned from California this morning? It felt like ages ago. It was hard to know where the past ended and where the future began.

"Later, okay?" I finally agreed.

"Sure."

"Will you call me if you hear anything?"

"Sure. The searchers will be back on the water at dawn. I'm sure they'll find them soon."

"Thanks for your help, Luke," I said, really meaning it. I leaned over and wrapped my arms around him, his now-familiar smell of cologne and soap, a reminder of all we had shared—even if Luke wasn't aware of it yet. I buried my face into his shoulder and squeezed my arms tighter around him, not wanting to let him go. I reminded myself that this Luke hadn't seen me in eight years. I finally pulled myself away.

"Crazy first day back," he finally said, breaking the silence.

"Feels like I've been here a month," I agreed, wiping my eyes.

"I'll call you the minute I hear anything," he promised, his strong but soft hand coming up and caressing my face. I felt too awful to even enjoy his touch. I said a weak good-bye and slowly made my way up the front step.

Chapter Twenty-nine

Once inside the house I pulled off my boots and tiptoed up the stairs to my room. My Prada bag sat on the bed just as I'd left it, my miniskirt tossed on the floor, the high heels I'd worn at the parade strewn across the floor. My suitcase lay open like a staged prop from a movie. It seemed so long ago that I entered this town, embarrassed and chagrinned to be here. I changed into a pair of cotton pj's and fell across the bed, not bothering to get in the sheets. I was exhausted. I closed my eyes, but couldn't get the thought of Kelly and Brandon, out there somewhere, out of my mind. I silently made my way down the hall to my parents' room.

My dad's snores filled the air. I was surprised they had slept through the noise of the boats and trucks. As soon as I crawled in the middle of them they both woke up.

"Marlo? Are you all right, honey?" my mom wondered through closed eyes.

"No, I'm not. I just needed you to hold me." I began to cry. My dad clicked his lamp on.

I admired his sleepy round face, his round droopy eyes and tousled thin brown hair. I threw my arms around him.

"What happened, honey? Did you have a bad dream?"

"Yes . . . and no." I sobbed through a short explanation about Brandon. My mom flew out of bed when I told her about the rescue efforts, her pink tricot nightgown—the same one she'd been wearing since I was a little girl—fluttering across the room and immediately called Melissa.

"You've been up this whole time?" my father asked as he glanced at the clock. It was the first time I'd looked to see what time it was. It was two in the morning. There were still several hours before the sun came up.

"Poor Brandon," my mother declared, after hanging up with Melissa. "He was such a lost puppy ever since you broke his heart. I was so glad to hear he'd gotten married. What a shame."

"And poor Kelly. And Dylan," I added, my arms aching to hold him.

"That's right; they had a baby recently," she remembered. "Well, I won't be able to sleep any longer. Anybody care for some toast and hot chocolate?" She wrapped a matching tricot robe around her nightgown and headed for the stairs.

The thought of hot chocolate carried me down to the kitchen. I grabbed a saucepan and set it on the stove, then I opened the fridge and grabbed a jug of milk and poured it into the pan. After a few minutes my dad came into the kitchen, a blue terry cloth robe tied around his rotund belly. I wondered how I could gently encourage him to lose some weight. Convince him that his life depended on it.

"It's nice to be here," I said, watching my mom butter the toast while my dad stirred the hot chocolate. Watching them work together was a testament that some marriages worked. And didn't just work, but were actually enriching in even the simplest procedures, like buttering toast and making hot chocolate. Two halves working in perfect harmony.

"We're glad you're home, too, honey. It's been a tough time for you," Dad said as he set a cup of steaming hot chocolate in front of me.

The three of us sat in silence. I dipped the edges of my buttery toast into the hot liquid. My eyes grew heavy. I fought to keep them open.

"Come on, Mar Bar, let's get you to bed," my father nudged.

I smiled weakly. He grabbed the cup from my hands and set it in the sink. He wrapped his arm around my shoulder. “Up those stairs and into bed,” he called.

“Thanks, Daddy,” I replied, trying to memorize the way his blue eyes sparkled even in the dim light of the chandelier, or the way his mouth was always turned up in a smile, even when he wasn’t smiling. I rushed back to him and threw my arms around his neck. “I love you, Daddy!” I cried, burying my face into his big burly chest. He stood surprised for a moment, and then wrapped his own arms around me. We stood at the base of the stairs for several minutes. At least he knew how much I loved him. That had to count for something, no matter the future.

“Marlo.”

I rolled over and pulled the thin blanket up around my chin.

“Marlo,” Mom said again, this time a little louder. “Luke’s at the door.”

My eyes shot open. I sprang out of bed, my feet barely touching the floor. My mother was showered and dressed, her hair in rollers. I glanced at the clock. It was just after five in the morning. A low bluish grey light glowed through my shades.

“Have they found them?”

“The boats went in the river a few minutes ago.”

“Tell him I’ll be right down.”

She nodded and left the room. I rummaged through my suitcase for something to wear. I grabbed a blue sweatshirt and a pair of jeans. I ran to the bathroom and splashed water on my face. My eyes were swollen from crying, but there was no time for concealer. I pulled my hair back in a ponytail, brushed my teeth, and then hurried down the stairs.

Luke sat on the couch in the living room. He looked freshly showered, his skin clean-shaven.

He stood when he saw me.

"Hi," he said quietly.

"Hi," I answered. He opened the front door for me. The minute we were outside I asked where they were looking.

"Down past the island," he explained as he started the Explorer.

The island was a neighborhood in the southeast corner of town surrounded by canals, ditches, and the river to the south.

"Did you see Troy?" I asked as we made our way down Main Street.

"No. He's probably already down there. I think he went down in a kayak." My stomach rolled nervously.

We pulled up to Litton Park near the edge of the river. My stomach sank when I caught sight of the ambulance parked in front.

I couldn't move. I went to open the door, but my hands were shaking too much.

"What does the ambulance mean?" I asked.

Luke shook his head. "Might be precautionary," he explained. He jumped out. I finally got a solid grasp on the handle. My legs moved like warm jelly as I stumbled toward the crowd that hovered near the fence just off the river. Several boats hovered around a large group of cottonwood trees that grew near the water's edge. My stomach dropped.

A white sheet covered something lying on the other side of the fence. I stopped moving. All the air seeped out of my lungs. I scanned the faces of the people. Several men, faces scruffy, eyes bloodshot, looked like they hadn't had much sleep. I recognized the man in diving gear from the fire station.

I forced my legs toward him and grabbed his arm. "Who is it?"

He looked over at the sheet. "It's the girl," he answered quietly.

The white sheet fluttered in the wind. A piece of white hair lay exposed. I turned away. My heart dropped to my knees. It was then I noticed Brandon's father standing nearby, his face watching the river.

I followed his gaze. A jet boat sat further down the river. For a moment my heart leaped, hoping all was not lost. But from the grim faces surrounding his father my hope seemed unrealistic. Two EMTs lifted an empty gurney over the fence. I turned my head away as they placed Kelly's body onto the gurney. Luke was suddenly by my side. He placed a hand on my shoulder. My body shuddered at his warm touch. I turned toward him and buried my head into his chest. He placed his arms around my shoulders.

Someone's radio crackled loudly. My head shot up. Luke picked up his radio. I still couldn't understand the muffled voices on the other end, but I did understand the collective moan that rolled in a continuous wave off the men's lips. The hairs raised on the back of my neck and arms. The man in the diving suit met my eye. He shook his head in disappointment. I squinted past the glare of the morning sun to keep from bursting into tears.

Ironically it was a beautiful morning. The sky was the color of robin eggs. Not a cloud to be seen. The river floated lazily by, an unassuming silent monster. A black raven drifted effortlessly between the branches of the enormous cottonwood trees. Its morning song echoed through the trees.

The EMTs loaded Kelly's gurney into the ambulance. Several other men turned toward the parking lot. Luke turned to me.

"They've found a body. Down around the Henry's Fork trail. Just off the cemetery."

"Will you take me there?"

"Are you sure?" Luke's sable eyes squinted in the bright sun.

I bit my lip and nodded.

The greenbelt near the cemetery was only a half mile south west. We parked just south of the cemetery. I steadied myself as I walked from the car. I knew I had no right to run, cry, or act hysterical. To everyone around me, I was a small speck in Brandon's life, barely a memory. But to me, it was much more than that. It might have only been a glimpse, but for one week of my life, I had been married to Brandon. I had cared for his son. I didn't do it great. I hadn't been ready, but I had learned to love them both.

My fingernails dug into my palms in an effort to stop the tears from spilling from my eyes. I stopped walking. My heart was in my throat. I took small breaths through an invisible straw as rescue workers pulled a tall, heavy body from the boat and laid it on the ground. There was no blanket over Brandon's face. His wet skin was pale blue, his body bloated, his lips drained of color and covered in a white frothy film.

The EMTs hurried past me, an empty gurney at their sides. My feet sunk in the soft earth. I couldn't take a step forward or backward. They lifted Brandon's lifeless body onto the gurney and covered it with a white sheet. I counted the casualties. One, two. Same number as in my glimpse, only the people were wrong. My stomach lurched. Troy! I'd almost forgotten. I scanned the faces of the rescuers, but failed to find his among those busy pulling equipment together or consoling Brandon's father.

"I don't see Troy. Are you sure he was here?" I said in a panic.

Luke looked around the familiar faces. He leaned over and asked a man named Bill if he'd seen Troy.

"He took a kayak down further. Probably pulling out downstream a ways."

"Does he have a radio? Does he know they've found Brandon?" I asked.

"The water's swift, so he probably pulled out about a half a mile downstream. I'll send a truck for him."

"That's okay. Luke and I will go pick him up." I grabbed Luke's arm and turned up the path. I could feel Luke's questioning eyes on my back like searing stones.

"I'm sure he's okay, Marlo. He's just pulling his kayak in," Luke said.

"No, he's not! At least I don't think he is." My face felt hot. I blinked back hot tears. How could I explain what I knew? What had Dad asked me last night? If I'd had a bad dream?

"I—I had a dream. I guess it was a dream, but so far everything in that dream has come true. Kelly drowned, but Brandon didn't in my dream. Troy died in the dream, though. So far, everything has come true, and it's even worse in real life, and I haven't been able to stop any of it from happening. So please! Please, just help me find Troy," I begged in small desperate breaths.

"Okay. Let's go. Better safe," he said, starting the Explorer's engine.

We turned west off Highway Twenty and wound down a narrow country road until we dead-ended just before the river turned south. I jumped out of the car. Luke was already crossing the head gates. We wound our way around volcanic rock stumps and large mulberry bushes. Across the river I could make out the group of people still huddled around where Brandon's body was found.

"Do you hear that?" Luke stopped, holding his hand up for silence. We both listened.

There was a faint sound, like a horn in the distance.

The sound came from the river. "It's a distress call. I'll bet it's Troy!" Luke said. We quickly walked along the bank, searching for signs of Troy. Luke called out Troy's name. I listened for the sound again. The horn blew after a few seconds. Luke took off after the sound.

As we came around the bend, the corner of a bright yellow kayak partially submerged came into view. Something moved in the water, and then all went still again. Luke ran ahead of me and clambered onto a large log that had fallen across the river.

"His gear is caught on something under the water. It's keeping him under," I yelled out to Luke. He stretched his hands out toward the kayak, but couldn't reach it.

"Melissa said that the kayak got stuck in a fallen log and pinned Troy underneath it," I remembered.

Luke seemed to ignore the part about Melissa. At least he didn't ask me about it. "I need to get out there and help him," Luke said, crawling further out onto the fallen log.

"Troy!" Luke called over the water. "Can you get free?"

The tip of Luke's mask showed over the water. He shook his head, and then the water swallowed him up again.

"He can't get free," Luke yelled. "He must be almost out of air by now. If I can get in the water I could help him get free."

Troy's face popped out of the water again. Something was pulling him under.

"What can I do?" I asked.

"Stay there. I'm going in," Luke said as he dropped into the water. He latched onto Troy and went under with him. I climbed the log and lay against the wet, moss-covered bark. Then I reached down and grabbed Luke's shoulders to keep him from floating away. After a long silent moment Luke pulled himself up out of the water.

"His hand has gotten tangled in some old fishing line. I need a knife to cut him free. I unsnapped his gear, but it's caught."

There was not a soul in sight, and certainly no knives lying around. Suddenly I remembered Luke's keychain.

"Your keychain!" I screamed down at him. "Where are your keys?"

"In the car," he yelled back. I reached down and grabbed his hand and guided it to the log. He gripped a branch, and I ran off to fetch the keys.

"I'll be right back!" I yelled, already across the log and running along the bank toward the truck. I ran as fast as I'd ever run, tripping over boulders and sticks and nearly losing my footing. But I continued running until I reached the Explorer. I yanked the door open and jammed my hand through the wheel and grabbed the keys. I glanced down at them. Sure enough, the pocketknife was still there!

I ran back along the bank, looking for the kayak. Luke hung on to a fallen log. I screamed his name, waving the knife in the air and slid across the damp log. He reached up and grabbed the knife.

"Nice memory!" he called before he flicked it open and dove into the water. It didn't take long for Luke to cut Troy free from the ropes, unsnap his BC vest, and pull Troy out of the scuba tank contraption. Within moments, Troy swam free. His hands were red and rigid as he attempted to swim toward the bank.

It seemed like forever before Luke pulled himself out of the water next to Troy. I leaned down and helped yank Troy out of the water. His hands were ice cold. His tank was gone, lying at the bottom of the river, but he was safe. The men dragged themselves to the edge of the grass.

Troy lay on his back, taking huge gasping breaths. "Kayak tipped when I tried to maneuver it to the bank . . . jumped in, but couldn't get the kayak free . . . I went underwater to pull it free and found myself hooked to all that crap that's collected under the log . . . I was glad to hear your voice, Luke."

"Marlo had a feeling something was wrong. You should thank her," Luke said.

Troy looked up at me. "Marlo?"

I shook my head, clarifying, "I don't deserve any credit."

"Thanks, Marlo, I was almost out of air. Such a stupid mistake. I'll never live it down."

"How did you remember I had a knife on my keychain?" Luke asked.

My face grew warm. How could I ever explain? "Lucky guess, I suppose."

"That wasn't a lucky guess," Luke said softly, watching me closely. I turned and looked across the river.

"Was it in the dream?"

I nodded.

Troy slipped out of the top of his wet suit. Luke was soaked from head to foot. We walked back to the truck. I found a blanket in the back. I tried to wrap it around Luke, but he shook his head and put it around Troy's trembling shoulders instead.

The three of us leaned against the hot metal of the Explorer and stared across the river at the slowly diminishing crowd across the way. There were no words to be spoken. My heart ached for Brandon and Kelly and at the same time rejoiced for Melissa and Maura and Maddy and Brayden. Eventually the sun filled the sky and warmed us with its eternal heat. Without a word we made our way to the car. Troy sat in the back, the blanket still nestled across his shoulders. Luke shut his door and stared at his keychain for a moment. His eyes met mine. I smiled. He smiled back, and with the turn of his wrist, he started the car up and we drove back to town.

Epilogue

One month later . . .

I rounded the corner of Bridge Street and crossed the river just as the early-morning sun rose above the Tetons. I closed my eyes and inhaled the earthy smell of fish and moss and fresh clean air. For the first time in weeks I heard the sounds of blue jays chirping to one another. And for the first time in months I felt hopeful again.

I had never been one for the dramatic, but the last few weeks had been nothing less than a chapter out of a Jude Deveraux or Danielle Steel novel. I didn't understand why I was able to help Troy and not the others. But I also understood that life was complex and I may never have the answers of why I couldn't save Brandon or Kelly. Maybe, like Melissa would say, it was God's will. Maybe it was their will. All I knew was I had heard the call of the raven and had tried to answer it the best I could.

There was a part of me that wished for a glimpse again. To hold Dylan and rock him to sleep, smell his sweet baby-powder skin and listen to him babble. But I also wanted to start fresh. Find a real relationship. Not one where I was defined by my partner, but where I was complete because of him. I could only be loved for who I was, and for me, that meant no more tennis clubs, fancy shoes, and expensive bags. That didn't mean I was going to give all my things to Goodwill. I loved my Prada bag, and I had a few fantastic shoes that would stay as part of my collection, but only the shoes that worked for me. No more trying to be anything other than who I was.

I had learned a lot of other things in the last few weeks. I learned that Brandon was Methodist. I hadn't known that. Even in high school. We had never discussed religion. It had never seemed important. But it was important to me now. It was nice to go to his church and hear how Brandon and Kelly had helped others during their short time on earth, ways that no one would have ever known until a funeral, when we finally acknowledge the good and forget the bad. I watched with painful yearning as Brandon's mom and sister, Holly, took turns holding baby Dylan.

Only when the funeral was over and the dinner had been served did I dare ask to hold Dylan. I took him outside. The sun was warm, and the sky was a brilliant blue. I'd kissed Dylan's perfect forehead, held his tiny fingers in mine, and breathed in his innocence and purity with hopes that I might take a little of his goodness with me. What would become of this sweet boy?

I hadn't seen Kale since the accident. He hadn't come to the funeral, or if he had, he had kept out of sight. I couldn't imagine what he was going through. I was sorry for him. He had loved Kelly. They shared a child together. Kale had just learned this before Kelly's death. It would take some time, but I imagined Kale might come to terms with his newfound status and wish to be a part of Dylan's life. Then again, maybe he wouldn't. Perhaps he would silently remain on the sidelines, unable to find peace with himself. I couldn't begin to guess what he was thinking.

I saw Amanda after the funeral was over. I was just getting in my car. She stopped and stared at it.

"This your car?" she'd asked with a bit of a smirk.

"Yeah," I had answered, reminding myself that she wasn't the horrible person I'd seen in the glimpse, and that I had no reason to hate her.

"Nice tires," she smiled. "Are they new?"

"Yeah, they are," I answered suspiciously. She didn't wait for me to answer. She had already turned and clicked down the sidewalk in her red heels. I stared after her in disbelief.

I hadn't seen Luke since the funeral. It wasn't that I didn't like Luke. I found him handsome and wonderful and almost perfect. But I needed time to find myself and knew I couldn't do that with Luke's silky brown eyes hanging around and turning my knees all soft. Funny thing was I missed him. I thought about him a lot as I helped my mother pick out new paint for the dining room or while I sat around the table late at night sharing stories with my parents. Or when my sister stopped by with Troy and the kids.

Sometimes late at night when I couldn't sleep I'd find myself at the Sand Bar. I'd sit on the stairs and watch the moon reflect off the water as it rolled peacefully by, and I'd think of Brandon. I would hear Brandon's voice or his laughter ringing in my ears.

I wondered if it had been some trick of the raven's to send me on a wild goose chase, or if I had really set everything in its proper order. There was always a nagging doubt that I had done the right thing by letting Brandon go in after Kelly. But I also knew that if I kept Brandon on the shore, like I did in the glimpse, Brandon would have regretted it. And maybe never forgiven me for stopping him.

I only wished I could have known Kelly and could have helped her somehow, but I hadn't even been given a chance. But I had helped to save Troy, and my father was still alive, and I was working to help him too. I'd find a way to live my future by living my today, just the way God intended. And speaking of God, I'd decided to invite him into my life. I'd even attended church with Troy and Melissa and the girls. It felt good. I might even go back.

I crossed Bridge Street and placed the earphones in my ears. I pushed play. The music rose like fog after a rainstorm. I'd started running again. My dad had agreed to join me for a walk after he went fishing this morning. I was even trying to talk him into an upcoming 5K. And I'd already asked him on a date. So what that it was nearly a year away, say the end of May for Fisherman's Breakfast. I wanted to make sure he didn't already have other plans. I passed by the tire store. I checked my watch, it was only seven, but one garage bay was already opened. I glanced inside and caught sight of a tall, dark-haired guy walking away from me. I wondered if it was Kale.

A car pulled into the parking lot of the gas station. Another crossed the bridge. A second garage door went up over at the tire store. Two women passed by me on the trail, busy in conversation. The Tetons stood brilliant in the distance; a jagged chunk of granite protruding far into the heavens, a reminder of how spectacular and mystical this land was. The river bubbled between rocks and jetties as it flowed quietly by. The desert earth looked perfect to me in the morning light, as if some strong hand had personally placed each rock and volcanic boulder strategically between large green sagebrush bushes.

A raven shuddered out of a nearby cottonwood tree. I jumped in surprise. It floated into the sky, dipping and circling before crossing the river and climbing into the deep blue heavens and disappearing into the horizon.

I had looked everywhere for the old woman, but she was nowhere to be found. The apartment was cleared out and empty. The only reminder that she truly existed and I was not totally crazy was the robin egg blue walls. Perhaps her job here was done and she had moved on to help another misguided soul.

A small squirrel darted between two olive trees. Its long tail fluttered like a ruffled dress as it scampered up the trunk of a tree. This place I had known all my life seemed to glitter like tiny pieces of crystal in the morning sun, hidden jewels welcoming me home.

Two fishermen stood just off the river. I slowed my pace, recognizing them. One was my father. I was expecting him. The other, a thin, tall man with blond hair and gorgeous eyes, was a surprise. My heart nearly stopped. He turned and looked at me. I took a deep breath. A small grin crossed his lips. I could feel a smile spreading across my own. The dark raven glided between us; he cawed loudly, and then soared into the sky and out of sight. I thought of that saying about how a journey of a thousand miles must begin with one step.

I took my one small step forward and opened my heart to a thousand new possibilities.

The End

CPSIA information can be obtained at www.ICGtesting.com
Printed in the USA
BVOW020106090412

287099BV00001B/3/P

9 781432 788278